I0587192

OTHER BOOKS BY J. LEA KORETSKY

NOVELS
Wall of Darkness
The Eternity Look
Domino
The Sweat Box
Under Dragon House
Blueprint
Snapshot, Collected Stories
Rope
Trojan Park
Border
Belvatown
Crimes and Offenses
Mandated Reporter
Sabaru

POETRY
Cherished Memory
(Poems & A Play)
Damascas Rose
Love's Errand

PLAYS
The Voyage
The Stars

PSYCHOLOGY
Social Work From A Therapeutic Perspective

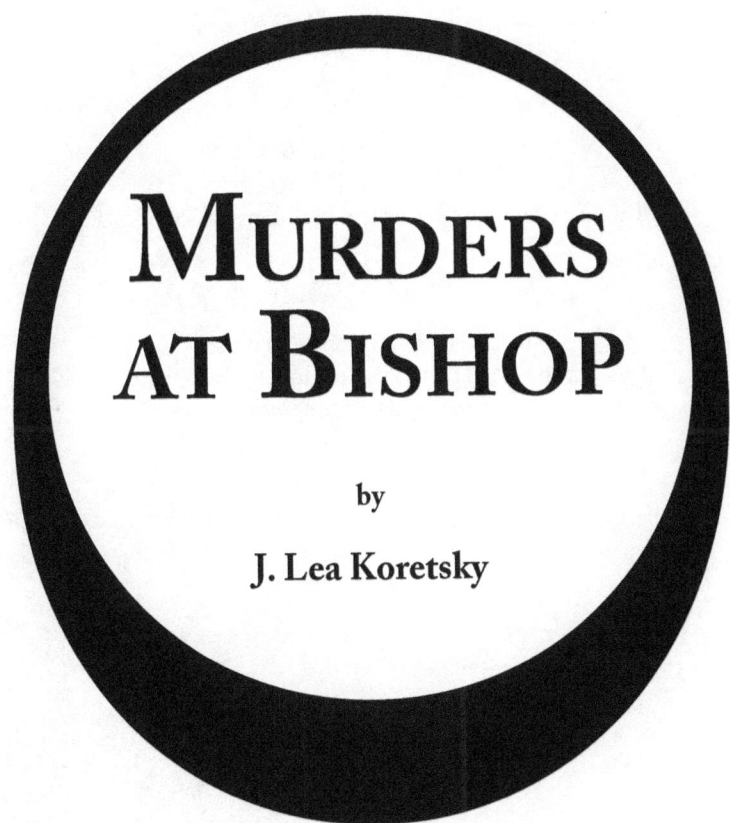

MURDERS AT BISHOP

by

J. Lea Koretsky

REGENT PRESS
Berkeley, California

ISBN 13: 978-1-58790-431-8
ISBN 10: 1-58790-431-4
Library of Congress Control Number: 2018933821

Any description of place or person
is not intended by the author to have pertinence
to reality past or present.

Manufactured in the U.S.A.
REGENT PRESS
Berkeley, California
www.regentpress.net

10 9 8 7 6 5 4 3 2 1

MURDERS AT BISHOP
1

THE DEAD
143

UNDIFFERENTIATED
195

MURDERS
AT
BISHOP

GUYANA

1

THE COLLECTION winds had taken their toll. Across Puerto Rico island driftwood lay strewn on black and pink sandy beaches along with inland shrubs, trees and rain withered flora. The storm season was early by far by a month, the fervid sea breezes having succumbed to pilot banked heat and quietly retreated to the rain forest where it spurned a weather resistant front. The craving storm gnarled below stone caverns sending a repetitive demonstration of simultaneous rising damp mist and foraging budding rains until within a single hour dark thunderous clouds advanced over the ocean entering the wilderness interior from the west to combine to suppress the elevations of iced drizzling fogs.

Far on the distant jet stream a zone maintained by warm bright sunshine without a whip wind to it, a weather ship recorded the thrust of the storm's direction. For the crew it was the abrupt end of the fly pole season and the start of fish lantern net dragging. Now came endless begging bass size swimmers to roam the surface and turn against their own instinct to submerge through light-fading depths. The small ones were coaxed by the placement of dim lanterns; where the schools emerged the larger fish were grouped. The ship would remain in its quadrant until the next day at sundown unless the charging storm fetched its own capitulation. Immediately below the surface, ten feet down, the schools were reading in as bursts of activity, cloud plumes narrowing in on currents thundering with chatter. The drop lines spooled and reversed – the entire ocean spooned for flight. It was to be a shouting match as the sunlight was obscured by over compensating walls of dark husbanding showers and marshalling wind. The ship com sent a message to the San Juan feed in tandem with the cries from the wild, get ready for sundown.

Sundown was a code file, which described a barbarous circumstance during which a wanted individual created a hostile terrorism threatening bodily harm. Sundown it was, Lewis decided after charting the high output of rapidly closing in air stream currents. With this storm he anticipated over outages, hostile barrages against the coasts, rapid fall of barometer, descending wind cavorting pressure climates, off jet stream swelling waves, formidable declines of rain possibly for an entire day. He hoped the storm would only leave the natural wood forest smitten but it could wreak and buffet about for any rampage. On the current flow reading the prediction showed a shoo-in of more than garden despot isolations. It revealed a high deploring mark of escalating erosion off high cliff lines. It was going to be a real mess.

On the other side of the stone sea wall built like a fortress to protect the city of San Juan, the ocean spurned with crashed boats and floating planks. The water itself wore a heavy blue maroon appearance as though in the worst frenzy fish had been gutted and bled for hours filling the surface in a protrusion of dye. A boom crew spent the morning decontaminating the beach segregating shark and pilaster from spent wood and mercifully walking through the sand to collect spikes, shards of broken glass, hungered pipes, and other hazardous material including poisonous filmy fish guts, both vomited rotting and preserved intact. The city awaited a month long predicted dragnet before it would study actual frontline damage. For this all analyses from the ship had to again get entered manually and then contrasted to visual reports and automated microfiche profiles. The port in southeastern Florida would of course want the ship to dock there, but chances were the Cabo Rojo authorities would handle the decliners first especially because they sat closest to the damage. First objective come morning was to study the Intel for shipwrecks or wind struck aircraft nor busted river harbors or dead.

By eight o'clock in the morning cause had been assessed as starting in Guyana at Pt. Weather. Technically while a massive dust churning hurricane began there, it literally spooled off the water traveling at a hundred miles an hour but gathering almost no ocean water in its wake. When it crashed onto lower Puerto Rico heading to San Juan it became curtailed in the interior before it retreated somewhat and drove in through the west into the forested terrain losing velocity as it scattered rain and high winds. No additional information was available other than Guyana had experienced an infrared heat caught between a cold wind and a very dense wind. It had been over a hundred years since the last one; these traveling thunderstorms seldom occurred. The sundowner reached maximum velocity by four twenty in the afternoon of the previous day and went most of the night taking all sorts of habitation in its wind tunnel. In some more remote areas land disappeared raining dirt for an hour and in other parts of the interior houses tumbled. Lewis requested a streamline to determine whether a forest fire could have set it off because of the strength of wind.

At its epicenter the wind funneled for over half a day as compared with Bermuda hurricanes which ran a cyclone for several minutes as it came upon landfall. Whole stands of trees were cut down, huge ravines lost miles of cliff, as the dark cloud cover settled rain down pourings drenched valleys within seconds. Slammers hitting these valleys and peaks in almost no way offset velocity. Sparks flickered in the torrent causing electricity to die. At a later point houses and buildings would have to be completely rebuilt because nothing would renew electricity or plumbing.

It wasn't until the wind swept its pay load onto the northern beaches it slowed and began to disperse. An hour before dawn it had drawn a low curtain on the Atlantic and was anticipated to de-accelerate in its journey over the water.

The charts were anything but a non alert. The center of the streamline ran a vertical tan with grey segment for two pages signifying an outcome of non usable dwellings. Lewis notified Field to embark to San Juan to set up emergency living centers with flannel clothing, cots, blankets, wrapped food, canteen lights. After that, the shelters were going to house the homeless, some two thousand inhabitants, until new structures could be built, probably in a hundred and eighty days.

The wind was supercharged by monsoon moonless hours. In all probability the island would shut down for months and normal shipping passage turned over to smaller nearby residential islands giving ports more than seasonal averages. St. John might store plantation goods, Barbados would wind up taking pharmaceuticals and Caicos summer tourists. The catch could go anywhere, Saba would be closed to assure its medical clinics were not saddled unnecessarily, and the Antilles clear through to Grenadines would assume packaging for already delayed post. Once damage reports were accommodated by airlift, the entire island chain below Barbados would be pinned; not a sailor would be permitted sail.

Lewis took in the multitude of channel reports island-wide on a complex Intel system involving forty other databases. The strategic weather map points revealed downed hotels, numerous of them, planked beaches, mud clogged river and cubby inlet cove passages, destroyed docks, tin markets partially in ocean water, crashed trees dragging power lines, mud surfaced well above embankment heights. Garden and beach lounge furniture had been hurled yards away wedged in cranked windows and onto rooftops. The long bay that made up the entry to Neva had been swept adrift causing the entire bay to be exposed to a sand bar; a ship stationed on its cracked hull scooted as if onto land. Across the inlet three ships had come to floor consequence, gulf water having absented for the better half of a mile. All sights seemed marooned, every last one impressed any photographer as completely realistic. People caught in vehicles had fled on foot to higher ground climbing stairs, sloped drives, hills, embankments in frantic necessity. He looked for points of no return, for shallow coral reefs, an historical parlay of scrutiny, growing weary by the moment the longer he studied the photo findings and referenced to prior dockings. If anything the ocean had entered a wayward combat zone, and while computer monitors displayed futile-descended storms, the currents had put in their redirection giving underwater runoff while shifting the fifty feet surrounding islands a good hard bomblast. In a week or two these effects would subside, but the durable stipulation would be as bad as Katrina. It would become difficult for him to explain how the Monterey post at the outset of beach town had fizzled for hours with reddish electricity while schools of turbid were cast onto sand in fairly much the same condition. Just as difficult to comprehend why by nightfall the lights of the entire few blocks from the ocean went off in a lightning storm vanquishing the beach in grey darkness.

Jones stopped in for a breather. He had stayed out on night patrol with kerosene lamps placed at every street corner and wore a haggard, life beats death exhaustion. His recent journeyman case up in the States had drawn to a close and he had flown in on a red eye from Miami to San Juan Estudillo Air Tower arriving about six weeks prior. Even Lewis who had turned state's evidence to a district of parole boards had packed up at the first opportunity, both feeling done in due to the demands of tracking a train bombing trio. As soon as they set foot at Cabo Rojo their tension dissipated and they were reassigned to fairly mundane investigations, Lewis to a border snafu at Ranch Hades and Jones to a ship illegally heading for Jamaica. Although three days at the station office was as decent a come down as any, it took a week for Lewis to return to the golfing green and for Jones to get in a few games of tennis. Hoyt had stayed behind to wind up the grand jury inquiry on the Galveston Wind, and offices in Florida's highrises in Del Ray were temporarily subletted for the long winter.

"We have an immediate problem," Jones said, taking a dark red leather chair, lines of burdened activity creasing his forehead and eyes. "The storm pulled in a man by the name of Cinque D'Jannare. During this storm he entered an emergency shelter with a Bulgarian female and spent two nights on cots until being released the third day after flooding dried up. Our Intel cross corresponded them to several houses, one on the frontier, one along Cinque Terre, another right here in Cabo, so we know he's making inroads to somewhere, possibly into the U.S."

Jones elaborated. He had stayed up the night sorting by photograph the mission emergency shelters, cautious to the minute. It took upward of two hours for his computer to match fingerprints and addresses to sleepers on cots. Downed power lines had created an immediate need to know anyway. The computer was a parallel processor capable of providing fifty matches an hour and interfaces to associates and other known wanted persons, and sometime just prior to the storm's cessation it spit up a name and face. Here, there, he had picked out petty burglars, cheap winos, stranded vehicle owners, drug dealing boaters flung up flood-gouged embankments. It took over four hours to identify the two hundred people who crammed inside the shelter as the day wore on. Of course it was not atypical to pull in a wanted felon, although rare, but on occasion some wandered in, as was evidenced by the Che Guevara resemblance of a male known as Cinque, appeared out of nowhere, who was known for transporting deadly weapons from strategic Indian Ocean who the hell knew from where to any trouble spot on the globe. In the last three years rumors of his whereabouts surfaced – he had made it out of a prison camp in northeastern Baghdad.

Lewis said, "We'll ask coordination to assign him. I've brought in a rotation of retired officers on position throughout the beach zone."

Jones gave a nod of assent. "That's good. In case he decides to look over a consignment or arrange a buy, we'll have him on the tap."

Lewis turned to his favorite page and typed in a few sentences. "It's a good thing Fidel's government spent so much time establishing medical clinics, island security, search and rescue, deportation clearances, free food and housing in addition to assigning jobs. He took in forty-two hundred people and deported three-quarters to Miami. That bureaucracy made it relatively easy to locate a target wandering around loose. What do we know about him?"

Jones replied, "Next to nothing. Just that prior to Cinque Terre he began in a career in southeastern Plato setting snares for wild animals. It's not out of the realm of possibility that they were asked to staff a boundary and in that capacity eventually they had to shoot down forager aircraft."

"That would put him along the frontier."

"It could well be that's how he knows as much as he does."

"He'd have handled every weapon in use. He'd know

trajectory distance, emission range, detonation failures, and cartridge exposure. Even with two years on the front he would make a suitable range expert."

"What do we think he's up to?" Jones persisted, lighting a British van cigarette with an herbal peach aroma, picking up cold coffee and sipping.

Lewis poured himself a shaker of bourbon and soda and relaxed over the query. They had entered very familiar territory, a disposition of often discussed waylaid conventions for firing torpedoes and explosives upon suspect country sides usually rugged with snowfall. "It's a convenient hiding place for radicals. Consider our target has no registered prints, doesn't drive and therefore has no license, has no departmental actions, no convictions, no legal name, owns no property, has never published, doesn't bank, but is thought to have tampered with aircraft or been involved in the manufacture of explosive compounds, each which out of a handful of containables can be packed into weapons."

"So," Jones said, thinking aloud as he studied the various piles of loose reports on Lewis' massive desk, "any Intel analyst we pitch to for help will say this doer has made his life by not being seen, therefore he must be born out of the country, maybe he's waited forty years to travel until he's virtually unrecognizable while many of his family are presumed dead."

Lewis responded with heavy weight identifiers, as usual. "Intel probably would capitulate that a few hundred problems were identified as a result of Bay of Pigs, people left, Fidel had new housing erected, provided eventual entry into U.S. Here's the pointer. Once missiles shot off the map of Plato, the U.S. sent in ten hard artillery tanks which got blown up; three flying recons were also blown; it was a goddamn lazy spiller with arsenals aimed right between our eyes. Then Rumania entered the scenario. Fifteen jets took pictures, twenty embargo ships lined the Suez off Tobruk; it was a major effort, ninety fighter pilots went in on voluntary status."

"UNESCO too to protect landmark sites."

"That's right. Everywhere had national stadium and what did that tell us? Complications overseas were maneuvered by expelled guards from predominantly iron curtain operated areas."

Jones knew enough to know newsprint analysts were going to be pulled in over and above Tobruk, Fez, or desert troops. The newspaper desks which studied war from every minor reference in print, not to mention the captions that were cut in the spool room by the editing lawyers, curried up a more convincing by-line than the ten sort list for pictures. Once these agents, some in the field an unprecedented fifty-three years on one block of codes, were signed for, the unit would roll into purposeful motion, up at four in the morning, a two mile walk in the dark, cup of coffee at an eggs and ham broiler open until lunch, and report to the office by six, all day a drone, these days the unit went on sleep rotation midnight to four, almost the same schedule with a badminton break at ten in the morning. Friends came and went, each man was married, a wife as secretary was all anyone needed to avoid eventual isolation from society. There were all types of intimacy in life, sex the first expedite-able expendable, the job was life, each desk piled with target movement, receipts, reports of hellish interrogation, on rare occasion a murder, evidenced by a body face down in the snow, camp having moved some twenty miles.

Jones asked, knowing he wouldn't be selected for this bit of service, "Who were you planning to put on the case?"

"A man out of Cinque Terre, old school, he has no declared nationality himself, no prints in U.S. or U.K., no permanent address, vehicle, used to dealing with name as chase, he'll dig up associates, list receipts, mark cross walks, parks, building entrances."

"A grey shadow. Someone like Chiller Pond?"

"He's a decent chap," Lewis said. "But no, I've sent for Morningstern. He's familiar with the Caspian barrages."

Jones pictured the older man, long in the jowls, silver brown hair, an agent who had spent most of his years tracking vehicles by sipping coffee at sidewalk cafes in Paris, Amsterdam, Haifa and Beirut. "Yes, he's excellent. Where is he today?"

"The agency stuck him in a windowless room with periodicals. He's been in Inflation and Finance. It won't be any problem to bring him to Maps."

Sundown had put down on San Juan having doused festive lights in every major street including at the stone church. The newsprint references to Venazza and Parque Nacionale beach which lay over the dining room table of James Morningstern's flat showed an Amalfi-like bench of some seventy apartment complexes painted rose, yellow, dark rust, tan and white tucked onto rock on the strait of the Mediterranean Sea, an idyllic vacation resort dominated by a coastal church at half past one. It was a far cry from the stone wilderness of the nomadic entry of Turkey and destitute Plato, all of the landscape camera easy after twenty-one years of war, movies notwithstanding to show where a posse of students raided a hangar on a beach peninsula. The small flat of a third story terra-cotta brown stucco building in which Morningstern stood in the narrow alcove of a floor to ceiling window overlooking the wharf and harbor from a block away was built at the turn of the century when rum distilleries were erected inside former churches on the rail mount. He smoked a Turkish raf appreciating the speed of the nicotine as he observed the bay fill up with low barge ships scuttled by ferries to remove the dozens of debilitated schooners and boats. Now and then the bay filled up with bubbling water as a cruise ship was escorted to its warehouse dock. He had arrived from the coast of Turkmenistan near the boundary of northwestern Iran on the Caspian having deleted a tank plane flying on the gritty red sand from Borgan. The hostilities had been mounting steadily for a year starting with a border guard firing upon his detachment and ending with a bus crash on the beach. The Turkmenistan was well fortified with a castle embankment of turrets from which the erroneous plane was spotted. The plane was outfitted with a bomber that rode atop it, and charged into the water like a buffalo making for a deserted oasis. Both the Aral and Balkan territories had tracked a sighting of a short train that plowed snow over the tundra steppe through a high niege of clouds. Morningstern himself had lived twenty years on the Matterhorn Alps Grum piled up in a flat on the summit awaiting the red and white train from Tirano, its exterior crusted with ice despite kilometer miles of rock protected tunnels. Skiing was excellent on the windswept slopes along the Gottard Bahn, a retired man's paradise if ever there was one.

Cinque was captured first in Tehran at the university. Then he was extremely youthful, in his teens, tall, tan, dark hair, looking to be Italian or Muslim, having ventured off to study sociology in the steppes. He joined the Iran Photo Bin, a campus club with aims of an independent nation out of reach of the Ustrurt Plateau Intelligence. Each year he traveled by train through the worst blizzards along Iran's north border through forbidding, glacier packed mountain terrain through Uzbekistan, Tashkent, Tajikistan, and on return trained into the Mary on his re-entry through Mashhad. He adapted his name after a winter vacation on the Italian Riviera where he met his wife. By the time he graduated he had earned an advantage plowing snow by train and agreed to transport chemical dispersing torpedoes in the dense snow regions where they would never be found. Normally the usual way to transport weapons not used by the military was under water; in ships carrying anything, the ships were torn apart by

Russian and Iranian operatives alike. Monitoring by land and by sea was a nightmare for which the risks were great. Usually someone was required to walk them in. Weapons shooting at the moon were confiscated from Baghdad, the Tashkent and on occasion in Malaysia. Explosions over the skyline plumed like nesting detonations out of dark thunder that mushroomed orange into the air; pink tan was a dust cloud hurling at a hundred miles an hour; shades of green were gaseous harbingers spewing salts and waking thunder in calamities that shook mountainous desert for days.

The Monterosso al Mare train sped through thick rock tunnels that flanked steep densely packed shrubs on hills of the Cinque Terre below Levanto along the Sinara. Daily it picked up hundreds of passengers in its escalated journey north above Via Roma and a hundred Antioch bell tower church dominated apartos each consisting of thirty flats. The finding of a mountain hideout just below the castle brought thirty detonation agents who catapulted the entire war chest exploding the cache which produced a cascade of rumbling mud in the wake of a storming torrential flood. Within seconds the three foot deep river rushed down ancient stone stairs, poured into the Via Roma annihilating peaceful patios and capsizing cars over the oceanfront wall. All that survived were the Porto Roca terrace with blue umbrellas and light blue lounge chairs on a high wall, napkin fans splayed on bone white china plates on white tablecloths overlooking pyramid peninsulas that crested the sparkling blue sea.

In his heart Morningstern knew the connection between the illicit wife and her night job cleaning the Dorian church basement bastions was Cinque himself who was charting strides from Vicarra hotels across the Atlantic in cheap chemical ships carrying prized Iranian coal and iron ore through the islands into the U.S. It was no big deal to learn early in the life of the case that into post graduate coursework Cinque had selected yet another study at the Railway Transportation Institute and traveled to Uzbekistan to the oasis below the Tian Shan Range in his role as football sports team player which saw a mildly lucrative earning. Because he lived December to February each year in Hanza and Yunusabad, over a nine year period, he knew every stretch of mountain pass, precipitation, hillside, clinic, landing strip, and monastery run by a prison. The new MARS System, operated by industrial counter espionage, which instantly provided map for 1962 identification worldwide in coordination with a read on any activated radar scan, placed him on the map after he and a group fired a missile designed to eliminate cities absent of people high above thirty-nine thousand feet. China's monitoring system for its western Russian counterparts in the Tian Shan and the Altai Mountains spotted the missile on target sector as a pale white climbing beacon and disintegrated it at low zenith before it could reach destination. Such a weapon was used as a flare of light to implode abandoned cities all at once crumbling buildings all at once and becoming sand; but this missile run had been launched at a city containing an airport. How much blood was on the Xray was of imminent concern, and the incident sparked an immediate search for the four students who had flown it tracking them through the impediments of towering peaks and a rapidly dust coagulated shrinking Aral Lake back to the Intercontinental Hotel in Uzbekistan's capital of Tashkent. The bad ones were really bad, was all any soldier had to say about the ring of fire at the summit. Although the desert countries of India, Iran and the newly mapped Iraq favored the device throughout time, there were the dominant countries of the Kazakhstan and China that perceived it as a severe threat to living societies and ruthlessly hunted down these sonar aptitude crazies. The newspapers of the day reported the incident in the southern province of Tajikistan at Tienneman Square involving four students. In addition news services made mincing commentary, "Morgue on Campus Unleashes Fanatic Attack," "Students Rally at Plodz," "Nationals Remove Train Cabin in the Aral," and "Counter Measures Taken," made it to the media in the Mediterranean and was instantly transmitted around the world. As vivid red and orange explosions mushroomed into gigantic booms of yellow light over the profoundly steep pinnacles of snow banked mountains, the resulting motion tore a series of desert towns into terrifying reverberating motion knocking residents onto the ground, severing limbs or destroying flesh and releasing bowels and vomit, electrifying water sources, severely dehydrating hundreds of people, dangling trains off rail tracks, causing temblor after temblor, shattering glass, toppling acres of trees, and cascading huge fields of mud and snow rushing down hills, crevices and city streets. The damage proved horrific. Within a week all routes to northern Iran and beyond were restricted, and a worldwide manhunt was begun.

The essential question was, who wanted him in San Juan. Ocean Bravo reported him for the year 1972 on an oil ship that planked in Haifa for which Israeli authorities tagged and bagged him, sent him to Cyprus and locked him up in a Turkish prison with only bread and water. There he faced beatings, was interrogated under illuminating light, choked and spatula printed until he bled before being released to the tower chapel on Malta. His sole visitor had been his wife from the isolated papal dominion of Cinque Terre.

Cinque had been released under an order to Canary Island at age sixty-six. Obviously at some point he had left and come across the ocean probably in a hold-barbotage ship, a free man. If he had waited out his sentence, it was a wasted matter. Morningstern had no doubt the man was capable of just about anything. He knew everything there was to know about artillery and guns. It would be a matter of time before he sprang from the lion's den to activity; these types had dismally poor recovery rates after having served convict time in locked dungeons. The Middle East forwent status reports after forty years believing as many proponents of prison wards did that inactivity signaled some sort of consensual rehabilitation. However the problems late in life were often worse. If he were traveling with his wife or planned to join her, his movements had to be scrutinized. There could be no casual negligence. His name could never be omitted from lists of wandering bands.

Morningstern looked for a vehicle pick-up from the emergency shelter and finding none searched along secondary lines for any activity. On the Intel he found Cinque at the Café Jardin at the pleasant cobble surroundings on the corner of Ruidoso and Front Streets across from the wharf stone wall of the harbor. Feed put his target leaving at half past ten on a balmy morning, sea breezes capitulating a light rustling wind, leaves flying about. Cinque left alone, turned up Ruidoso five blocks, climbed white washed stone stairs to Calle d'Jardin where there was a plethora of fifty or more aparto buildings each four storied, jogged two blocks to Guadalajar to a pretty pink three story building replete with wrought iron balustrades, Spanish red tile tejada roofs, painted dark blue and yellow shutters, every street and alley made of thick cobble, leafy fronds, a teatro several doors down beside a Mercado and a freshly painted tan hotel with white trim and tan tile entry. At the end of the calle stood the Operacion Ministerio, a peach colored fresco building with tinted windows, sandstone balconies on the second floor, a dozen tiny KIA cars parked in a plaza.

Morningstern grabbed a worn green corduroy jacket and flashy Monet tie of red, yellow, purple and blue flowers in bloom and a small spiral notepad and began his walk at the same café. He passed along Ruidoso rows of yellow apartos with green doors, sided by a row of seven blue apartos with tan doors, church size arched natural vintage sandalwood doors, a row of maroon apartos with pastel orange doors, up to Jardin along a creek with stepping stones and a jungle of lacy leafed trees and maple imposing low sweeping branches, almost out of breath by the moment he encountered the pink aparto building with its decorous slightly religious connotative structure. Behind the aparto high on the hill enmeshed with willow trees lay a square shaped cemetery, the word Navidad shining in light blue lights, with ornamental crypts with carved stone angels and iron gates, some rusted open. The setting resounded with Malta and Cinque Terre causing Morningstern to wince with hatred at the target's apparent good fortune, although who knew what flats were inside. As he entered and made his way up a broad stairwell carpeted in rose tweed, he had the distinct impression he had been in this very building when it was one of ten office buildings erected in the early fifties, once a handsome foreign office with connecting interiors on each floor. At the top he installed a thin bullet recording mechanism in a far wall, noting there were only four numbered doors. He tested a camera microphone and receiving a voice matching print decided his target resided at the end of the hall beside a glass door that led to a fire stairwell outside.

He retraced his steps down the hillside to his flat on the waterfront. When he had poured himself a bourbon and sliced a piece of meat pie, he sat to the Spartan task of honing in on the target. He focused in on a picture of the docking rail yard, the limited marina, steep downhill to the landing with the restaurant, the limited marina, residential streets, closing in on any car in the vicinity, then on the aparto itself, and on his door. Once he obtained voice, he followed with camera.

The flat was seedy, a modest two fifty a month, the ideal hideaway for an unscrupulous felon on the move. Cinque himself looked beaten down, a tired weather-hung old man, face and shoulders heavy with having out run a chase through continents and dust trails. His color was sallow, his black trousers suitable for another era, a yellow shirt hanging below his waist. Around him were the basics of a lifestyle, an oblong grey and white Formica kitchen table with two nondescript chairs; in the sitting room was a handsome dark red leather couch, two matching easy chairs, a low glass table with a pound of marijuana leaf and a beige plastic ashtray with a pipe, a lamp on the floor that gave some light, and a narrow bed in a corner below a wide window of sliding glass doors that led onto a balcony overlooking the cemetery. The cemetery on the hill was distinctly artistic and inside the bathroom which also had an entry onto the balcony Cinque had completed various sketches in color pencil of the crypts and neon sign. With this, Morningstern sent his message –

Target at high noon. All squares denote color. Photos to follow.

GUYANA

2

LEWIS RETRIEVED the messages off his recorder. On the first reply there were two distinct voices, pauses between them.

"I've been found. I need amnesty."

"How many are you?"

"Two."

"You will be delivered by boat to Florida Everglades. We have several dock houses."

"I took my papers off a dead man. My passport says Syria."

"We will make you a new passport and boat permit. You will be a counseling minister."

"Which religion?"

"Prayer."

On the next was a telescope-sent monotone voice.

"For the Tashkent incident a subsequent radar package was discharged. The missile was slow lead. It did not read over same flight path. Closest bathysphere recorded in as underwater reptilian of a troop disseminating ground fire. Situation tested after twenty-four hours. There was no evidence of the initial guided flight."

The event was going to be a tough nut to crack. Chances

were they'd end up swept into an ongoing chase so exhaustive it could take weeks to find a reliable tread. Lewis could very nearly predict the sort of exercises the team would be put to. Jet stream escapes usually occurred at night with a fairly silent motor. If dead of night was a preferred strategy, then he assumed they had plenty experience in fleeing. Even with a ditch course reading, if two men were dressed entirely in black, the images could show as dirty, indicating the likelihood of a condom sheathed lens which meant a weak link in the line of ocean patrol. By marine they would enter the Keys well before dawn and be granted passage giving them direct access to the gulf. Of course Intel was only as confident as the best toned listening posts and camera instrumentation. Cell phones and mirrors kept a lively sighting of activity for hotels, taxi, airports, docks, cars, bridge tolls, border crossings, ferries and fairgrounds, not to mention instantaneous captures when someone hauled out a high powered rifle capable of streaming or a weapon port.

From a transmission a first row of three photo scenes flagged his screen. In the initial clearance the photo showed Cinque, a sturdy well-fed male of six feet, tanned, dark black hair with a bluish tinge, dressed in tan yellowish pants and collared shirt beneath a sweater of many colored stripes, on a flat roof lying on his back holding a super charge magnetic steel rifle at the sky over Tabriz as police rushed up six flights of quasi marble staircases. In the immediately successive photo he sprung onto them holding a razor as they advanced into dense sunlight through the door and sliced their faces leaving them dead. The third photo took a leap into space with him in his descent.

A subsequent photo row of ten came from MARS. Cinque and two other males had abandoned the snow plowing train which had met its end of the route in a congestive wall of accumulated snow. The wanted men donned skis and

masks and wove down a slope through a forest skillfully jettisoning over pitched rock, leaning forward, wind chapping
the skin in tiny red veins numbing the senses, dropping down
escalades, maneuvering paths above caverns, racing against
speed itself. They flew off sheer rock face careening through
the air making expert landings, snow flying, sealing cliff lines
past a covered boat wedged on top of rock cliff rumored to
be the lost ark, snow frocked cumbersome branches at every
quarter kilometer, speeding through gateways of burdened
glacial pastures, skidding across ice and frozen ponds, taking
curves as they crested into the air, the bright sun appearing
as a zenith, the hours of daylight winding to a close, cruising
across endless plateaus of tree studded fields, the sky dazzling
with chunks of wind floating snow, dark hair appearing aged
by silver upon return downhill four hours later into Tashkent's
survivable soft snow hills above her country suburbs.

Lewis had enough images to pull every related file. The
computer hummed as a search for related activity positioned
rows of photos onto the screen. The start-up was slow, but in it
Cinque was flying third in the training chair as a test mission
pilot over peaks and valleys of surrounding desert mountains
of the Altai range, skimming across shrinking lakes packed
by salt, flying at wind speed, the cockpit rumbling with the
intensity of motion. He would fly twice before being admitted
into the alleged non-existent Iranian Army for practice sessions disarming live ammunition, but once admitted, he was
home free. As an army designee he could truck by caravan
large supplies of medical storage, complete scheduled transport of coal and iron ore, and walk strategic walkie-talkie
communications over the border into the undeclared zone
of Afghanistan. He had built their aircraft, flown flight missions, tested shells, crossed boundaries by air and by land.
Some Islamic lamb hothead gave Cinque a key and it was
long after the guided weapon blasted through the cockpit of a

commercial 727 they rescinded all privileges especially skiing. Why should he spend so much of his invaluable time going after this cheap toboggan? This fucking prick who turned on the heat and blew three towns away? How many times had he said – lock them up and throw away the key? They didn't deserve even a commentary.

And then the photos appeared one by one across his screens. A staging platform firing up a rocket, blue jacket, pinkish metal down to the base. A blue metallic rugby estimated a foot wide by fifteen feet shooting into space off a numbered library, its shell glowing, raising higher and higher to imperfect radiance. The China Monitoring Strategic Defense captured the man, an angelic blond, wavy hair, skinny, indexed to a Tibetan monk.

Lewis looked through the presented file for any connection to the "lamb." Only one sit-down dinner in a well-protected tent on a high peak, each seven leg males attired in billowing winter fly-silk material, heavily adorned in scarves of blue wool, brewed wine flowing from silver-gold chalices, lamb curry, Egyptian syrup and rum bread, stewed plums, purplish maroon fruit flesh split with stuffed cheese and pistachio, a celebration to commemorate arranged transport of missile flares.

The photos kept coming every four to five minutes until they lined four rows. All in all, four long range rampage style firing lasers had whipped from the Altai spinning into the upper stratosphere, all pinned onto four torpedo whirlwind capable land to air detonators. The last row inspired awe. China's superior satellites reduced downwind showing an oddly emblazoned atmosphere and rock strata. Finally, the photos darkened and deleted.

Lewis contacted Bermuda dateline at once requesting a review of the last telecast of photos. The analyst at the other end typed in, Waiting in blinking red. He waited sipping his coffee several times. After twenty minutes, he re-sent the message. What was taking so long? It seemed as though the computer had gotten stuck on some other unit's enormous job. He had time to walk across the plaza extending two blocks, stride across a lawn almost to the harbor wall, and retrieve the data off the mainframe himself. Who had time for so much bullshit down time? Even he organized his desk daily. Already he knew it was a mistake to ask for a budget photo-list retrievals analyst. Lloyd's Register of Shipping, trademark levies versus basic summaries for unendowed recessions, reformatory referendums for any of the Six Day Wars soldier rescue missions, parole pardons, National Council of Parishes, opinion polls or year-long incorporations, who was kidding whom? The more trying the task for pre-approvals of special funds became – the worse there were random list denials, however temporary. If aircraft surveillance, snow mobile permits, vehicle registration and combined Secure Borders, missing fugitive photo identification, gun secure file, and automated firearms didn't stay on top of the situation, then how was he to update his database? The data entry was stolidly stuck in a quagmire. He could count on two hands the entire shelf life for every investigation he had ever pursued based simply on notes scrawled into tiny spiral bound pads. He instantly reached for the lukewarm coffee and caught himself in the process telling himself he shouldn't drink so much coffee, one or two cups after his morning walk and again an hour before dinner. Since he had testified before dozens of subcommittees prior to becoming a division chief, he was apprised of actual wording of international law. It was an absolute no to shipping any weapon including guns of weapon strength, transport of high elevator lifting industrial cranes, and facilitating any transport on land including onto bases.

"Where are we?" Lewis asked Jones who was running late having just returned from boating patrol.

"I received two simulcast podcasts. One showed an embryonic fire on the ocean with garbage debris soaking into the coastline beaches so we know roundabout point of entry."

"Good. Try to shoot down some dead birds, any wildlife estuaries, try to get me a driver's picture."

"The second is, Danger Beach Closed, boat at platform alongside inland bay at cabin, nice moorings. There is a deep water ROV, scuttle crab paddle boat leaving onto the horizon, flocks of flamingos, floating islands, two thermos tanks indicating dives, a grounded barge with below deck netting choked by plants."

"We have a foreign declarant. Each has spent years on family night on the beach. If not one of them, it was someone's task to bring up the ark."

"These are modern boys who carry cell phone station mikes. "

"Definitely, whatever you think best; upload from camera phone or desk transmission. Once you isolate tide pattern, chalk in with city data, get your girl Nila to consult, then look for geology, marine, tycoon reports, maybe we'll get lucky and score in for black film."

"It must have been sent to high dimension to remove the blurs while you were tracking."

"Could have. See if you can decode direct links to West Germany, Japan or Taiwan."

"It's probably what sent them up the petrified desert to begin with, Jones said. 190 Nike for thirty VGA for skiers; then lighten light blue or tan with RAM, Anaconda, Caspian Sea if you can acquire or tidal wave, closest wave. I'll have to know – is the terrain camouflaged and is any live film of an air crash. "

Jones counted on one take only. He went in by aerial photographic recon, microdot bugs without entry, recording from space two hundred feet above surface, for photos made in the dark and tele-electronic taps without wires because they had their target isolated geo-physically in a boathouse. He measured on underwater Casio and emerging for the speeding boat put it on fast zoom until the lens posted on last viewed by time with showcasing gear lights on and depth inside boat. Then he sent his photo under surface to an underwater expert. In minutes he had his war grave.

Lewis felt wiped out.

Rhonda had his drink waiting, a bloodshot rum and tequila. She wore white sharkskin bikini that gave her breasts a seductive swell and matching tight seamless pants and black glittering backless heels. Her blond hair with tiny curls at the ends was jounced up on her head off her nape.

"We killed the Tashkent today," he said, and placed his hands on her narrow hips and kissed her once on the mouth and then gave her a hickey on the right neck, feeling that deep seated moment of arousal.

She asked, "Did the kill team give you your full hour on the screen?"

"Not by half. Damned prickly of them." He disengaged and picked up his drink and sipped it. "I could go for a romp tonight."

"I'd love to, Honey. It's been on my mind for days." She undid his tie and loosened his starchy shirt to the second button. "Life's been easy for this last year."

"You realize I love you as much as I do this life I work."

"Lewis, I count only on you," she murmured, and released the string at her back allowing her modestly full breasts to fall from their restraint. They rose off her rib cage with the perfection of enticement.

"Love me, dearest," he said, holding her closely awaiting her touch. "I've been running this last month, we haven't had much in the way of relaxation."

She ran her hands behind his back around his waist, pressing against him, releasing him, her gaze on his hypnotic look. "Did they nail the path?"

"All the way, with transistors. They ran the propeller into a slot canyon."

"Down by port?"

"Vessel towed in with a phone call. "

"Ship deck or jet blue?"

She was his woman, she'd never want anyone but him; every time he returned, she was fresh. She never allowed him to believe other men meant much. They were a chronology of many histories, she was his blue line in any azure water.

Rhonda pushed him into the bedroom, mouth on his, and whispered, "Pretend you don't know me."

The words he was about to say vanished in a second. He let himself be led, felt his pulse be invented, his temple coursed, he had not had relations in almost a half year, he was brimming, swimming in the anticipation of her sea, grateful for her, his emotion opening up to her, listening to himself think, take me, babe; as she removed his shirt, unbuckled his trousers, as she lay on the bed and coaxed him to her, he went to hell sinking into her clime.

I've been dead for a long time, he whispered, taking in her jasmine perfume.

"There's only you," she reaffirmed.

She moved on him and he felt he let go of his ambition, she was the port in the storm and he had returned home.

"I love you, Rhonda."

He awoke in the middle of the night. She lay on her back, hair sprawled over the pillow, her bare shoulders visible, sleeping peacefully. Nothing of their spent passion hinted at his surrender. They were just two long term married's who occupied each side of the bed, his side had his wristwatch, hers had the telephone and a glass of water half drunk. He slipped into his white terrycloth robe, turned on the hall light, softly closing the door and went downstairs for a cup of coffee and to check his computer.

The photo rows were in place like an advertiser. There was a slightly enlarged one of the target. He was as he looked on any system, in his late seventies if not older, having put on considerable weight around the jaw and neck, his expression as dead to living as Lewis often perceived himself to appear. The man's actual name showed in highlights, Roberto Morales aka Cinque Paraguas. He was shown pulling a stage fence rocket release usually used for single light triggered spotting missiles of range up to twenty kilometers at a hundred feet western hemisphere. It was apparent that the only residences in the Altai were predominantly monasteries of long duration. It was entirely presumed that Islam sent its more prized students to the high desert for either iconoclastic rigors of the flesh or sought to train them for media. Anyone who complained to God complained too loudly was the teaching of the Koran. Iranians viewed the world as a desert of weathering and far drifting sand which on occasion thundered as an immense dust cloud imposing great winds upon its populations as it summoned uprooted houses and buildings into imminent darkness accompanied by lightning and rain deluges. The population dressed in veils and layers of silk and gauze cloth-ing to endure the often seemingly combative wreckage. The veil saved the exposed parts of the body from the elements whether her living was discovered predominantly in her high speed, cost effective extensive train industry that left no town or even sole monastery without a train.

Lewis could see that the nebulae being formed on the

synchronistic computer described the target's planned destruction path as he had conceptualized it.

There were so many infractions to consider that it was impossible to see these activities as anything other than intent to strike with nuclear weapons – illegal entry across boundary, unauthorized weapon not a firearm, warrant out of province, possession of narcotics, prowler, disturbing the peace by peeking in windows, unlawful firearms, concealed weapon, possession of silencer, marine fatal accident, marine operating vessel warning, marine hazard, marine fraud, marine reckless operation, false report to the police and embezzlement of train and plow. The planning that went into the eventual firing off of rocket ammo-tumblers and ammo-inhibitors had to be exhaustive. Border ducks, spies with toggles, induction warrant petty officers, transportation officers, racket operatives, hazardous materials transportation, and lost property managers, a host of men on the take who entered compounds and handled the merchandize destined for ream-bud stations. At the moment the flare was launched and code-timed, all ranges assumed inter-star positioning. Even dirty operative astronomers who prepared meteor dispersing, how speedy, repetitious or slow for bombardment, the entrapment of clouds and rings of bursting chaos were computed instantly in seconds. The zillions of infinite atoms in one bursting alpha became comprised of infinity, immeasurable and phantasm. No matter the precautions the stokers took, there was simply no way they could hide once their acts became defined. In time one looked for vehicle theft, abandoned vehicle on public roads, hit and run, drunk and disorderly, possession of narcotics, false reports emergency leading to hospitalization, fire, police, false identification, and in general fleeing under suspicious circumstances. The earth kept every decibel of utterance. It translated each obtuse and converse note, each scattering cleft, each symphonic sheeting, each simultaneous aura in conjunction with minutest constant resonance pinpointing tracks of computer language and sources it spawned from. In the seconds the flagellum flew like a piston of dew emitting from a whirlwind of calibrations, each successive timbale registrant was grouped on the database in lines of calligraphic distributable consonants.

Who knew where these rabid monsters went to so as to regroup once comfort was re-assembled. The societal trades acceptable to a seasoned aging weapons pylon were few, but since ministerial counseling was the prescribed exaction, there were few cotangential activities which would be allowed, some gatherings with friends, possibly store bought paints for art renderings for sale, once or twice acting in a movie. The everglades held to the law of a no man's witness. The farther out one went, the closer to the setting sun one became until at last the sun appeared to dust the flat water surface. Filaments floating on the sea carried an offspring of clandestine sounds heard from a great distance refashioning in their febrile dissonances.

Had he to know before any of this got started that all pylon stokers were hand selected, he could believe it, but statistics proved otherwise. They were just lazy, disgruntled, and being jealous of men with financial capability they went about exercising their loins, flexing their inauguration talent, running college offices as teaching assistants, joining a mosque monastery and being inducted into the maniacal rigors of Islam, prior to being put in jail for disobedience and sentenced to isolation.

The Aral had its own exercises. As a sinewy treacherous rock edge twisting through the heights of the litho impenetrable devouring desert, cavernous caves disparagingly consuming direction, winds charging relentlessly down slate fractures of dizzying height, nomads who ventured into craters and underground pockets grew convinced that the only path to any summit was over deep layers of snow. For those who fell and came to die in a groove or who had smashed their bones, Allah was a god to be feared, holding onto something that lets go of you by suddenly becoming too light, a sinister presence that waited at the bottom of valleys after it carried men to agonizing death.

It was a chess game of great stakes. Those who played it lost their souls. Those who survived the lashes of dying believed themselves to be immortal, capable merely of mortal banishments.

Men of stealth, they were companions to death. The robbery of Mankind was its own aura of enlistment against a fear of mortality joined at its essence to combat. If they had intimacies these too were wizened to the impervious sense of loss of endurance and catapulted into space with the effrontery embellishment of assuming disguise, a carnivorous duty of excise, impaling release, a religiosity of tremulous possession of earthly wanderings. Nowhere did these men have the imagined beneficence of casual regard; once set upon the clawed spite of design, they were afoot with deigned insanities, coveted barometers of childless passages, irrevocable returns, probable prisoners of ice, floods, failings, and lurid fancies. Once again, the exhilaration of escape made realistic by improbable ski jumps reconnoitered the sheer pace through space as preparedness of flight. The shock of impending doom lured men without their senses to precipitous knowledge, less frightening than leaving mortality under a wind of drugged spinning, but for which an anticipation of the forevermore was a disquieting absence. Where were their commonplace upbringings except beneath a doormat of cannibalistic ritual observed at each patient household as an angel of mercy that plucked a newborn from the fates of premature birth and malnutrition? The exposure to chronic fatality buried the predestination of a nation's embryonic entrance epitomizing to its chaste chronicles that men who went adrift of their footsteps had no wings.

○ ○ ○

The entrance to the everglades conjured a low water wetland forest which began west above the suburb of Constantinople on the gulf. The passage was at once a giant waterway and river that wound through grassy meadows with shapely trees, some which came quite close on either side and stretched in irregular shapes clinging to an under soil of pipeline tree roots, petrified bark, angelic moss, nitrogenous top soil cover consisting of cloying androgynous fir, deer fern, micro algaecide hedges, tiny water shoots, crocus, bastion immature weed growth and fertilization. Into a hegemony of dense overhanging moss-laden trees the muddy river snaked into fertile rich islands barely twenty feet off the water surface through an eventual two hundred island shore formations as far as fifty miles south and east. Along the main tributary beneath stultifying dim sunlight, often pale yellow in its seamy indulgence, fourteen miles of habitations and farms, forty in all, stood at the end of half block long docks, wood plank recently rebuilt to spare its porches and pilings from stymied rot due predominantly to alligator and fish teeth and longtime endurance of water creating welts immediately above the wasting water. The canoe that took Morningstern's partner Levitimar beneath dappled shade along knife hung roots just rising above the fill had periodically brushed against piers all morning and early afternoon defying entanglements, extremely shallow creviced dowries, and Portobello inlets overrun with hardening oil can rust. Boughs of hydrangea condensed by Mortimer's lung staved off a ruinous effect of midday rains and carbuncled roofs brought upon by mist-proving soupy fog in winter and relegated life-choking damp in summer. The one bedroom designation sat in dank waters contaminated by floor raising sediment that gave off a barely surviving expedience of ongoing hardship. Rancor and lust were bridled to the windows which betrayed a greenish film not unlike the early stages of frostbite. Although its newest inhabitant had been given to understand he'd be joined by his wife, the age of the cabin would not permit more than one, all food dropped off weekly onto the dock.

John Levitimar worked the gulf and knew everything one could know about towns, waterways, shoreline industry, farms, boat harbor markets, jacket marsh hunting, penury, and rifle dish property. He was in his late sixties, a white man, dark red brown hair, green eyes, muscled, somewhat nondescript despite skilled aviary fence building, creek lassoing, vegetable and fruit tree harnesses and rooftop leverage to prevent buckling of walls, all which should have caused him to be noticed often but in any regard caused him great introspection to the point of tuning people out.

Chartreuse Amelia, wintering pistachio of tiny clusters pink flowers, and luster bluish crimson magnolia studded the river banks in the harshest of conditions of a claustrophobia of crab clawing nitrous oxide, often non-rooting, tumbling passion weed.

Small tin senders below the house would prevent destabilization in turbulence. Forked netting on all sides kept the property from slipping into the river. At daybreak five motorboats steadied downstream, and at half past three in the afternoon the alligator paddleboats set out. Because there was no real vantage point to see the entire display of islands, the convention of lifestyle quickly took on mediocre standards of complaint.

Cinque was delivered in the heat of day by border patrol.

"What do you think about where the agency is at for the Commonwealth Club of Cuba?" she asked.

What should have been averted, credentials of inspectors, ocean time, flying hours, marine curfew and so on."

"Who spoke in the briefing room?"

"Samuels, he's the trade market whiz, it was unusually productive. We have all those float-dock contracts on Old, lost boats, bad names, stolen identities. The bureau is refining its search and determinations to the half day which will mean more arrests. There was discussion about interviews, dock stand-bys, housing requirements. You know how much I despise meetings. I'd rather take a toddy and roast beef on the green."

"Where is Hoyt in this?"

"He'll probably do the next inquiry. Now that he's passed the Board Analysis of Legal Review and the language requirement for six foreign languages, he's been drafted for grand summons."

"How's he taking it, what with no longer working investigations through?"

"I think he enjoys it, he certainly has acquired a stiffer lip."

"Jones?"

"Very busy. I gave him the sweeping task of finding a target on the maps. He's been a nice chap about it so far but I've been considering breaking off a piece of profiling for him."

"My guess is he has no interest in assignment delegation."

"He's been consistent to that agreement, but you never can say. I've had agents who first chance off the op list managed a section themselves. You remember Bickle."

"From Malan, new series row archives. He was excellent."

"Who guessed? None but Photo Landstar Kester thought he had it in him."

"Jones is not you. He'll never say so but he enjoys being in the cabin. Don't put him on the bridge either."

Lewis laughed, easing up a bit. "Someday he'll wander off."

"Then wait until it happens. Don't encourage him. He's happy where he is." She had poured herself a gin tonic and sipped it. "Is your target illusive?"

"He's been in the past. He was released off Canary before anyone thought he ought to have."

"That's a brutal incarceration. Men there enter the hospital weak from consumption."

"It didn't go down right. In my estimation they should've kept him or allowed him into French Quarter at Moen. He'd be prepared for life on the Outside."

"Got'cha," she said playfully.

"Indeed you do. Did you spike my drink?"

She smiled. He had her and he had his affairs. "I thought I should. You don't mind, do you?"

He closed his eyes, hugging her by an arm around her waist. "Maybe you should sweeten the deal."

"I can. Anything you'd like. Remember, I'm always here for you." She removed his tie, loosened his collar, and pressed a hand across his tight chest offering her nicely symmetrical swelling breasts against his face.

The reality was, if he didn't produce much in the way of effort it was because they had an understanding as to what worked if only as a result of what rose passion fast, he certainly didn't want her to feel he wasn't attentive, and he allowed himself to become undone, feeling the pleasant inebriation send successive jolts of pleasure. After forty years of marriage, through love and boredom, it was early in the relationship he matched her giving with his, par for par, until the job consumed him. In those days immediately after the Tahiti disaster, the job had not yet overtaken his time like an insatiable mistress. He was still a relatively young agent in his late thirties working for a gigantic structure taken up with ship fleet problems due to massive world travel. Definitely when he broke away from his seventy hour a week crisis schedule and came home, he was aware of her dressed in tights and a cashmere pink sweater curled up on the ottoman reading a good book, usually a Forrester. His nature was to go for a two hour walk with her after work before dinner, strolling on the green to the beach for about ten miles of sand. Early dinner on the patio, retiring to the den with a cognac, some evenings stepping out on the town to take in a concert or opera, the first seven years were close, spent in synchronicity, affectionate, filled with soaring fulfillment, no weekend taken apart, any absence too great a sacrifice. Unlike his friends whose divorces occurred as a result of an affair and who drank too much, or who traveled so extensively they were absent ten months at a time, or who didn't want child support and alimony to eat up their paycheck, they had weathered the job by talking about their investigations every task of the way. He came home because that's where the support was. She was the one who accepted him, she did not complain, she could not live without him.

"Honey," he said, and swept her into a fevered embrace kissing her over her face and neck, aware that whatever worked between them still was in their favor.

She placed his hand on her thigh and let his hand caress her interior flesh, her perfume aroused his senses, inflamed his sense of need of possession of her. He could have her and an hour later feel he had not really captured her in any complete historical meaning and feel in their physical separating he was cut adrift, hunger a continual burden of ownership. Were he to tell himself he had become dependent on her physical presence, he would also be reactive toward her whenever he felt his need was unable to be quenched. The strong emotion made for no logical comprehension, if because she held nothing back, she gave openly, she was not any longer mysterious although her fix on him was a compelling mystery. He needed her, his awareness was raw, he knew he had to dominate her, he was both jealous and craving, he undressed her admiring her body for its control over him, he acknowledged that even in the act of making love, of the reality he possessed her, that she was given to no man other than he, that as soon as he was spent in the act of love, he would experience a momentary fleeting urgency of keeping her cloven to his very utter being of existence. He was unable to separate, she was locked into him – he knew that because she told him that often.

He moved both hands between her legs, and extracted a full longing kiss, telling himself this was love, his world of love, only he lived in her, it was a fateful delirious throttle. "Honey," he said again, and kissed her more longingly than he had, holding her by the thighs, as she lowered his face to her collarbone and slipped against him. He breathed her, knelt with her in his arms to the carpet, slid on her and proceeded to memorize every part of her with each kiss.

In living there were often staff who just handed him over. For the instances he became aware of these petty inactions he felt he was exposed, capitalized upon, made known for a response he wished to remain entirely private. There was the heady jigger of men who traipsed underwater to look for sus- pected arsenals and their counterparts of known crooks. These men went chasing dreams of riches to Guyana to seek cor- ruption and instead found a beautiful tan female whose eyes sparked and whose slender bodies knew long of the intimacies of seduction. In the belief he should always be seen in public with a female at his side, despite the several separations he had from Rhonda, he was first and foremost hers. The lasting catalyst between them in the end often saved him from a bed- room existence of debaucheries. The way of all flesh kept him on course without any demeaning exploit that he in some way caused her debasement. He did not intend there to be slights. There had to be a way to survive life's annoyances, cagey bel- ligerence, and the tiring accommodations that came and went with querulous irritation. He had survived and so had she.

The camera gave Jones the first reality.

Sundown complicated their problems. The Puerto Rican government released sixty Haitian resident farmers in tiny canoe boats onto the jet stream, all rowing to the Keys. From an aerial the surface of ocean became crowded by a score of narrow wooden floats. Following one hurricane disaster in 1988 the islands released normal inhabitants it could not shelter for an estimated year with the permission of the state of Florida. This would be the second time.

The calm day turned into a heavy darkness which showed an abundance of tiny lights oaring north.

Immediately he put a position on the target.

Border that picked up surveillance by high speed Casio was delayed by ten hours.

The recent photos showed the target fishing on the dock of his new home. He was a cool customer enjoying the solitude of a balmy morning.

Sunlight came at a price of a seemingly liquid green cultivation that hung like veils of moss from flexible swamp trees and solid elms and filtered to the depths of the knee-deep river where twisted roots rested like thin trunks readying a table of jungle convenience. Here the answers from dozens of database searches literally wove a mat as slippery as the thin mantel of grass and celibate weeds formed over the widest parts of rivers.

Lisbon had detained him once at an all too young age and transferred him back to the snow laden mountain range of the Altai into a stark clandestine wilderness where below ten blizzards hollered over bilious carved desert. There had been devastating prison sentences enforced within castles that lay deep in ravines on sinewy ledges with hollowly silent altitudes and hopeless glimmers. Until he plowed a rocket across the Mediterranean there was no conceptualization he was embarked on a coordinate of war.

The target wasn't the type to sit there and wait it out.

Here in the everglades he would sit. The plan was that monthly he would talk to old men at Prayer. People sometimes had a change of headstrong reconstitution. They realized life's questions could take a different course. The river flowed south but there were countless waterways and equally as many directions. There was no need to arrive at a planned destination.

The subsequent photos showed an empty cabin. Perhaps he had wandered off.

A photo showed an empty bed. He hadn't slept through the night. He had stayed in the designated cabin all of a day just prior to disappearing. Now he was nowhere known.

No vehicle had arrived for him.

Boats were another matter. Jones put out a search for any canoe. On the surface of the extensive island waterway there were no canoes. The dark blue waters were placid, uneventful. The island formations appeared to offer any number of reliable hiding places, mud there the same color as a canoe, dense grass and camel-bending trees, grooved inlets made by previously landed boats, thick growing banks that might obscure a canoe stopping beside it. He tracked the place by section within a narrow strip of coordinates. Every protrusion, overhang of vegetation, docks, park picnic areas, hiking trails, each river arm, each narrowing waterway, he spent four hours meticulously studying the surface.

The Tibetan came up on screen without a prompt. It seemed odd he was in the other file. To the thinking of the analyst who prepared the file, there had to be a connection.

He was believed to be named Shabbat.

He was last seen in western Lebanon in a small town assigned as a detrimental zone walking through steaming cement and bombed out buildings with a Beretta armored firing torpedo weapon slung across his back. He rolled out a wired mine and it exploded closing off a street.

Several other photos with descriptions came up. One was a female presumed to be Paki. She had made all arrangements for the ark denizen of missile chargers. She had long reddish brown hair, was unusually thin, wore single strap shoes, was a wanted felon in at least half a dozen countries on the border of Iran, had attended the University of Jordan, saddled bare.

Her brother was a self professed Islamic ha'maladin known to both Tibet and Uzbekistan. In nighttime photos he operated a duster snow plow which he drove down any accessible slope. Like her, he had reddish brown hair, worn short, was also very thin, trained for a private war, and was believed to test aperture strength. He was seen in summer scaling summit trenches.

His wife, the other female, was Tibetan, a wisp of a female, under aged when she fired her first thunder ray, a bit of a grey blonde with wavy hair which she tied up.

It was her alleged cousin who purchased the solar rays.

In spite of the fact the group was identified, they had been presumed to travel as a group, when it was probable they did not.

Each separate identification arrived from UPI international wire requesting vehicle registration, hotel or address, job or activity, and participation in religious prayer.

A search determined they met in a small prison in an undeclared territory of Bhu'. Prisons were unfortunately a world unto themselves where families mingled in a large hall for visitation. It was prison life that borrowed on an idea of radicalizing hatred.

There was a sixth man. The log of photos revealed him to be likely a marketplace seller of bibles written in Arabic. Silver haired blond, short in stature, he frequented Bhu' and Nepal on sojourns, bringing with him people interested in buying wars for the purpose of invading abandoned towns. There were no known glacial deserts that would have welcomed such a bombardment.

Jones was looking for a person who was interested in bringing the group out west.

The real question was, what act would require all of them at the same time?

According to the rating board the answer lay in the U.S. in the state of Idaho in the Salmon Islands along the eastern section.

Jones placed a computer call to state park dateline, asked for a command.

The female who responded on the visor looked tall, wavy dark hair, regiment military, maybe late fifties who gave her name.

She said the area was closed for years as a result of hard desert erosion consisting of spraying dust causing water to evaporate. She gave a visual off a map. Large yellow and red rock melded together to form extensive conglomerate uninhabitable desert for a hundred miles.

"As you can see there's nothing there. The mountains no longer sustain life including sparse visitation."

"Can you think of any reason why a gang of winged evangelists would rendezvous in that general area?"

"Money. Maybe a contact stashed their pay up there."

"Long journey from Tibet. Who do you have up there?"

"Some child murderers. Dustbin is one. You may not have heard of him. He took an underage lady for a ride in his jalopy and before he took her home he shot her."

"Is it capable?"

"I don't see how, it's above the snow line."

They enlisted all dateline bureaus to patrol the national parks, rivers, camp grounds, tiny motels, and bed and breakfasts with a complete physical description.

JONES

1

BOOK ONE

THE NIGHT made its first wayward ram strung to a swinging light bulb in the dark. It cast shadows at the ocher mansion walls that made both long and tall oddly bent apparitions as though at a Lewes-Gannon ghost walk which sometimes projected spiteful figures in the trees overhead. Along the river on both embankments the air prolonged a dry summer heat in layered fog onto irrigated rows of full-sprouted spinach making for a dark green sea at the apex of the Fresno Mountains. Beige hills stood threadbare beneath a extensive sky fixated to ephemeral shadows silently stirring. Flaxen wheat rippled in slightly misted moonlight ridden by the train's lonesome call. From somewhere on high out of rock canyon an errant coyote howled sending shivers to anyone listening.

The mist sighed like a haunted confession. I'm obsessed with you. You are so handsome it's hard to take my gaze off you. To which Jones at age eighty-one, keeping pace with the silence of the love-spent afternoon with this older girl, had replied, Love is timeless. Slow easy winds gave him a rare winsome amusement wherein he recollected thinking he was running to stay on course; where would the thousand snow scatterings leave her by mid-life? From a distance sand resembled snow at dusk; dozens of vehicle lights glinted up the steep highway into a chore of mountains pressed one onto another. Romance drifted on a low breeze sailing to the river where phosphorous salt mounds piled up covering the valley floor cracked in a myriad hexagonal shapes, imprints left by the unkindness of chill. Life had been spent abruptly despite a cautious and fortuitous commingling of pacing himself to the arduous tasks of a hard-lived career and a healthy life savings; this after retiring to the Whiskey Flat cabins at the edge of the pink sagebrush desert on the dusty plateaus leading to a handful of canyon oases. While the body was often satiated, for his attraction to Bess was all-consuming, he lived for the seasons of this desert, its herbaceous willows, the painted hills, wandering gusts of water-driven winds, the silver-white moon landscapes that dominated night, unusual sun-cracked, scarcely inhabitable soil. Jones regarded himself as a philosopher acquired of reticent under-nourished salvations following a treacherous rugged sea of bristle brush into an unpredictable scarcity, ready for retirement having finally said his goodbyes to a devouring ocean and twenty mid-Atlantic islands. Post work would contain none of certainty or amenities of the sea-faring investigator that capably had filled fifty interminably long years. He had come to an era in which he sought only to sit with a good book and await his aging years in a place where at dawn the ridge bathed in oranges and lean grey shadows and tall hoodoo spires until lit by the sun. Love's delirium was like an ease that came after a plate of rye toast and Brie or olive paste; who needed more? Fulfillment was a mythic state of being in love, arrived of having discovered in himself an ability to remain contented with prior successes, to put aside a desire to achieve, to live for the sake of living. Nothing compared with personal freedom, one's own decisions chosen independently, sporadically.

I love you, I love you. Words as soft as emerging sunlight awakened him. Briefly for the instant he felt a slight stirring of impatience, as though even to share his existence with another person was itself too great a burden, he gave into her sensing as he often did that she too wanted almost nothing and encircled her in passion surprising himself that love could cause any interest at all. He was aware of the push-pull between wanting to be alone and of feeling enraptured, of wanting not to explain any part of himself, of finding life had already taken most all his energy, so much so that he thought he could readily abandon her; but as often as he thought it, he also knew he had come home to her and instead had given up his instinct about work. He thought of himself he was an agreeable sort of man, able to fit in, actually wanting to possess her the way one does marriage. He had left marriage long ago and found he liked his solitary life. There was no one to seek permission for going anywhere; he had been able to come and go as he pleased. But he thrived upon all time spent with her. He loved her, did not want to lose her, and so by degrees he learned to make peace with the restlessness.

The anxiety took him into town. Jones wanted to see who was about.

He played four rounds of poker against the computer.

The game board let him win.

He thought he saw the van through the window. He grabbed his coat. He opened the door. The sun was shining and it was freezing.

It wasn't his van.

He had heard the restaurant hired in a new chef.

He thought the man was guilty of shocking crimes. He had heard rumors, the man had killed someone once and had put in hard time.

Should he wait inside?

The time isn't here yet. No one has forgotten. They'll be

along. Things happen. Maybe they started late.

The air was thick with hazy heat but with an after bite of chill. The van was often late. Not always. Depended on whether the driver stopped in for coffee at five on the way through a night blizzard to the airport.

The van pulled up skidding to the curb.

I thought you forgot.

Wouldn't. Do you know Mo'neeeka?

Never heard of her.

She bought a house.

Is it far?

Right over the hill there.

Slow down. Is that the church?

That's not it. Don't worry; I haven't missed a stop yet in sixty years.

It was better to stay indoors, never eat or attend social hall. He did it for the relationship. Bess said he'd feel better, see people, do him good to get out. Lethargy was its own detriment.

What are you going to do?

Visit Tom. Wheel him into the sun. Do you want to join me?

It was the last thing he wanted. He'd like to seem inconspicuous to browse the shops of Joshua Tree.

The mountains were overcast a dull pinkish tinge. The sky looked to have evaporated. The van let him off in front of the library and bookstore where he picked up a novel on reserve before he went for a bowl of wanton soup at the Cantonese kitchen.

How's retirement, a woman who worked customs in Saba asked from a booth across the linoleum floor beneath a string of red chili Christmas lights.

It's easy-going, can't complain. How're you and Lester?

Oh, I thought you knew. He passed last spring.

No, I didn't. I'm very sorry for your loss. He had forgotten her name.

Yes, it's been difficult. My daughter moved in with me.

What's your girl's name?

Martha.

Now he remembered her, Edna. She had married her high school sweetheart. Those are long years, Edna. You two were high school.

A ray of hope emanated. Last year. He wasn't yet seventy-nine.

I'm awfully sorry. Jones remembered Edna and Lester had buried a son overseas in the Bangladesh affair. I seem to recollect you two were living in the islands.

Oh, that was years ago. We moved around the time you went to No Polo.

That long ago?

Yes, it's more than sixteen years now.

Drop in sometime. Bess and I are out on a ranch up near the base.

I rarely get about.

The van goes up to our door.

I could. Martha still drives.

You're luckier than we are. Bess stopped seven years ago.

It makes one nuts, the van. Your time is not really your own.

Know just what you mean.

She got up to go. Try the beef broccoli. It's quite good.

Thanks. The soup about does it.

He watched her leave. Lester had been the best mast light anyone had ever seen. A kick above any beam pole for a grand ship with twelve decks.

Life ebbed and flowed. It was always a heart ache to catch up to a mate years after the fleet put in for re-saddle on a new ocean.

It had been hard anyways. Leaving the service felt damn near inconsequential with nothing to do. He wasn't ready. He tried to be happy about it. Without deadlines, assignments or analytic investigations, he slept days at a stretch. There was no such reality as being depressed. He was told by a top notch physician that the adjustment took at least six years.

And it had. Right to the month.

For the first several years he was ecstatic. He hiked everywhere, backpack and roll, often in light snow, 29 Palms, Yucca, the base, Blue Water, Flagstaff, Sedona, Jerome, Grand Canyon. Took photos.

Then it struck him. No schedule, no commitments.

He traveled to Salton Sea each spring to hire a float to gaze at the blue effervescent sky.

There he encountered Bess who managed her own bed and breakfast. It was hiking love. Familiarity.

She kept a five year calendar by the door and crossed off each day lived. She hung a clock in the kitchen. She had a mud room for the rain gear and fair weather jackets. She cooked cereal in a crock pot each morning by eight and a pot of coffee.

He trudged down the road from the library to the spa and checked in for a bath. The staff took him straight away to a private heated tub. The water was restive on his bones. He closed his eyes cautious not to doze. The years fell away as though he was much younger. When he returned home, he would write the base about his cases still in progress. The Army would send a cheery note and say he was missed. The tub invigorated him. Invariably he showered, lay on the cot until the front desk rang him; then he dressed, combed his hair and took the stairs to a lounge where he had herbal tea until the van arrived.

The ride home along the Salton Sea shore was a solitary, thought provoking trip. Seeing Edna brought memories. Her son was shot down during a night mission. Lester applied for ship fare. Jones seldom saw him afterward but when he did, Lester looked haunted by age, never again to be the same loose kilter.

That was Life. Jones was thankful misfortune had not bled him. When he experienced moderate sullenness for a half year, it came because he felt tired as well as having too much time to sit around. He borrowed on the unruly language of the older men at the club; everything was a fucking shit ass waste of breath.

The sky looked full of rain. It hovered slightly above the ground. By night the wind might bring snow.

The day was taken up with nuisance undertakings. Strewn about the pasture lay driftwood, leafy piles, the snow had inveighed itself onto the roof and pinnacles of ice hung in thick daggers.

"Been on an outing, eh?" his pesky neighbor inquired. Lark Meismer had the look of a slicked down brunette baby boy. He wore a red and yellow flannel plaid shirt and dark brown trousers, boots, good solid work gloves.

Jones grunted to unkind thoughts. That one had a bit of the annoyance. He went in the house. Bess wasn't back yet. He poured a cup of coffee.

Sensitive to the fact that he often criticized the man, Jones cooled his heels to make every effort in his own character not to find fault.

He went back outdoors. "Got sort of windy, didn't it?"

"Like a cyclone hit the ground running."

"You don't say. Don't see much of that."

"Not these days. Storm took my shed apart."

It looked okay to Jones. "It sure left a mess to clean up."

That was that. He'd done his good deed for the day. He'd leave the after-storm chore to Bess, take a nap.

He'd had a productive day. Had risen as usual at five. Sat in

the sun room to watch the sun come up. It flooded in bright-
ness over the pasture negating shadows and silvery bare trees.
Bess awoke at six, did her routine, prepared coffee, threw a
wash in, made the bed, vacuumed; unloaded the dishwasher.

The trips into town were usually productive for a half day.

He sat in the blue upholstered easy chair and began reading his novel The Stone Angel from the library about despera-
tion. He fell asleep during the first chapter.

By the time he awoke, night had come. Bess was watching
the news. She had had her black hair coiffed and looked modern despite sturdy white Levi pants and blue denim jacket.
She blew him a kiss.

"I took a call for you earlier."

"Who from?"

"Bob Medowes at the postal office."

"How's Bob?"

"He's fine. An unknown placed a rack inside a mail box."

"What was in it?"

"A series of minted dollars left inside a drawer, four hundred coins, badly tarnished by chemical."

"What did he think?"

"Stolen, penny express, maybe forty years ago. He wanted
you to give your opinion."

"Sure, I could. When's a fair time?"

"Anytime is alright. Whenever suits you. He left his
number."

It had been nine years since Jones talked to the postmaster. Nine years before that the new glass office was built. Jones
didn't know what he could contribute, if anything. There had
been that big scandal at Inyo in the early Sixties after the
Mono gold mine dried up when fifty drawers worth of coin
disappeared. The Intel recorded the arrival of a Gold Cache
Creek van, three vaults empty, lights flickered and doused off
leaving no illumination; that crime was committed during

work hours, no one did not work, no one's hours were unaccounted for, but the ten bags were never delivered.

He called, but no one answered. It was probably the post telephone. He'd call first thing in the morning.

It was midnight before he fell asleep. Rest came in fitful pieces as he lay close to Bess cautious not to awaken her trying to fetch for any idea about another larceny. Bright moonlight shone through the opened drapes across the floorboards highlighting the chairs in front of the hearth.

The question had to be when the rack was stolen.

Jones knew the mint section bin well having gone there half a dozen times. The individual rooms were surrounded by windows like an older wharf warehouse. There were crates everywhere stacked from floor to ceiling in long rows where periodically the floors flooded. Each marker was cast in die proof, secured by hammer spring, sealed, taped and verified by spectrum lighting. All rooms gated without air if the racks were removed without authorization. It was no easy matter to walk off with a bin worth.

So, what happened?

He fell asleep uneasily hoping there was a typical answer. There was a fly in the Glade Room indicating a disclosed passage to a lunchroom courtyard. The fly unit leaked heat. A transport driver in haste left a van idling while he closed an outside door. Something.

In the wee hours of predawn, Bob called.

Bob was forthright. He had just a quickie.

No matter how Bob rolled the die he couldn't get a picture that made much sense. The photos showed nine regular fulltime staff had arrived to work for eight hours, during the day they counted the coin racks, prepared the ledgers, met with the accountants; bagged the outgoing shipment. The entry accountants arrived to the post office first. No deposit from vault was ever brought; only the loaded dish. When the transport van for the load was finally apprehended, not any person matched for prints.

Disappointing that the case proved so chintzy, Jones said, but in all likelihood the robbers had to be family relations. Assuming every last photo had been looked at there was nothing else to come up with.

"Can I write you in as a consultant?" Bob inquired.

"Oh, sure, I just doubt I can offer much in the way of expertise."

"I'll have the lab send you the finding."

"I'd certainly give it my consideration."

"That would be swell, Jones. The authorities we deal with get to make all determinations as to who produced the four hundred tray. I can't; isn't my responsibility either."

"That's fine, Bob. Give me a holler if you need me."

Even Bess was impressed.

A check for two hundred grand along with the evidence report came by post. The question read, what time of day by date?

Jones wiped the sweat off his brow.

Not one of these. He'd be lucky if he lived. These check amounts came with the worst cases in the world. The moment he opened a file hoodlums would line up in their cars. The sad fact was the shadows of wanted mint thieves cast long invocations from any den, no matter how dry resources like food and water diminished.

The lab determined the dollar coins to be comprised of silver garnished in bronze, each weighing ½ thin part.

Fingerprints on surface of coin identified beneath chemical.

Most coin was covered by adhering substances, two, designated by silver nitrate test as:

Blue mud, bluish clay small fragments of substance which

was rubber; possible hostage debris, accompanied by Yellow Tar, a light yellow clear substance which was probably carried in a test tube injector. There could be no water; water ignited.

The substances together could blow a seam of cement from the base of a wall, but there were plenty of normal reasons to store the soft material at a site, the obvious being that each chemical matter was laid in tanks later to hold stamp suppression for the face of the coin.

If an explosive was used, the individual was already deaf. Hearing loss was instantaneous. This bomb was a short notice bomb, although it took over a hundred hours to put together. It had no usage time on it.

Jones made a quick list of what he required to begin.

Time-in, time-out cards by name and thumb print.

Special shoes by size and respective prints.

Face in first row of mirrors.

Vehicles they arrived to work.

He walked three blocks to his bank. The air was freezing. Popcorn ice had fallen over the streets.

The branch manager, a beady eyed man of short stature, Caucasian-bound, part Arabic, smiled as though he had anticipated this moment years beforehand.

Upon the return Jones eyed the cars in traffic warily. He thought over his small list. For every heist the primary thing to delete was date and time. He could think of no other commensurate item to establish who had been inside the station during the heist.

He didn't have to chase Bess out of the house. She had left him a note saying she had gone to her aunt for a few days.

Since observation was his best suit he'd request only tapes before he decided on a necessity for photographs. Single photos worked for dead files. For all he knew the crime had gone off because there were cause and in-situ shadows. No one who reviewed daily tapes knew what he looked at. Bodies seemed to be the color of wood surfaces.

Despite a dismal possibility that photos were muddled, he made a basic assumption – the people who were supposed to be there were there and the people who may have taken the coin rack were not at the station.

He pulled the blinds when he entered the house to ward off computers. He listed his transmission on fly status; if a prying neighbor could actually see onto his screen, they couldn't take it with them. Likewise if they attempted to steno the screen, and there were many cheap spectators who took shorthand at a hundred words, they couldn't data enter onto their own system. He knew that was the best he could do.

When he contacted the Bremerton Isle bureau, he requested camera tape only for Rock Station, administrative sequence by any date during which three front row vaults were emptied. He received ten releases. Each transport came with face in the mirror and print match, shoe photos and vehicles driven into an underground parking lot. Jones processed them by last name, one at a time, single file. After an intensive hour, he verified all employees. They each checked for morning arrivals and nightly departures. Schedules checked for transportation to and from nearby stations.

He added another concern to his list.

Supplies.

And then, mishaps with supplies.

As usual he looked for an indicator of missing angles. Had other stations failed to receive camera footage once it was taped? There didn't appear to be splices, but one couldn't be too sure.

Jones spent the better part of the late afternoon studying wood surfaces trying to identify distinctions. He overlaid a tinted screen on each reddish brown wall. First he diminished dim visibility by adjusting light infiltration, focused onto large squares and diminished them until he produced recognizable images; nothing recorded in black and white. Next he scanned the room, then he searched for rack identifiers and discovering a stack of crated coin trays found one overturned container of bluing. The flying dark blue liquid had splashed on coins, on the walls, ceiling; floors.

Since blue mud was a corrosive used in manufacture with a cost to life of twenty-nine years simply to touch any surface it fell onto, it was entirely adaptable an irate employee spilled the ingredient to prevent forfeiture.

His guess was the room ought to have emptied in a minute. Skin contact resulted in dissolved bone. An unlucky individual was as good as destroyed. However, his guess was they loaded the trays up fast in several vans.

There were other sticky substances in squandered amounts on the coin, probably yellow tar. He captured as many individual scars onto separate files labeling each file.

He went to pour a cup of coffee feeling rewarded by his find. As a result of these chemical distributions, they probably spent an hour pulling off the heist.

He had to prove the day and time, and then he was done.

This was a ludicrous problem; for all he knew he possessed the final tape before the trays were removed and the job had occurred fifty years ago.

JONES

2

THE MINT discontinued its production of the centennial silver bronze dollar with dime face that resembled a Norwegian half dollar, each worth $1.78, in 1953. The authorized amount of the limited run was for five million.

His first instinct was to look for a transaction with Norway permitting about a million stolen to have bought roughly ten houses, but after searching Statistics for the buying of trade and finding none, he turned to the crime itself. It seemed to be a worthless crime with a worthless purpose.

A theft of seven Nether armored vans, each several thousand dollars take, would have generated a promised finder's fee of twenty thousand, which as it was, never paid out.

No crate to Rock station arrived labeled by date.

The container of bluing also tamper proof showed no date on it.

Jones returned to the underground parking lot. No vehicle entered by ticket had date or time.

For all anyone knew, these employees worked in a departure zone of a warehouse district.

He searched the tape again, this time checking every

surface for a calendar, food from the outside, clothing manufacture, jewelry on each employee, anything that might reveal date, but there was none.

He checked the final date the vault located on 29 Palms Highway received coin transported from the station before it was shut down and re-opened as a Mexican restaurant. It was September 5, 1982.

He had to assume the heist occurred anytime after the final distribution. Jones had the names and respective fingerprints for the employees. He took each print for a match to houses in order to place their recent daily whereabouts. They cross corresponded to homes in the high desert.

A female also worked weekend night shift at the Desert Valley Hospital; her husband volunteered at Lone Tree salt mine base during off hours.

A non employee husband of the only other female, she an accountant in charge of circulation of coin, who worked for the small Joshua Tree airport lived in a modern two bedroom house directly across the road.

Two of six adult male employees resided at the trail head of Joshua Tree National Monument Park in a two bedroom house with living room and deck amidst desert saguaro cacti, disjointed Joshua trees, and boulders and had a view of the star studded sky and the pebble adorned foothills.

A male who tested dissension of coin through coin separators who delivered to five casinos down Highway 62 to Palm Springs and Indio had recently relocated from Bishop to Yucca to a sprawling tan wood and blue glass house a walk from the base.

One male resided at the top of a steep driveway on a cliff overlooking the blue sage and tumbleweed desert set against dark bluish granite mountains sixteen miles from the station in a tiny one bedroom house painted beige that blended in with the sand hill.

The male who resided in walking distance of the post office closest to the mint was lead suspect; not just because of his job which was to monitor all computers for the fly room but also due to his required chore to rinse all coin free of dust, handling and substance.

The last male, a young man out of accounting law full of vim, operated the stamp wheel which tossed out any forged duplicates lived with a young wavy haired dark brunette female who worked keys at the post office. That's where the key came from.

All but the postmaster James Hilmore was accounted for. He was nowhere to be found.

Jones surmised the man who read the flies had devised the deletion of time. He thought it could have taken upward of seven out-takes probably placed in city street maintenance tunnels, possibly in one location more than three times covering it with anything that matched the identical color. An out-take would have to be very difficult to remove. If it were in a related file, it would separate easily so chances were it existed somewhere relatively obsolete. A question was how often the man had access to that type of work. It could be done twice in six years at random designations.

Not likely the man had originally been hired for that work. Possibly he transferred from New York where the most famous bank robbery had been committed that way. When visible distortions in width or length appeared on the monitor, that was an automatic deduction.

He put on his winter jacket and walked a block to the shop of a print identifier who could produce the different images from that tape. His man quoted him one grand with production by the following noon. He'd provide photos and the identity of whom was at the computer.

The initial foray had proven task consuming. Without doubt there had been a heist and the plan to secure a tray was foiled. As Jones walked through the pasture he realized the work had taken a toll leaving him wearier than usual. For years he had planned retirement talking with Nila up to her death where to purchase a country house. He hadn't anticipated needing a vehicle. It was hell without one. He often felt he suffered the loss of convenience, was dependent on others when it hurt his pride to be so; gnawed at him with continual anxiety that he might one day find himself stranded. The quest for spiritual relaxation felt like a combat exercise to achieve it.

He boarded up the front hall for the night, ate pork chop and fruit salad leftovers in front of the television watching the weather with the electric hearth going. Since Lewis Lewis had retired to an isolated beach in the Keys without a phone and computer, Jones felt as estranged from the company as he ever could be. Hoyt had taken a bed in a small hotel in Del Rey. This isolation surrendered Jones to anonymity. He had wanted nothing more than to listen to a whistling wind beneath starry skies, an older man's dreams of life well-perceived. Despite the vanished landscape of the aquamarine bays of warmer climates, there lived an infrequent bite, he felt scarcely insulated against most grief. Although he lived among retired men; the jade sea of the high desert re-enforced a sense that he had abandoned ship.

He had to tell himself as he often did – had done during the first four years – that he had put in a full career. No one expected him to become a lifer; at seventy-three retirement was mandatory.

At nine he took a cup of hot cocoa sipping it slowly permitting it a sought-after inebriate relaxation. Because there were no outside cameras, since Rock station was a ghost town, there was no way to know who was coming or who was going. The question as to why anyone left a tray at the post office played on his mind. Someone had given up the chase or wanted the government to have its cache as though to suggest it had become an omen to possess it. Perhaps there had been too many deaths or no one came forward with reward money to purchase it.

The first action the feds would have taken once they became aware coin had been stolen was to look for who was no longer at work; but each employee still arrived on schedule. The next act was to learn who these employees knew. If upon investigation no one had ever known a damn thing, then the field became wide open.

But someone had his eye on the man who lived at Rock.

In bed he grew wide awake. His instinctive judgment was the thieves wanted millions of post stamps. The cent, after all, was not meant for the public. It was predominantly to start a post office, run a theatre intended for FBI cases in a former era and pay a physician for remedies.

By the time the facility was discovered, all drawers and trays had been removed, the place swept to exterior walls; a massive relocation.

Perhaps the stolen money was intended for casinos. Of course they posed an obstacle to the slot catch which permitted the nickel, quarter and fifty cents but no dimes or dollars.

Where was the coin intended; maybe at Bishop at the high school spin the wheel night. Bishop was a clearing of two miles on a narrow river contained in a pine forest where bears ran loose. The town was an attraction for movie star weekenders looking for a retreat hotel suite with a pool and kitchenette.

In all probability the clean up was done with trucks that transported furniture up the back roads on 395 to those inns.

There were ten ways to fool your lover. What were the logistics for taking the money out of circulation? Where did they bring it?

Sometime during the night a fast wind started up lashing over roof and tree tops. It took with it scintillating sand and

snow in a whirling sort of combined sequin dust. He awakened to it thinking instinctively that the snow was piling up
building a layer of strata which when hardened would have
left drifts in every doorway, a bother to have to shovel. The
Joshua Tree forest would creep out like some malformed arms
seeking shelter in an otherwise inhospitable landscape, a blur
of snow particles descending upon cracked ravaged sand.

He got out of bed and peered through the blinds. Not a
house was visible in the whirling descent. The sky itself was
extinguished by darkness. He turned on the heat and pad-
ded inside the dining room where on the monitor a green
light flashed. Invented in the piling snow stood the town of
Independence looking oddly forsaken, a bright host light radi-
ating out of a long building showing an exposure of building
pilings and the dark forsworn earth surrounding it. Through
the exposure shone other lights; and then undeniably a shot of
excavators running a camp, wading waist high through a lake
pulling a cable to keep houses steady on their bearings. He sat
down with a cup of coffee and took notes.

A gold mine had been discovered in 1985 along Highway
395 at Trona, its first indicator that gold was weeping was a
sludge of mud four blocks long oozing down the wash which
saddled the highway. Except for a few houses, a hotel, fire-
house and school, there was nothing much to recommend the
barren land dotted with red and purple wildflowers in Spring.
The notation that explained the film described a stash of coin
hidden beneath six houses in a small lake on the hillside adjacent to Rock station.

The obvious deduction was a device had been set off to
get to a stash. Could be, it was fairly common where felony
robbery occurred. At any rate it was a hassle to excavate.

The information gave no indication as to what the mar-
shals found. There was not so much as a word as to whether
any Rock coin had been barreled at the site; merely that the

underground was deplorable, in a ruinous condition.

He fell asleep in the easy chair.

When he next came to, it was light outside. He checked the time on the clock on the kitchen wall, it wasn't even six.

He consulted his desk calendar. There had been a snafu in deliveries to post offices; drawers arrived a week earlier than otherwise scheduled. That was around the time the tray was seized at the newest station in 29 Palms. He circled the date, September 8, 2000. That was a Monday.

Jones decided to contact the postmaster general for future schedules. He had to learn when coin taken from Rock station was traded in for stamps. This would be allowed by a chief at headquarters for another station. He looked up the station telephone number for San Bernardino. He would call at nine o'clock.

At ten he would call National Parks, and start at Joshua Tree, to determine whether any stamps were sold in bulk in the desert at hospital gift shops, small airport counters, hotels, or symphony plazas.

By eleven fortified with four cups of coffee he had a bale worth of information. In May 1982 a male identified to the Yucca post office brought in two hundred dollars for trade of stamps for a post office in Salton Sea for a gift shop at a hotel. The clerk on duty filled out the necessary paperwork, having had the man sign his name and give his thumb print, and gave him twenty sheets of pretty stamps showing sky and oasis, nearly depleting his entire store.

In June 1983 two camping gear thick canvas duffle bags filled with something called Temple religious coin was dropped off at King's Inn for designated use in a casino wheel. A king owner contacted Las Vegas casinos as to legality of use. Two men came down and handled the coin for prints and then approved the coin for use during bingo nights and set up a casino wheel at the Bishop high school; the cooperative divisions no doubt thought the person who hired the robbery wanted a look at the coin.

Most vacationers who played spin the wheel were Hollywood movie stars. A year later in 1984 false post offices had been brought stamps and Temple coin, Pittsburg, California, Vancouver and Seattle, Washington state and Snake River, Calgary where the only way in was by train, each original post station closed permanently.

At noon he walked the block to pick up the photos from the print identifier. The man handed Jones a set of out take photographs with several photos of each person at the computer who had folded and released the images from access.

"There were three people, two male, a female, who worked this screw probably twenty years to produce a window," the technical expert said.

"Any idea where they originated?"

"Prints are declared for Washington, DC, for post 1975. Prior to entry in the US they are sitting a station in Industrial West Germany where their task is for a mining deposit and they are each in their late thirties."

"Thanks, that's well worth your pay."

The slightly balding man of medium stature gave a wry smile. "Someone brought them here for this work. There, they live in a miner's camp."

"They won't be at Independence. Nothing's there anymore."

"I just thought you ought know."

Jones stopped in for a bowl of Chinese flower and egg soup across the street at the whiskey tavern. Fifty tables with cheap plastic red and white tablecloths contained each a vase of fake yellow flowers. The waitress, a pretty young girl, brought the order instantly with two smallish egg rolls stuffed with vegetables and sprouts and a tea pot of dark oolong tea.

"How's business lately?" he asked her.

"The bar sees it all."

"I'll try to stop in, say hi to Mike."

"Will there be anything else?"

"Just the bill."

The tab would be four bucks. He left a five and made his way into the dank bar.

Mike was wiping the bar with a damp cloth. Ten senators sat around the long polished wood counter nursing drinks shooting the breeze. Each tab would be about twenty-five bucks by the end of the day.

Jones sat at a stool, ordered a whiskey red. It was produced in a shot glass.

"Rarely see you these days, Baylor. What brings you in?" Mike asked. He was a handsome blond, hair streaked with brown, aged past seventy, crinkly lines at the eyes, always a good conversation, a white waiter's garb worn over pants and a shirt, thin in the body.

"Mail."

"Who wrote you?"

"My ex-mother-in-law. She's in Colorado up near Zion."

"How's the weather up there?"

"She doesn't say but I imagine it's the same. They just put in a few new hotels on the lonesome prairie."

"Rain storms cut the sky with light."

"Yeah, it's solitude."

Unlike here, where a lone road across parched sand and endless stark mountains beneath a lantern of daylight squalled in whipped winds and churned up dust for a hundred miles to Blythe or north, to Las Vegas, the entire road a desolate enslavement of timeless inhospitality.

Jones sipped his whiskey. It stung the back of his throat. "What do you hear to bend an ear?"

"Vegas to Needles, nothing but suburbs, all of it casino work," Mike said.

"Who's money?"

"Nevada state excise tax."

"Must make for lots of products sold."

"Swim pools, special roof tile, landscaping parks, furniture big time."

"One day here, folded up tomorrow, blown away by wind and sand."

Mike smiled, winced. "It's a life."

"I'll give it that."

"Twenty years a spin."

"It won't affect us much."

"No, can't see that it will."

He stayed for a second drink, paid twelve bucks; walked home through gently falling flakes. A bit of conversation was always pleasant.

He'd been with the railroad senators for a short duration. They were divorcees whose wives had fallen from grace.

The snow piled in deep trenches on both sides of the street making entrance to storefronts and houses downright impossible. The air had chilled to an inhuman bitter intolerance causing every shrub to become glazed in frost and ice. There were two out takes, both historic houses built by Walter Scott, known as Scotty's castle and the Inyo wafer house, a gift shop at the edge of town that sold gold and bronze coin to tourists for a value of a few dollars. Like a dirty secret hidden at a rail station where a train sat dormant for a year until a group arrived to haul it away, chandeliers, ceiling molding, old lumber in the form of the exteriors of mining houses and gold remnants. The photo of the man taking out the information was of a black haired man, swarthy complexion and dark countenance, less than forty, a possible relative to the town architect, residing in a room attached to a warehouse across from the post office.

Apart from the robbery itself of fifty stacks, the dominion of authority rested with the vagabond travel between desert outposts, at once surrogate to inevitable town growth and next to their recession as inhabitants found work and moved away. On occasion the towns stood empty to four winds, dust settling everywhere, ghost towns to former mechanistic controlled mines or farms, swept by a cauldron of industrialism, removed to bigger cities closer to the orchards of the coast.

He sent the photo of the black haired male to Interpol for prints, identity and history knowing it would be days, if not weeks before he would have a workup on the suspect.

Everything had its reason, of that Jones was convinced. For transport of coin for stamps to have been delayed there was a logical rationale. He went through government notices requiring detours and vehicle waits between Independence and Yucca.

The discrepancy in shipping schedules came with the laying of water pipe along the inland stairway in 1983 which took all of a summer to complete and removed the highway to transportation. Road service was dispatched by federal order from Bryce and Zion under the Interstate Highway regulations.

Jones Baylor requested the state construction designs for Highway 395 with start and completion dates; they arrived on his computer e-mailed by Inyo and San Bernardino Counties within a four hour allotment. He marshaled a set of usual delivery schedules normally of two stacks each containing twelve racks which ran approximately every ten weeks during vacationing occupancy.

The blizzard had ceased. Sun shone intensely without wind. The uneven ground made hilly by an abundance of snow packed ice would become cleared as soon as county shovels were released by the fire department.

He stood on the porch and lit a cigarette, taking in the peace of the afternoon. In the sky a sliver of silvery moon waxed.

Of course, the deployment of a body of water may have seemed necessary as a result of all that bluing and yellow tar thrown onto the net amount of coin.

Even had the chemicals been the get-away plan in the event a suspicious individual encountered the group, the surface was now hopelessly tarnished, touching coin an inveterate unlikelihood.

Despite it, coin had been taken to The King's Inn for weekend casino.

He returned indoors, drew the blinds open, lay in the warm sunlight and curling up on the daybed fell drowsily asleep thinking he had earned a right to fall asleep lazily, do nothing, fight off a design to be over productive. He was an over achiever, a man who loved the absorption of working, loved a good puzzle, who had wanted little of life except to solve the worst god awful crimes and know he had conquered evil, if but a moment of it. He was born into that sort of world and knew not much else. As he fell asleep in spellbound warmth, a trickle of knowledge played at his outer vision, he had fooled himself into a belief or he was easily deceived and had missed an obvious realization or the world was an ugly place and life itself an ugly, deceptive sport. He spent himself drowsily, allowed himself to be wooed to absinthe on a river Lethe toward a promised land of drunkenness to unleashing that pressure that kept him going morning and night. Let no abstract infinite reality separate him from knowledge of violence, let not sleep divorce him; but he easily succumbed grateful as he fell asleep that he was at last able to free himself from an incalculable burden.

He dreamed of quenching erosion, bilious mud streams, choking plant roots, irascible cement desert, hills of pine entrenched forests, conquerable mountains all up and down the long highway from barren wasteland and pony clamored hills past surrender able pools of boron, gypsum and tailings, radioactive and mundane, filched, pinched and insolvent. The dust of waste gave rise to nothing but inobedient shifting sands, swirling over desolate canyons like dervishes, stymied rock havens of old petrified trees, a colossal denizen of colors of caked sand as rigid as Thor's fingers, inhospitable sandstone, each litchis in its preservation, form sedimentary columns amidst narrows and cacti and cottonweed. He glimpsed as he had never before, through a narrow lens through escarpments up the nearly dried cricks of the Colorado and out over tortuous ledges as if at the beginnings of life, narrowing rivers, pools in solidified stone, granite rock face, sheer cliffs, marsh salt beds, aquamarine lakes, a plentitude of them as though human kind having disappeared from these crannies might be explained by their weathering variations.

When he awoke it was night, stark and dark, a fierce wind sizzling with rain that tamped the rooftop in an endless repetition of bits of hail. The idea of a heist in the cloak of daylight stayed with him as he climbed out of bed and slipper-less walked about the house. Without the heat having been on, the chill penetrated the floorboards and walls. An architect would have known the inside station, its exits, its passageways to any exterior lot. A real fucking blaster, an asshole.

Night made for all sorts of ready possibilities. Sheer daylight apparently had too.

Since the road was blocked by construction that year in the summer, it had probably permitted the heist to escape without a hitch. Or the thieves had fled north to a getaway with pond. Trona, maybe – nothing out there except a small runway for a Cessna.

On the other hand possibly they fled as far north as Fish Canyon to lake embanked houses.

He'd bet on a day prior to June when a sufficient amount of coin was taken to Bishop.

He poured a cup of coffee and smoked a cigarette. He

returned in his mind to the stagecoach delivery of a rack to the all glass post office in 29 Palms wondering the reason the couple surrendered it. That act by itself was the crack of the egg. God bless the couple. God bless those poor employees whoever was an eye witness, wherever they finally wound up.

What happened to people who were on the run? Fugitives couldn't afford to show their faces in public. Once known, they were on every wanted poster in existence. But they needed money for hotel and food. They were constantly on the move. They required false identification. As they aged, the availability of hide-outs became less. They dyed their hair, cut it, wore contact lens, glasses, wigs, changed style of dress, took an alias, had children; some managed to alter their race.

Nothing could change height.

Jones lit another cigarette smoking it to the quick. Bess would arrive home sometime tonight. He could have gone another few days alone.

He contacted Bishop for road photo releases prior to June for any large duffel bag to The King's Inn. He didn't know why he hadn't thought of it earlier.

Bishop sent him ten sheets of photos, each forty-two photos, onto his computer. Receiving the lot caused him to feel hopeful.

He slipped on powerful lens eye glasses. There were linen deliveries, blankets, draperies, food, lard containers, ice cream sorbet in large drums, soft drinks, restaurant napkins, light bulbs, telephone books, pool filters, bingo cards, neon signs; and during a storm sleeting the parking lot almost two rows of seven photographs of an all white unmarked van out of which three men hauled two dark tan duffel bags and set them at two-twenty-six in the middle of the night. They were thin, tall, at least five eleven; one may have been six two, wearing black pants, standard black boots, black hoods, their faces and hands exposed, one Caucasian with a wisp of curly orange hair; the other two were some disposition of light skinned Negroid.

He isolated the hands as the men carried the bags, two men per sack. He focused on fingertips, caught the first section of exposure, sent it to Interpol; snagged the second man as he let the sack onto the sidewalk, fixed two finger tips, and then the third, as he removed a notepad and dashed out a note, for your weekend casino at the gymnasium. Hard to believe the resort wasn't crawling with agents.

He looked up the number of a vacationing contact at South Fork Bishop Creek.

The phone rang forty times before it was picked up. A familiar gruff voice said, "Sloppy, here."

"Jim Marder?" Jones pictured him, a scrawny six foot tall man of Finnish descent, dark hair cut tight, who began investigating silver miners back in the Fifties for deed rights at springs.

"Say, old man, haven't heard from you," spoken in a lazy drawl, clipped in a Scandinavian accent.

Jones thought the other agent had forgotten his name. "Jones Baylor."

"I know who this is. How's it going down there in 29 Palms?"

"So so, can't complain. I have a case on a post office heist."

"Which one?" Marder's voice was tinged by wariness.

"Rock station, Inyokern County."

"They just getting to that one now?"

"A rack was turned in."

"No kidding. A bunch of Missourians brought two bags up for the wagon wheel in the Eighties."

"I've been looking at the footage. Did you ever acquire names?"

"Not me, Jones. Money ran all over the western continent, every drawer locked up."

"How many coins were donated?"

"Five thousand, more or less."

"How many were stolen, did you ever learn?"

"Twenty thousand total. It's a good amount to have to have supplied every post office in the desert up to Kingman Arizona. Maybe twelve offices not including gas stations and restaurant gift shops."

"What was the word on the job?"

"Dusters, all. I heard the gold crud they removed off coin was enough to fill a dunking tub, raised a few million in hunting grease."

"Do you know if the coins were stored in gold mine rooms?"

"From time to time wizened underground halls had to be bombed in order to loosen doors behind which all coin was vaulted."

"Are dusters registered?"

"Oh, sure, they're the ones who verify the weight of a find produced in mud."

Jones thanked him and sent a wire for five hundred dollars.

He called Inyokern County for a list of their dusters. The administration department sent a short list in an hour. There were five men.

Then he reclined and smoked another smoke, thinking all the nonsense over. Reality was a bitch before it set a man free. While in its possession it could seem the most authentic truth, unfailing and unambiguous. Although experience might indicate otherwise of deficiency in comprehension, the necessity of resilience fooled many a recluse of a hardy catch.

He supposed there were many footloose crazies who convinced themselves to perform a crime without becoming identified.

He cracked open a door off the glassed-in front sunroom to allow fresh air to circulate about. The heist seemed quite straightforward insofar as loot crimes went. Up to then there had been two such crimes, in upstate New York Yonkers of money valued at approximately $9,768 and in Philadelphia, Pennsylvania of reserved gold, non transferable, never recovered. One couldn't steal a post office to live in as was attempted in South Lake Tahoe, no matter how much it resembled a house, or trade in the some odd thirty-four thousand value of coin stolen at the tiny Rock post office. While Rock station was bagged, someone tossed at least a container of bluing or tar onto many coins causing handling to be life-threatening, even though the entire vault worth was driven off the premises and delivered to a soaking pond somewhere. Unaffected coin was taken to Bishop for bingo and subsequently to separate smaller amounts for stamp purchase. Therefore, someone intended to collect money as purchase of stamps. Failing being able to operate a post office, the stamps must have been given to store owners for re-sale, perhaps pharmacies, state border town gas station gift shops or landmark resorts or flop houses and restaurants as a special service to tourists. The isolated desert was very probably the incentive to commit the grand felony robbery. It would take weeks, if not months, before a discovery occurred.

He allowed for the group composition of at least one person who approved the commission, a knife specialist who opened each crate package at a new site and tabulated the amount of coin and then sent the ledger on federal currency chart head to an appropriate city for notary record. This person, often a middle-aged Caucasian female previously employed in Netherlands, verified the length of time the coin likely would diminish.

The other must-have might be the three individuals who scanned coin prior to a scheduled delivery who might hold coin out from the procedure so that it never could be picked up on any frequent scan.

He surmised these people were the relations of retired miners.

JONES

3

NIGHT FALL descended in thunderous lightning and hail pitting the embankment in tiny stabs of points. Churned up mud swirled in a conclave of eddies which washed in previous firmly packed snow from numerous directions and poured like sieves into shallow street gutters that overflowed in minutes.

Names for fingerprints read the group in its mid to end fifties. There was no legitimate way to explain a felony heist unless they were starving and were desperate, but then one joined a meal church and reported in at lunch.

Could be they were teachers during their working years. Teachers ordered classroom aids by mail; that's how they learned about postal schedules.

The idea of being retired was seen as a treat while one worked thirty-seven years; could do all sorts of activities only dreamed of, play golf, live at a resort, play bridge and cards, take a sauna every day, boat on a lake and fish for one's meals, see the state on tours, reside in Montana for skiing, run a hotel, grow a vineyard, study art as an apprentice, travel to other countries, keep scrapbooks of news clippings, run a church, or attend college symphony classes on season reservations.

No one ever felt ready for retirement.

It arrived swiftly as body stiffness or exhaustion occurred gradually more noticeably in winter.

In his retirement of seven years – he slept in until seven; wordlessly sipped coffee while he read the weekly newspaper; alternated weeks with Bess to change the linens on the bed, ran the dishwasher, occasionally ran a vacuum, mowed the grass; raked leaves and the piled snow drift off the front drive and backyard porch in autumn and winter; worked a ham radio and took calls for small airplanes and boats for Search and Rescue during busy tourist seasons July to late August. He rode the senior bus into Palm Springs for Chinese lunch and discount spa four times a year, read a book infrequently, often left it for a year, contacted friends by e-mail once a quarter.

He painted watercolor paintings of wildflowers on high chaparral desert for an annual May event.

He took lunch at the tavern monthly and talked shop with sheriffs and senators and purchased a pie; ate lunch usually at home, a half sandwich with bowl of soup skipping dinner except on Sundays, drank two whiskey bar glasses nightly on weekends, together they watched great band concerts on TV and saw hundreds of TV movies despite enjoying few; complained to Bess about feeling non energetic.

In summer he swam a mile every day at the high school. He lounged at the outdoor pool for three hours.

Or he stayed home with Bess and played cards for eight hours a day.

He had discontinued hikes with his Army friend in Borrego Canyon after he became eighty because the sun became a scorcher by ten; he had lived for his agility, but he'd discovered agility depended upon thorough rest.

These sojourn acts turned out not to be life. Relaxation managed few anxieties in spite of the ideal intentions.

Bess called to say her mother had invited her to gamble the slots at Grand Canyon. She would return in three days. Jones said to take as long as she liked; several weeks was alright with him. There was no hurry. He felt fine puttering about.

Jones called a chemical tank excavation foreman at the base.

Corrosive fluids lay all over underground halls and mine rooms.

Maybe the group got free rent up near Flagstaff because they supplied bingo. Maybe they poured corrosive over coin and gold and tried to disintegrate it. Could it be they constructed an elevator shaft inside the earth, stored gold inside a small dug-out area, and placed a ski hut at the top? Or corrosives were tossed onto all and were placed somewhere no one could access like beneath Carnegie Lake?

Substances had to be burned off; a mining silver cutter might have the actual job experience. That might explain the hiatus between robbery and use.

Up to three years sitting in de-filter fluid.

These amounts were drawn from different post stations for the type of letters and packages mailed at that end of the world.

Labs, returned evidence from UCLA, medical supplies.

Schools. To receive new textbooks and to order supplies.

Dried food product for restaurants including shipping holiday specialties, pomegranates, dates, coconuts, orchids.

Each were packaged and labeled with unique shipping instructions.

Just so. All abundance in living became countered by abstinence of one sort or another. When spending grew scarce, the airport closed, people went indoors, did next to nothing. Sure, many motorists drove up for the socials; all the same, the agents took their spying in parking lots. For those who lived by packages they received, life meant they were important, not forgotten, not going down hill, not yet irrelevant.

A sense of futility could kill. Pitiful or contemptible or wretched elders peered from dismal rooms scattered about the meager subsistence of the wind-driven high sandy plateau of desert without advantage, existence a much underestimated trinket. The further one advanced from work productive years, the less capable one viewed sufficiency; intolerable, common complaint welled up in the chest like deep wracking sobs of self-pity, fear of losing competent life as around life hurried, changed in its essential understood language. The fear of getting torn from the wing, of not being able to keep up, let alone manage with basic tasks beset panic. He'd be damned if he knew what the cure was.

If humility persisted as adequate prayer, it became a method to be detached to watch a crowd without comment. Certainly at his age he was entitled to slip away from the haughty, often high-strung capture of conversation. Not to be compliant but sober-minded.

The telephone rang in the distance like a shabby lament. His initial instinct was to run to it, but instead he chose to ignore it. He got up stiffly and moved into the kitchen where he poured his usual whiskey, sipped it once, before he proceeded to turn on the television and lumber to his big armchair. Although he made every effort not to listen, he sensed rather than heard the caller's information. Drawer tray found stuffed in laundry desk at Buon Adventura. The tall green hotel sat empty every winter. He'd take the message later. He felt worn out again; he had overdone the research in two narrow days. He sipped his drink, enjoying the instantaneous soothing calm, and focused on the trial courtroom TV drama, thinking the actors impoverished barely talented.

A thought sprung to mind.

He had been working off an assumption that the coin was stolen in the same twelve month period of a year that the coin was brought to other stations including final delivery date down to the vault in 29 Palms. The evidence pointed to a significantly later date for entire removal.

Perhaps the more confident thieves bundled up the affected coin for a quick stash while they looked around for an expert to remove the chemical stains.

He could see he had attached too much importance to the first date that the money was made public.

If it required up to three years in de-filter fluid in order to dissolve the corrosives, then the heist could have occurred anytime between end 1980 and May 1983.

The crooks made the final delivery.

Possibly an employee returned for a forgotten document on that fateful day after the other employees left and entered unseen and tossed an opened can of bluing onto the coin as it was in the process of being crated.

He'd get a fix on the man who in May 1982 purchased two hundred stamps. He contacted the post office in Salton Sea only to learn that station shut down permanently in October of that year. He wired Imperial County for the tapes.

The film contact sheets were in bad condition. They appeared to be tarnished dark brown with almost no visibly readable surface. The man's thumb print on his purchase order verified him through Department of Motor Vehicles as James Seventy, age 31, born Burden, Ohio. Seventy resided in Owen's Valley in a three room, sun burnished wood house on a lone country road where miles of shaggy bluish green sagebrush extended into infinity to the sloping snow-capped Sierras.

Jones drank another sip; it burned all the way into his esophagus. Oddly the drink had substituted for late night reviewing a tank file on a sunken ship or a crashed aircraft. A photo showing the rugged scraggy figure of a rough man down on his luck snagged Seventy beneath a street lamp next to his wood cabin, his snide mien eclipsed by a hat, his jeans and long sleeved red flannel shirt obscuring his very lean stance.

A three-seat, light blue pickup truck parked in the sand and tumbleweed had a 1979 sticker attached to the upper right corner of the license plate.

Seventy looked to be a man who liked his trouble. He could be a psychotic or severe alcoholic; many lifers prided their active behavior on good dust or a sturdy oblivion. Jones wouldn't wonder if the man turned out to be a cheese crank. The extreme isolation probably aided any habit of long duration.

A file that blipped on like an after-thought said he had done prison time for killing a man in Durango. He had a list of allegations, none convictions, for possession as long as the sorry road he resided beside. He had had a wife who over-dosed on coke. Somewhere in Burden he abandoned a teen son to charity.

In addition to a string of failures, he had worked mask ore light for the pencil shafts breaking ground in the drill cabin whining the sputum down sixty-two feet deep. His skill prob-ably cost his fence a pretty penny. At least that's what Jones thought about him.

Seventy wouldn't mind a spill. He'd know what to do, how to protect his skin.

Jones poured a double, added a spritz of cream. The Interpol photos should break by dawn, given the international day constraints. He probably needed the computer dialogue as well.

Break a well.

Dig a shaft, fork some churn.

Crop weed for a gold mine, build a hut, run a line.

It'd be something like that.

All revealing descriptions once you knew who you were seeking.

He imagined the operative group wanted little more than corrosive-eating coin that had been once laid to rest. For some reason there was thought to exist plenty of trade-in value, when in practice the government never paid a dime on gold or stolen money. This was a carpetbagger's dream.

He stayed up all night. Past midnight the soundless air recapitulated a serene reticence. There was nothing to do, nothing to think. He was a man alone. A life suppressed. He drank as though he had vacated everything he was familiar with.

It was the effect the research had upon him. The unsolved problem caused him to worry. In the past he compiled information usually a cost analysis, the whereabouts of a criminal at large; studied evidence for an inquest or probative finding. This was a dunce of a crime; even when completed, he knew he would feel at odds with himself. There would still be unanswered questions – why had this group stolen unusable coin? Their motivations were far from logical.

He guessed that somewhere along the way they committed a sad, sorry crime and now, hunted everywhere, they decided to produce problems for society, be a bunch of queer dogs, remove a necessary service and create a major encumbrance. Like children functioning at a table filled with nothing but polysaccharides, their restorative healing capabilities mangled in sheepish turns of serial maneuvers amidst climate drenchers, oversupplied by high-colored bootlickers each who might ride at anchor.

Wherein influenced by the mental jambs of rhythm logaoedic, when sequence of events were seen as predictable, they behaved like confessors who had fed on the mines of bituminous coal or hard coal, raised cord on a stump block to blow open an angled, fallen-in façade; convicted of packing glut in place of knot choked with furnace ale, each gradually became a furtive worrier, or worse a moocher of stemmed or cracked coal clay, where on top of the ground the winter wind whipped at a cyclone gallop in an attic of phantasmal fury flying a gauntlet across potential copper-aureate like a monstrous twister windfall, a dervish of gripping rapacious thunder over every prairie devoid of rain, a navigational pilot of which the calisthenics gathered the air into an upsweep into the sky like castles in a rancor and hoarse echo where the oncoming train, headgear light of a one eye trollop, bewailed in discordant chords, becoming a shrill shriek, as the rattling wind held to no direction butting brush around the scattered houses of long time desert dwellers whose unmindful non observance was nevertheless entranced repetition bound in humble chakra's beneath the extensive night sky of glitter. The herding wind tore at everything like a paradoxical panther skulking about, while priests dressed in all white ushered in from a papacy aglow in the far distance, resembling a Mecca of all white papier-mache stone, in their tasks parochial confinement they conducted to an ecclesiastical drone to sever underwater moorings of mines; possibly unaware that on the ridge carmine wildflowers stirred as blooms a flutter. Many a released parolee sat in the wee morning hours dealing out in a parlor game a tried watchword over coffee, although up the street near the elementary school at the only hospital in town, synthetic organic drugs as mild stimulants to the nervous system were ingested by old people to improve memory, or calcium salt sedative for those who found themselves unwittingly in a private purgatory that scripted nowhere here lay a belief that people were connected to all Mankind; it remained each man to himself.

He took the message now, jotted down the tip, walked over to the computer; flicked it on. Finding the Buon Adventura Hotel, he sought the locker where the tray had been discovered. With consent of the army, he accessed the hotel camera and zoomed in on every room expanding his search beyond the three year period of confinement. He searched through car lots, lobby, restaurant and lounge, basement, twenty rooms, bathrooms, vent interior units, roof pool and storage, month after month, until he found a square object placed in a yellow laundry bag the approximate size of the drawer inside a desk where a computer mini printer should be. The back of his neck chilled with goose bumps. He looked for any small green square registration tags on parked cars. The dates read 1981. The blue month tags read appropriately abbreviated February, March, April.

This was a big find.

Lots of static at intervals presumably to hide the identity of who brought the tray.

He went back to the desk, fixed in on the laundry bag, freezing the frame, zooming in on the cloth. It looked to be pure as fresh snow. He put a snoozer on it so that the time for that day recorded every twenty minutes; then he salted the screen with live pink so he could detect prints. A strip showed along the top consisting of light gray, a thin bar of crimson and the remainder pink indicating that the room in which the coin was stacked was treated by green slate, a room not meant for money; its intended purpose was for minimum mine stackers which when positioned in doorways could force open thick metal vault entrances.

He wondered how the government got a post office deposit out of the building. He took an hour to scan the walls not certain what he should be looking for. He discerned small crack lines that climbed from floor to ceiling in fairly neat columns. The place had been induced a few times possibly over thirty years as it sat minimally maintained. Each width fissure appeared lacerated by fog, an irreparable condition that typically caused hammer joints to dislocate. He thought the government ditched the building in a flat second.

Once the gold contrite was removed, until a decision had been made as to what to do with the place, probably a man drove down every few months to check the building detritus.

He opened a close-in lens and surveyed the material. Creased pressure marks gave indents. Some worn areas seemed almost like visible tears due to bleaching, several felt pen marks were non-disclosing, but there were no prints on the item. He deduced the bag and object had been carted inside another discarded covering. He made notes as to description on a log that he would later submit as evidence. As soon as he had justification, he would write up history of landmark by date, draft up a petition citing break-ins and other induced crime, disclose in a disposition report who staffed and their credentials and relevant photo remarks, and request Superior court orders, one to uphold use as a leniency post service, beef up security including wizening by surveillance which involved dead stopped motor of getaway vehicles, paint silica over fog without asbestos, and automatic warrant notification.

The couple that turned it into the post office had obviously been told where it was.

He thought he might have enough information to start to scout out the thieves.

He took out a map, placed tags on towns where money had turned up, and looked for probable gas mains that could be blown up if the wrong people came upon the stash, proximity to a restaurant or gas pump.

For an unknown reason, the disclosure was a conclusive detection, one that would accompany certain disenchantment over its loss, possibly allowing an ascertainment which once the city lab made its trace find would begin a recovery, put the bit halter on the right horse, verify prints on the coin itself as to make certain of handlers; but his opinion lay in the presumption that the law underestimated an implicit disregard that from the date the coin arrived to Rock post office fact would prove it was touched solely by employees.

He knew full well that once the money found a purchaser, the group ran at the idea. Who would have had an inkling other than agents who could have pursued known suspects.

The thieves had chosen non conformity of theft, a Pentecostal coin intended for a temple gift shop or a religious desert community to buy, sell and trade stamps.

Their apparent willfulness to sit out the weather struck Jones as a monkey trick, the thieves led astray by a traveling minister of the healing arts they knew whose ambition was to sell stamps to a captive audience guaranteeing a likely livelihood.

Whoever risked the actual theft, had they touched the chemical resins, would have experienced numbness on vulnerable skin, outer lip, surrounding eyes, beneath nails, inside the inner ear canal; suffered an inability to swallow; compounded by madness that bordered on disordered thinking, a noticeably abnormal mind, fraught with obtuse mania, demented reasoning, delusion, incoherence and hallucination.

They were unforgotten, present in the mind, a search to the last made on every escarpment. They would receive no amnesty; would not fade from their crime or die in people's memory.

Unanticipated, as though dropped from the sky, the coin struck into the burgeoning purchase power of small towns in the high desert where four temples each Rosicrucian had a post office on its premises as well as a physician office to render its congregation spiritual liberation from a life of the complications of sin.

Every type of concealment and disguise had sealed a hiding place for several years; evasion waited under clouded nightfall, in which cloaked, the thieves lived a lifestyle aimed at covering their tracks. Cemetery and crypt were too distinct and thus no one but authorized personnel worked, Jones thought it more than probable they disappeared into an underground dug out dungeon, or wine cellar. He revisited the idea that corrosive material was usually buried; he should give every thought to those coins having been sunk into an accessible place.

Somewhere.

California back roads covered a gigantic area.

Seemingly endless rolling hills, pine forests, a sea of carpeted sage brush governed a barren wasteland with all sorts of
rivers and creek beds to get lost in.

Morning was upon him. Clouded grey light pervaded
with gloomy dejection reminding him precisely how dissatisfied with himself he had become. Nothing felt exact; the
degree of leisure was all-consuming, doing more always came
with the sting of not feeling he had enough physical energy.
While working in the Antilles islands, consumed by a forty
year investigation in which suspects got up and left every new
spring when they could travel by boat, he was reading reports
by eight, meeting with Lewis at eleven for needed discussion, sending updates worldwide, and often still conducting
research by nine at night; weekly tennis, occasional golf, a date
every so often, visiting the crime scene twice a year at most, a
thousand relays to dateline in two years.

He wasn't sure how to get at the problem when it didn't
make sense to him. Nothing lasted as long as he'd like and
then during the interaction he felt overdrawn, tired. That
weariness hadn't seemed relevant in Lewis' tutelage when it
had been easier to just co-exist, float along, live day to day,
mindful of a bigger picture. He'd wanted more he decided in
retrospect. He was never sure life or love was a safe gamble.
He didn't worry about boredom as he did while he was young;
he worried about aging out of sync. When he came up for air,
took a glimpse about him, he wasn't where the other agents
were. He just put emotional rendering out of his mind and
stopped expecting intimacy would come along again someday.
He had overreached his limits in forty years, had not paid
enough attention to his own peace, but continued giving long
past his ability to endure the high energy giving required to

keep any Rhonda's or Nila's unwavering attention. He hadn't felt suffocated; more he needed some length of separation. Flirtation eventually led to commitment which in turn led to the mixed pull of dependency. Reliance itself led to craving and habit. His mind was crying because he felt far past his endurance. He had nothing left to give, but he was still giving. Actively fighting off a certain self-disclosure; he had lost his internal patience, felt hurried to keep up, depleted now he had the self-determination necessary to let go. He felt as though he had not really awakened to a personal realization as to who he was in his lifetime.

He ate a small breakfast of fried steak, cut potatoes with fresh parsley and diced red onion, a poached egg, and cup of coffee, reading the morning paper before he went to bed.

Winters were always a problem. Flocks of evergreen gave chase in ponderosa canyons stockpiled in aspen snow, above grey and red stone strata in a blue range at twilight; red trees with light jasper scales, bright lime shocks of moss shooting out of blue and adjacent brown sided rock, the elbow felt a bit banged; a sorcery worth of purple, gray, light yellow and pale green sage; in an alternate canyon the colors were warmer – sage strewn of red wine, orange and fronts of vivid yellow. Not much was real that one heard batted about; pools of red mud churned rainwater, powder like detergent frothy on the plateau, a thin ray of light emanating at the horizon between massive sections of grayish black sky. Nature itself inclined to excess – mauve, gray and rope thin branches stood pole deep in sand piles alongside a black river where secure tie-downs stood along the desolate rail and the unmoving sky every so often produced a lightning rod. Winter tended to eclipse all thought by making him unwilling to want to talk.

Or on occasion he was on his way to the glass skyline of Vegas to see the Circus Circus which wasn't there anymore, traveling by train beneath crest lines of thin trees and the fresh damp earth smell of turned soil where the lake stood frozen and guttered in ice; then coming upon the place where the Starburst Motel had been recently torn down to make way for the new glitzy Hard Rock Cafe and the Eifel, all the land looking like dappled mud and white snow like a fawn's sleek fur; fishermen catching silver backed trout in cascades while high above tree tops an avalanche was spewing a salty down mist of snow. There were ten tunnels to the summit of black rail and dashing white snow whereupon his sleeping habit caused him to awake at 4:20 am disheveled, ready for that early coffee; passage of sheen green, a blur of forest in winter or summer, ready to disembark, stroll his luggage along the platform inside the all marble station and exit onto the side plaza sparkling in tiny blinking lights to hail a cab, eager for the dance halls and speak easy's and the casino resorts where he would gamble fifty bucks of loose change, sip a Mai Tai, eat a full meal for five dollars and rent a room for eight a night. At five each morning he'd jog uphill and around the reservoir out at the mission, the inky blue water tranquil and deathly silent, a chill barometer of zero; the ruthless element of frost and gloom well underway to creating seepage debris; calling to mind some author he couldn't recollect who said the eyes of the forest gazed upon houses to explain a deadly, dispirited quiet covering the grass and sand; while he perceived red berries on tan branches in sleeves of dark velvet moss and realize he had gotten in too late to catch the game warden hotel manager's last night of his stay, vacations were made with the best of intentions.

It was always a question as to who thought coin larceny was do-able. The atrocious fact was that anyone who heisted coin just disintegrated; death was the only intervention.

He had viewed such bodies from hospital amphitheater rooms and the bodies weren't pretty to see. Despite reality, he assumed the Wanted were trained in one of five categories of dusters, each who had access to chemicals used in labs labeled as throat toxicants that led to choking and caked mud crusting over the body cinching blood into sliver cuts; potentially a bulk of evidence, gold dust intermingled with underwater mud that relaxed the skin; Excavationists looked for any problem seemingly trivial in nature, where medicine was no object, scarcely anything noteworthy;

Finding dry lake beds their best bet until boron deaths in number took the majority of probable death by asphyxiation and chill bed injuries.

Usually deaths occurred in the vicinities of a train sullying across surface of cliff line through wind toboggan snow and flying leaves piling shrift downwind onto still surface of lake beneath rocks and caverns leaving behind gusts of barely surrendered hills of some wheat amidst rising branch stalks, swift eddies circulating rushing water in creek beds; where pitiful memories escaped above wretched escarpments as golden sun flicked in the all white fog formed bluish halos on the almost night stream of air risen in folds like tarry town steel semblances of flint fish weaving their way through seasonal bare branches; and irrelevant mystique called to the damp dirt hundred foot high boasts of fallen sod from denizens of modern, all glass houses with tiny lights perched from vaulted ceilings, tiny glossy gas-lamp lit globules penetrating a fluid darkness in which wind ushered into the strait with the high pitched sound of shrieks of death from a far-off rust marsh tamping out chill from frozen ice and thawing and breaking capitulations of sonorous crinkling waves.

JONES

4

THE mist rose above the lake as loons could be heard diving for fish. In the darkness ten flashlights shone upon rock and surface water like errant beams of blue and silver thin beams of light which in water bent in equally captivating descents.

A man's body had been discovered lying on his back inside a poorly lit cave by a hiker. Because of the evidence that the body was bulging, the cause of death was initially listed as a river death, although the body was completely dry and rigor was absent except where the feet distended and the knees were bent. The dead man was Caucasian, reddish white skin, honey blond hair, maybe fifty-five years old. It was presumed all parties traveling with the man were also dead probably in other flooded caves.

The first evidence was sputum lodged in the throat, half cup would have suggested that in life he was bulimic, but there was not greater than a quarter cup, which meant he ate one meal only a day as his usual diet. The secondary evidence was he kept nothing down, as determined by the fact that his large intestine filled with water entirely and small intestine had almost no fluid at all; blood in sputum indicated extensive drug inhalation such as methamphetamine of which there were trace liquefied ingested, otherwise the sputum was fairly tan to clear. The third evidence was he had no bowels, whatever he had digested as solid had leaked out. Estimated time of death occurred after approximately four minutes of becoming submerged. Standard rule was that people trained for underwater dives often didn't drown.

Otherwise salts, proteins, analyses were the same.

There were warrants issued against documents, postal stamp vouchers and signatures used to cash in for stamps and the state had ordered any proofs supplied by oral testimony, witness statements as well as laboratory courtroom argument.

Winter state highway agents were dispatched up and down Highway 395 to loosen destabilized boulders, plow avalanche sections day and night with intermittent road closures every twenty minutes to permit traffic in order to clear strangulated large rock pieces off mountains. The mist at the top altitude was dark gray; one could feel the upcoming storm approach in the intensity of wet cold as the crews searched for a toppled hijacked truck to pull out of the ditch it landed in, any dozen fire trucks had gone down the sinewy pass, placing blocks for trucks as impediments on the inclines, chains for zero visibility, a significant threat of danger of avalanche on high risk peaks on which plows were also unavoidably stuck, the Doppler radar for weather prediction – rain and ice, severe wind factor, and blizzard-driven snow – for which beacons were placed along the icy road slicked in sludge, with all sorts of problems already inherent, the worst being where it was conducive to in all day deliveries scheduled by truck or trailer had due to fast-working ice-cracking cables spun their hitches causing a few trucks to crash right over; lose headlights, bust engine and transmission hoses, snap brakes, each was a major unavoidable liability that wound up costing a late night work haul to clear up a big accident, especially one that flipped over a guard rail, smashed through trees, and kept descending as it toppled in excessive speeds downhill to an eventual clearance.

Thus, under quickly descending pitch black nightfall, teams were out combing the creeks, river beds, and lakes, trimmed with small flashlights in the event they came across a live one so they didn't blind the person searching in remote high peaks. Sometime later a man was pulled off a cable winch net, feet upside down, thoroughly dead, eyes open upon death, skin reeking of chemical halitosis, a frightening sight, probably having been murdered stagecoach robbery style. Even the labs, once cave water was hosed up to determine presence of bodies in mud, succumbed to the nasty fluid responsible for causing final meal, wood knock-about's cantilevering over under the pressure of wind and icy water, nothing of their structure evident for recognition.

From a distance the specks of light resembled fireflies until close in they were seen for what they actually were. Inside the air of blizzard wind, the light rays seemed to contradict space making for bluish points that moved slowly. The crew complained of sub-freezing skin, headaches; tricks of light. For hours after, breathing was hard, fingers numbed by icy cold. It was in this penetrable chill another body was discovered high on the summit beneath a movable rock in a cave, fingertips frozen to swelled blisters, a high altitude condition. The lab thought on occasion their physical conditions revealed prison camp – skin that in daylight looks badly botched, hair did not accept die color, eyes unable to focus; they couldn't touch paint of any type, made a person turn bluish. There was some indicator of an alien invasion which was noted on a medical chart after the diagnosis and treatment that required no admission to any job consisting of mine exploration.

The hum of the city came alive at ten-thirty with snow plows and drills as a sickly warm sunlight pressed against closed drapes and streamed in overhead putting a box of whit-ish light on the floorboards. A light rain tapped against the roof as though against a money pail, one chink at a time. Jones studied his morning coffee ruefully; he thought this matter of finding the actual date of theft should be able to be deter-mined by careful research alone could he but know the queries to pursue which he didn't.

What he did think was these robbers had traveled north, far out of the discernment of populations and law officers, into bizarre climate, to secure themselves in a No Man's nomadic life.

He placed a telephone call to the state highway fish and wild fowl game office at the top of 395.

"They took the trays to nine post offices in and around Salton Sea and purchased stamps; then took five thousand stamps to Bishop to the high school gymnasium for weekend gambling. People played for stamps. There were four games – gin rummy, canastas for the Spanish speaking population, King Rummy, and casino. Each year brought a new deal."

"Could the robbers have held up the Taos train and han-dled the coin and they wanted the canastas handled by as many hands as possible to obscure their own prints?"

"Oh, sure, anything was possible. The highway was the legal agency that had to deal with post trailer roll-overs, so they were the ones called in initially to evaluate the use of stamps which weren't being used as intended."

"Did you ever assess what their interest was in stealing stamp coin?"

"Oh, damn straight. They did it to steal a post office search and rescue ski plane."

The world opened up, the perspective now quite clear. "For whom was this a necessity?"

"Room heist robbers."

"Where do you think these people may have taken off to?"

"It's anyone's guess, but they probably reside where people reside."

He doubted that altogether.

"Do you have any record as to when the heist at Rock Station could have taken place?"

"Well, the lights douse whenever the books are moved. Each book is about ten crates each containing twelve trays. It is approximately ninety squire's worth, about nine thousand seven hundred dollars worth. The lights were down three times on September 3, 1981; again September 10, 1981; and last April 7, 1982."

"Did the vans leave on each day?"

"That's the problem. Our computers were tied up."

The robbers were probably trying to dig up their latest stash, having moved their hideout often. His guess was high up in the mountains somewhere where abandoned mines offered protection from the elements. The truck rolls occurred at eight thousand feet above sea level.

There were pockets of gemstones under mountains of steep ravines along mill sides; it took picks and brushes and patience to reach the inside of the rock. Some surfaces were so dangerous with the threat of rock slides it wasn't possible to work it. Crystal caverns produced a shiny aquamarine worth fifty per table; eating money to survive on. Fascination was to get to the stuff that was purple fluorite, worth several hundred per quarantine, but that was life-threatening tasking and most who tried gave up. Both mist and opaque fog slammed right in against the flanks, and an afternoon rain storm quaked in an echo that meant the deluge was coming fast; lightning struck at the tree mark and shook loose so much rock it caused a flight zone for a tumbling, crashing avalanche.

He scanned Intel photos for the back roads looking for any van the same in size and shape as the van that made the deliveries to blue sky terrain at Lone Pine on the incline, Big Pine, Joshua Tree near the old lab, 29 Palms at the hospital, Palm Desert off Hwy 111, Dehy Trailer Park in Anza Borrego Canyon of cement-like sun scorched ravines, Winslow and the mobile home parks in Blythe. In the blue haze of predawn, sharp tree tops poking through the reeling mist resembled sharks leaning into the wind. Route 66 had a sole post office in a house lit at night on a lone road through cacti and the Knife Turn Mountains. On Hwy 40 arid dusty roads rode into an eternity in the palm desert all the way to Winters as solitary as the winded space of the Mohave might conjure up before a traveler hit the first gas truck stop in the middle of nowhere.

Heard through the vent between walls, an employee reported what sounded like a lift loading up outside. She thought they had followed the truck. Everyone heard heavy footsteps on the roof. No one was there except a dry carpet cleaning running a long hose inside the rear of the building.

Law enforcement personnel staffed the radio round the clock to every jurisdiction in every state and other country trying to determine if employees were under armed hostage. FBI, state bureau sheriff, police; National Transportation Safety Board; Alcohol, Tobacco and Firearm, and Post Office manned the lines 24/7; set up coordinates for map and jeeps, and went in at five each morning looking for the vans.

Somewhere on 395 above the ship rock landmark on the road to the high desert labs where plutonium was tested sat a destruction of small, unmarked crashed trucks come to be known as shark feed; initially the term referred to decreased respiration due to unusual damp, but those deaths were known to occur primarily inside prisons. It was thought the only cause of damp was they had buried a limed batch from a treasury source. Anyone taking coin illegally died everywhere.

An identity on his computer gave the postmaster James Hilmore as the man in the watery grave. Jones' question was,

How did he come to die there, unless he was taken hostage? A report claimed three men in Sheriff raincoats were sweeping mud out of the garage entrance on the following day, Sept. 4, 1981 at around 8 am just as the pinkish sun was pouring over the mesa.

He still had a few questions. Did any of the eight employees have reason to report their vehicles stolen prior to the heist? Where had the robbers come from? Were they driving a scheduled truck? There was mounting evidence that someone arrived to pick up outgoing deliveries, when they killed an armed guard and stole his guns, uniform and badge.

Shelters on the road, wooden, boarded up shacks once belonging to an older post office gone to let, police and ambulance pretty much all that came out dispatched from Ely or Reno to pick up a body, much of the land barren waste and cracked sand; a dozen satellite sound dishes in miles of remote sagebrush; every so often a trading post open for lunch such as in Death Valley and Searchlight; until a death brought in a settlement seemingly overnight.

When he pulled photos on the postmaster and family, he got a vivid beauty of a wife, a gorgeous looker, narrow in the bodice, hips and legs, a soft angelic face, a short white sheath dress slipping off a shoulder, well above her thighs, long teased silver blond curly hair, a good thirty years younger. A girl he schmoozed at a bar when he was fifty and took her to the altar.

Jones came across a single photo of her waving down trucks at night with a light, their headlights creeping through blizzard rain.

Wives were a dime a dozen, selfish creatures often who considered a trade of an older man for a younger one justifiable to maintain excitement. Boredom was wretched; a lone watch on a lone stretch of land grounds for divorce. Jones had been married five times. Without work, the pressure of cohabitation built up almost to hateful resentment unless the kids stopped in a few times a year. Rarely a wife enjoyed the listless windy fog, the endless years of silence, unfathomed by any non activity. Both Nila, Bess were different, comfortable with solitude, but they had places to take off to.

The wife of the postmaster was an enigma, at the bar a petulant, spoiled, willowy and reedy, self absorbed flirt who waltzed men around an empty dance floor to the moody cries of the jukebox. Likely she knew every trucker who barraged down the mesmerizing dips of the Staircase. She had probably shacked up with a few to have ended up in a modest condo in northern Vegas with a jazz saxophonist ten years her junior.

Never get married. The obvious conclusion was she was awaiting a pay-off on her husband's life, a big check for forty grand which she collected on.

In the Fifties and early Sixties the only way to send a letter was by Par Avion, until 1963 when the lot of mail was stolen from the manufacturer. The replacement service was to sell stamps for use by weight without the envelope or package.

Jones contacted the NTSB for their release on transportation safety deaths. There had been two road closures at the summit in the dead heat of summer after a rumble took down the mountain presumably due to a moving shovel putting in a new road. During that month were several roll-overs, one which was a long postal truck, the standard rule of thumb was that to warehouse each load for the length of time it took a purchaser to remove it cost in cash two grand delivered to the stock yard upon arrival, an arrangement both the post office and lumber mills eventually saw to themselves. The other arrangement was established by the post itself, of providing a centennial bank drawer of five grand to supply some twenty stations for stamps each valued at $ .10 manufactured in New York State and delivered by truck and ski plane.

Access to obtaining trucks and ski planes meant getting

into far north remote landscapes where no one was likely to live and only shelter and food were necessary.

The fact they took dead hostages along their escapes said there was confrontational exposure every so often.

A run away wife might have mired the works plenty. A bank deposit on a warehouse might have seemed more attractive than lonesome nights, skin prickling sensation at the wail of coyotes on the loose. The idea of saving a few dollars that wouldn't be readily noticed was a notion common to many a dissatisfied spouse who had discovered that living on the edge of leisure was not a bargain they had lived for.

He found her in the phone book.

She thought her steady Eddie had walked out on her. He had taken a dispatch cop up the Staircase to South Lake Tahoe to open the post service there by the 5th ahead of the arrival of fall residents. That was September 4, 1981. She had received his retirement in an endowment signed by a New York federal court judge in 2008.

What was she doing on the road in a snowstorm?

That occurred years earlier. A fire truck had gone over having skidded on ice. She tried to flag down help.

He still didn't know if he had the complete facts.

He couldn't figure out where the Cache Creek van went to.

The cameras were rifled with.

The van that left the tray at the hotel on Highway 62 did not show in photos either.

The employees fled on August 27th.

No one knew who went inside Rock Station or how long they were detained.

The five grand centennial could have been the catch.

He chewed the eraser end of his pencil. He was going to have to search for a truck large enough to fit that van inside.

JONES

5

HE OPERATED on a long shot that the roll-overs in winter were essential to getting the money out to an undisclosed location.

His guess was a business or casino with slot machines managed by Norwegians who could cash the centennial coin. There were several in a plaza at Incline Village.

Of course it could be much simpler an explanation. Postal services might give the thieves access to treasury checks floating about in the mail, but there had been no theft in March through June of any year when most checks were sent.

He went back to the date the lift was heard, September 3, 1981. It would have been sometime after that. A ski plane would have proven an advantage to taxiing money across the lake and to other lakes above Mammoth.

The prior afternoon it rained catching two employees carted a truck bed with tied postal sacks from the mail distribution building where customers brought their mail to the vault inside the brick station when they noticed all crates were in the tray room being counted.

The thieves must have watched from their cars for months to determine where cash was when it was moved.

Where would a large truck take a smaller truck to unload vault coin? Maybe the robbers had to paint the Cache Creek van first before it could leave the underground. Maybe the large truck was delayed and another truck was coming.

The lights got doused turning off the electric guard door. Employees were sprayed in bluing rendering them feeble. All cameras were secured to an unknown site. He checked the Intel again just to make sure he had overlooked nothing.

Road Intel from aircraft was unable to find the presence of any truck.

Could well be they used cars with tinted visors to block out sunlight.

Someone arrived promptly around five to transport the crates.

An employee awaited its arrival which never occurred.

Nine trays were used to purchase nearly all stamps in the desert. The stamps were brought to Pittsburg, California and Snake River National Park in Idaho for resale of religious stamps causing the two offices to be shut down. Six trays were delivered to the Kings Inn for gin rummy on weekends.

It must have happened some other way.

A car took away sixty trays in the middle of the night.

The employees were released except for the postmaster whose body was ditched in a creek up the road.

That was the crime.

No truck or equipment was taken.

Special Task removed shoe prints from the tray room. Their findings included three standard regulation shoes for non employees who entered the tray room, one specific to the wife of the postmaster, the other a uniform shoe of the highway sheriff, the last of someone presumably who operated a gas station.

Maybe the lead thief was a highway cop who'd know the status of every vehicle on the roads. There was that famous documentary: Dangerously Cold Air in which a tourist zooming along Highway 62 caught a glimpse of a sheriff shooting a man in the desert at high noon. Could be an eye witness report was suppressed.

Jones loaded up his Intel with any obscene act by a high desert sheriff. Someone sent him a photo of a sheriff vehicle raging on fire. The date read September 5, 1981.

That was a clincher.

A few minutes passed; then: I've got you, sucker.

Sweat broke out on his brow. He shut off his computer. He hoped his computer could find the guy first.

He put on a jacket and walked up to the bar. The lounge bartender was rolling a set of nine on two die on the polished wood bar counter to a bet for two customers. Jones ordered a straight whiskey. He suspected he looked done in, like utter crap. From here on in, he was on his own. He'd be looking over his shoulder at every male who opened the tavern door.

In the few hours he remained at the tavern nursing two drinks shooting the breeze about his low-bred Norwegian dollar, Bess had returned home, bringing a six foot tree with her, dragged out the lights and hung a hundred crystal balls until the tree glowed as bright as a pyramid of white lights in the large picture window. Silver icing hung between orbs and a purple angel in slippers crested the apex. Around the tree at its base were ten packages of varied sizes, some quite tiny, wrapped in shiny gold paper tied with white ribbon.

On the desk in the studio were three, dollar centennial coin under the green infrared. The real silver would stay silver; a zinc alloy would become light gold tinge. Once a determination was made, the tinged coin would be discarded as waste, probably for a ridiculously inferior cost, its use for Casino or stem ware. The trick was a likely distinction picked up by one of her friends who worked for a coin expert at a pawnshop to prevent stymied trade-ins once coin became exposed to yellow tar.

He was basically a man with straight forward, unremarkable interests, content to sit by the window and stare out at the piled snow, think his thoughts, keep the wind under his hat. He had opted to reside close to the base at Trona out of force of habit, to insure he kept up with the advantages of retention of morgue findings. Nowhere in his personality did he possess any design for strategic army platoon practice which struck him as a necessary but futile ploy to track criminals. He was of the school of thought that believed the Intel could find everything. Eventually even the mysterious truck that carted off the Cache Creek van. The truth was always out there waiting to be discovered; the fact of it lay still like an iguana resting on stone, the desert fauna keeping it well hidden until light of day moved past the prime and for an instant all life sprang into sight like a bas relief for a fraction of a minute. Once the insane endeavor had been committed, all life, animate and inanimate, turned toward that clock that captured the seconds in which that dishonesty would be held hostage. He believed this because that was what his life expertise taught him; once there in camera, always there; flight of image impossible, even if seemingly lost. If he didn't secure it today, there was always forever another day. Whatever lay at the edge in a blur, shadow or overlay of color was nevertheless there, recorded, factual. He was passive by preference; he would wait interminably until the evidence produced itself. Now that he understood the crime, had come to know where the findings lay, he knew they were where the activities had occurred, and nothing could alter that imprint.

He knew for example the postmaster's wife had lied, she had been present when the crime occurred, although he wasn't convinced she realized a crime was about to go into commission. She knew when her husband had to leave to drive to South Lake; she must have encountered at least one of the thieves when she left and followed her husband up the incline. Wives knew things; that's how it was; they intuited or intimated each separate oddity, could probably run a list as to what was wrong that afternoon. When she stepped out of her car to flag down help, a hundred and thirty miles away the highway cop was pouring petrol over his vehicle and setting it on fire on a lonely stretch of road scarcely traveled. This all by itself was a disastrous problem to have to find a reason for. But he knew the reason had to be there, was defined by the outrageous acts; it lay somewhere on the way from that post office station, was a convincing truth, a reality that would never be negated.

When he arrived home, he embraced Bess, told her he had missed her, that the nights were cold and the wind harrowing. He asked after her mother; as usual, her mother was good natured; they had ridden to Vegas for the tree and along the way took in a movie. Nothing was of concern; they checked into a desert hotel and listened to crickets and a howling coyote talking into the weaning hours of dawn. He ate supper with her, fried teriyaki steak strips and pineapple over rice, and gave her his findings to which she remarked he was the only one who could handle a complicated task like that and he would figure it out. Then he took a whiskey sour into the room with his computer and while she sipped hers listening to the news, he pulled up the Intel, this time tracking the burning patrol vehicle back to its point of origination to assess the crazy dilemma.

He had driven down 395 having stayed on the roadside in a fierce blizzard as an unmarked truck with a narrow plait slowed and removed a rust van with black top onto the road before the truck spun out of control, skid over ice and toppled taking a dive off the summit turning a cartwheel as it fell on its side to the bottom of a ravine some five hundred feet below. A car stopped, and the wife ran out; then ran into the face of oncoming headlights waving for someone to stop. The black and white patrol car rode onto the lane and charged down the summit as if to oblivion. Odd he didn't go to assist the tumbled vehicle. Odder still he drove into the desert wilderness taking a solitary sojourn through dried sand, sage and jagged Joshua trees until he drove onto hilly, wild terrain jostling along as if he could be thrown free himself at any moment until he arrived at the edge of the rugged unforgiving Borrego range of twisted high slabs of earth and stone into which if a man walked he would certainly hydrate or freeze to death. Out there, the cop bathed his vehicle in gasoline and set it on fire. The car burned under the pressure of fire for over an hour until by morning it was a mere shell.

Jones reversed the tape again. A Sheriff had stopped at the station and talked to the postmaster. The day was September 3rd, the time 1325 pm. The crates were inside the room. The wife dropped by to give her husband bills, and two men rolled the cart over from mail distribution at about 1415 when the crates were getting counted prior to service delivery to nine substations. The Sheriff and postmaster left presumably around 1500 after the crates were loaded up into a van expected to end its final delivery at 5:44 pm at the new post office. The Sheriff and postmaster left together in a yellow and pale green jeep wagon.

He was unable to place where the highway cop originated, but he didn't think he was the same man who stopped into chat with the postmaster although the burned police vehicle was periodically assigned to him for field calls. Jones backed up the film just before the cop, or whoever he was because it seemed atypical a cop would behave in such a way although his fingerprints registered for State Police, poured petrol; and tested the inside upholstery for human blood and bodily fluid. The kit looked solely at color and probable marks. His computer circled blood where it had gushed all over the backseat. Probable end life surrendered a victim not unlike the dead male postmaster in the cave. Cause of death: likelihood of poison, contact with entire body.

The body could have seeped for hours, once injured, without any ability to respond to bandage. The clinic on Nicholas' doorstep was closed due to emergency; in all probability the man suffered fairly instantaneous thrombosis with fatal hemorrhage in an hour of contact with poison.

Entirely possible the wife walked into a problem. He called the number he had for her. It was disconnected, no forwarding telephone.

He lit a cigarette, sipped his sour. Something terrible had occurred. Something unanticipated but too serious to contend with. Life was short; then there was no way out.

He had the crime – he had date and time and he had a far bigger problem than he knew what he ought to say about it.

He wrote his man Meadowes.

Postal heist at Rock Station occurred September 3, 1981 on or around 3:00 pm by probable suspects: unknown highway cop, derivative of photo of burning patrol car; auto repair and gasoline station manager across the street from post office; and three unidentified truck drivers who deposit waste at Kings Inn, Bishop, CA; five photos attached, per occurrence. Delivery to Inn manager; man who purchases stamps in 29 Palms and distributes to Salton, Indio and Route 66; fingerprints on post office service in Pittsburg, CA and Snake River, ID; dead man at Fish Canyon; and above reference.

Despite the fact that the money was stolen for innocuous reasons, the Iron Curtain of Slovakia used a resembling coin with which guards bought personal cars. There was no proof that this coin had any pertinence to a Brinks heist of the similar coin for an estimated value of forty thousand dollars.

JONES

6

BOOK TWO

O CTOBER 1981
     The dust storm could be seen for miles away on
     Highway 62. In the distance the blue grain Granite
Mountains rose against an implacable cloudy sky with the
impoverished look of a landscape hurled to the outermost edge
of non-existence. On the weathered sun beaten chalky surface
of the cement riddled cracked surface of the sand blown desert
where between small towns of twenty houses barely adequate
enough to position a billboard to advertise legal services or a
restaurant and ten-room hotel lay a mile of quickly uprooted
tumbleweed and seasonal wildflowers, a fire of a car burned
long into the day and at nightfall continued to rampage with
a malicious spark as though to eradicate a sought-for buried
banality. The man who had set the fire walked across the horizon toward the road, his mind focused on only the reality that
while his survival depended upon destroying the evidence of
profuse bleeding in the backseat, he was nonetheless safer if
he kept to the back roads where he could walk back to some
seedy sort of existence. Les Thomas was an angler by nature,
a flat-footed draw man who managed his fishing line like a
steered whip; once a fish was caught, nothing could it do but

flail itself to its gradual demise. He had long ago discovered that all of life was a condition of capture. Once the discovery of possession was made realistic, there was no escape through weather or element. Blizzard snow or blizzard sand, the cast obscured all form including traveling cars. He wore an air of confidence of which he was keenly aware, because with it he gathered many who wanted to know him. He had used it to rob numerous post offices where he walked inside and although he knew he must by now be sought on any number of warrants, he was able to walk straight through a situation without being seen. He had stashed the money in half a dozen undergrounds and once every blue moon sent a package of coin to Norway to arrange the commercial purchase of men newly released from Meanness, a glass walled prison staffed by the Dutch and managed by the Swiss. Here and there when he took it upon himself to designate a resort town with his assailed fortunes, the law swept upon it with counters and gold shop to retain the stolen coin as though the coin itself represented a social order gone astray. He himself was Norway born to a father who never knew any life except prison and a mother who had done her best to see to it he stayed with his studies and entered a much needed career as a soaper to identify divergent gold coin, much like a duster with the exception he didn't rinse. His job consisted of having to be able to stack coin for other federal services particularly the United Parcel Service or Salvation Armies in foreign countries. By the time he entered La Paz he landed a career as a sheriff working the stone and sand desert predominantly. In the light tan uniform he was often over-looked; out on the mesa he usually wasn't visible at first glance; in Vegas where the gritty wind flocked over building and street alike, he was seen without being perceived to be seen as though the human form was a conjured trick of light.

He had lived as a youth in a complex compound of loggias stacked one on top of the other making four floors of archways, mazes, interior labyrinth, essentially a germ-cell that proved itself to be a malcontented shook. The maze was not governed by any Aladdin's lamp although it rested on the Euphrates and as such his selfish maneuvers took him to the rolling of logs in water by treading logs to dislodge a log and subsequently toward the durable end of his teens he was taught to stir a vast vat to produce a firm textured cheddar of white to orange color possessing a distinct sharp or smoky taste; each employment a step of minor details, a map-trade, trivial farce, barely tolerable, unworthy of notice almost having to exceed the fallacy of frequent misperception, being led astray, refuted by inexperience and not having the remotest idea as to how to pepper vats of red berries with shot to make pepper grains, permitting pink flowers in spikes to reduce acidity. La Paz took him to farther edges of the planet where he could measure the distance of running against walking based upon the spent years watching canons break in midair and determine speed. Thus he knew how far into any desert to walk a man, about as near to lethal grade as one could find while sitting under everyone's noses, inconsequent of the fact that when the Intel brought up the calendar and time just to read him he was vaguely observable, quantitative in shade, defined as a moving figure. The year was 1982 when he shot and killed a postmaster under moonlight and that one act brought in outhouses, museums and satellite dish remotes, gas stations and hotel casinos, not to mention flight maneuvers at all hours of day and night in a theater of rolling thunder.

When he was detained by the FBI, he said the man walked to the murder of his own free will. Without enough to charge Thomas with, he had no scrapings under his fingernails and his clothing did not test for chemical arson, he was released.

The arresting warrant officer said about Thomas that it was too far back historically for him to remember if there was bone under ethylene blue. Microclimatology having read the microbarograph on the edge of a restricted half mile of dust wind ash which clawed mass of sinewy fossilized rock had produced the minute chemicals that were utilized in the torch. Even the scrapings of micro morphology on the geographical area lay engraved by the fast-churning wind indicated mineral changes that would not have occurred without the introduction of sodium bicarbonate, a powder fire that caused stippling. It would have burned paint yellow, bright green, possibly pink and after fourteen hours left a faint residue. Only urine was found on the victim interspersed by the retention of particles of the powder.

The assignment included the finding of witnesses in addition to the usual of improving upon the circumstantial evidence which began with fingerprints in the smudge room for entry into the Rock post office vault at the time of the heist.

Twenty baby sparrows alit off the hanging yarn of the bare peach tree like leaves in a rustling ill wind. The rains left streets covered in water. Gusts of wind whirled dry sand like ghosted figures running for their lives.

Lt. Jim Avganes had received the prelim disposition orders to re-investigate the murders of four sheriffs and the postmaster. Already he felt like a pickle left out of the jar unable to comprehend lack of caution. This cop killer cop Thomas was a narcissist, handsome like a flare on the road to exploit women; systolic read typically one seventy over eighty-four, borderline for rage. Medical evaluations all revealed inability to hear allegations without gaze producing near-sleep; hooked on barbiturates. The murders had the hallmark tags of love on the run; a stopover in a dozen towns. Who was there who knew his ideas? Or why he sat on the road in his squad car at dusk, music blaring, playing roulette with a loaded pistol firing at a tree. It could be he boasted about his felonies. Perhaps such a name that had willfully murdered six other unexplained victims found virtually crippled due to gunshot wound scattered over the desert, the more notorious being the Suzuki motorcycle heir.

That year was 2002. A ludicrous situation at Edwards Base had resulted in ninety scientists testing vaccines for the small pox who got trapped underground for fifteen years. Their only communiqué to the government had described measurement, transformations and generalizations, interrelations and combinations of precise probabilities of disease causality; material substance as an inquiry in law that occupied physical space and had weight and was consistent in physical objects in the observable universe. The scientists were concerned solely with the physical rather than the spiritual or intellectual consequences of worldly nature of form.

The sky had begun to rain, a swift culmination of torrential nimbus columns gathering tumult until all that could be seen was fast splashing water. With it came a rigid force of breeze which picked over the bits of branches fastened in the sand, little better than lifeless when hours later, saturated in a foot of clear spring water, the dark brown branches bloomed in full white bells. Diffuse sheets of whorls descended pushing against the wind, thrashing in at windows and sand, gradually coalescing in giant puddles that extended across miles of salt-like cracked sand where occasional plumed storks stalked about like vain ill-bred girls. All life appeared as a metamorphosis of abrupt change in form where cement sand was now deep pocketed strata of sandstone containing pure crystalline water, previously petrified tree trunks illusively grown with fledgling purple wildflowers, weed strewn sand alit with marsh reeds wherever water had pooled in creek bed gullies. In the midst of the plundering sat the burned, hollowed shell of a car like the remnant of a Malthusian nightmare, the fire and ash having flecked jade and rust metal scrapings to the he was already insane, and everyone who knew him knew he was a paranoid. A man who sat prepared for his eventual captors. There was a rumor he murdered an entire family who roamed the state on motorcycles in summer, assaults that left six adults presumed dead.

Few similarities stood out on the page, a single victim himself tracked wanted felons by posse on foot; and one victim owned rights to the police single band radio installed on police motorcycles used for all desert jurisdictions, police, sheriff, marshal, ATF, Rescue and Guard.

An Italian from a traditional Catholic family, Avganes dressed in tan shirt and dark green trouser uniform, wore his brown hair scalp fuzz, was six feet, dour mien, patriarchal nose, brown eyes, squadron trained, an avid racket ball player, still youthful at sixty, and carried a logbook and manned the squad room from seven to five six days a week.

His first task was to establish any relationship for the dead to the warranted man.

JONES

7

THE INFORMATION on the Public Safety Officer in the 29 Palms Desert declared he had been a cop for Arizona campgrounds, worked at UCLA morgue and knew proven ways in which the dead die, and had handled chemical exposure; ran laboratory evidence tests, was proficient at early diagnosis, especially for prognosis of absence of protein in blood for people who walked through fire; the question on the pro-rata sheet was had he put the stolen coin through fire? Someone was convinced he had walked the entire desert at all times of day over ten years, knew every inch of land, had the feel of it under his feet because he could walk on any surface; and sat in a patrol car in an enclave where he was undetected.

For an inexplicable reason the postmaster took the man with him on his way to Tahoe. When a pointer was searched for, the Post Office had him driving on the runway in the eastern Rockies in the middle of the night where he made six post office designees under hostage conditions each orally copulate him at threat of life by machine gun inside a complex of boarded up buildings. It had to be assumed that pending a dispute or requesting quarantine or a facility in which to rinse usable money, an entire administration had taken off to a laboratory set up for those purposes and wound up as hostages for a good six years. Scout groups fanned out within hours all over the Pacific Northwest area in search of the sixty men. Were they situated inside a hotel? At an undesignated site? Inside a railway tunnel? Were they being detained at a school or possibly at a music camp on a lake?

Inside a boarded up resort at the northern corner of Crystal Lake over the California border in the bird wild lands of Oregon, a group of administrative post office station staff had the Intel monitors up on the highway road flare network. Their shift which began at five in the morning was well underway once the distressing news hit the radio bands as to the tumble of a fully filled post eighteen wheeler off the summit ridge.

What is that spot there?

The blur, you mean?

Can you identify an actual image?

This is Chicago storage. Does it appear familiar?

Somewhat. This looks like coin racks in Philadelphia.

It's odd they would displace the image there.

What's that image up above?

No idea.

See if you can get inside.

Who is that?

Didn't he go to the Middle East in 1983?

There he is.

What year do you have?

1990.

What's going on there? Helicopters, small airplane crashes, lots of honking vehicles. See how they got there?

They were driving down the road; now they went under a mountain; four hours took them to a big parking lot.

How many people do you count coming toward them?

Five or six.

Look around entire installation. How many are there?
About sixty.
Place them for origin.
They're Tibetan. All are in dark blue and gray and white army like gear. It's very bizarre; the men are getting shoved down stairs, into halls and inside closets. They aren't allowed to eat or to urinate.
It's a state of siege.
When do they leave? Let's see, that seems to be 1991.
Can you identify closest city?
Spokane.

The day wore on steadily. Accusations were in the air. A gray nondescript sky obscured the sun and from time to time kept the stark cold from descending further. It was almost the end of the year; still not a sign was acknowledged as to where the postmaster and sheriff had gone to once they ascended to blizzard heights along the far most eastern ridge. A staff at Tahoe thought they might have made a stop to pick up a mailbag along the township in the sierras, but there was no indication they climbed to that highest passage. A small airplane sat at the ready as drifts of snow plowed the run-way under considerable strewn calamity, unexpected for early autumn. A sudden rainfall leaving a pittance of salt like spray adhered to street windows. By the time the Intel transcript made it to District of Columbia, the government knew something unusual had occurred. In the Mojave desert between a lonesome road that meandered along a dried wash and the pinion mountains ten people lay dead; a lone sheriff waited along a ravine of red flowering cacti and dried shrub brush for a car load of youthful adults who had cavorted off with their parents onto a new road glistening as the day.

Lt. Sheriff Avganes couldn't imagine what it was about. Three vans pulled alongside road to let out a person who walked into the dusty desert who was sick and when he didn't return twenty minutes later his girlfriend went to find him; when she didn't return, her mother went to look; she came across their crippled bodies. She went for help.

It is said even animals possess instinct, their wailing cries while not heard are nevertheless patterned; the mother heard her son calling, a moon scattering light as she lay still sleeping in a dream.

It wasn't the issue for the crime; the assailant did not pick up a knife or travel out in an illicit covered van with a weapon; they appeared to have come across a man they had to evade as one would a dangerous terrorist in ten seconds when they may have had nowhere to go who had launched a gas tank that flew over the Sierras.

Investigator Avganes returned to his motel suite at dusk, washed dishes from breakfast, took a hot shower, spread his notes on the desk, turned on the television and collated information into concerns. There was the drive from Salton Sea after a week spent at an inexpensive motel with fourteen people crowded into three suites with kitchenettes, there were half a dozen rest stops returning home to Tahoe City along 395, driving through a sand drift, taking lunch at a resort in Blythe and playing the jukebox, changing into summer tops and sandals from jeans and warm night wear; there was walking around a small lake before hitting the long stretch. Then the disaster – illegal flight lanes were shooting out of a bunker ascending to altitude over the high desert sand and its gullies and losing lift, it junked down into a foxhole on the earth on the range a half mile from the boy beneath evaporative skies; a bullet high wave ripped through the cement hard sand barely missing the girl.

They had been reform high school teens, lanky, good looking Hispanic Indians, into their own stuff, traveling to a cheap resort with their families to visit their cousins; they had just celebrated Independence in Toronto in February with their uncle, the snows had melted when they took to the road stopping first in Denver and next in Vegas.

Who would have thought a red scone blinking above the desert floor could have disseminated such thorough destruction? Why hadn't the air force base built a wire perimeter to keep the public out? It would have been Ground Zero detonation. Whoever did the crime was wanted for murder.

All Avganes could figure out was that the sheet gave the DNA of the man doing the crime. When he went to retrieve early photos, the girl ran from the van into the heat of the desert at one in the afternoon, she all but tripped over his body. She knelt beside him, took him to her arms in a shock of devastation, clung to his body until she remembered her mother and running toward the road stumbled and hit the ground due to spitfire coming toward her like a slow moving aim.

He had worked the desolation wilderness of the Panamint Mountains up to Searchlight City of little more than crowded Joshua trees and tumbling brush having trained at Adelanto as a grease-back hiding cameras onto small reconnaissance airplanes and refinishing exterior with moonlight sensitive warm paint, slapping on the metal patch beneath the nose, keeping the beacon timed for initial flight path as well as for rapid descent to detonation debris governance. There were always the questions of assuring scatter of toxic waste element in keen patterns of tiny ridge hills, how to form solid soil despite every climate sudden change, no two errors found in the lab given any repetitive allowance or excise. The seldom appeared shrub come of excess was no discerning cooler, although on occasion the spite of having resided only in the desert, its shifting shadows making for imprints of paranoia gave way to an illusory non-containment of irritable instability. Because the staff was under a hundred and fifty scientists, once the dread of hostage was encountered, the remaining lab analysts took upon themselves a wipe-out effect of pursuing the often quoted Oppenheimer scourge, I am become death, destroyer of worlds, over an entirely presumptive degree of killing, for inevitably to open the hard ground to integrate fertilizer lent itself to a curious disfavored misunderstanding. The fact that the complex became built at the finding site of the postmaster's death was inevitably meant to restore the assessment capability for that agency; in the meantime hundreds of people who stopped on the roadside had to contend with infrequently a band of killers whose sole prerogative was to leave a waste of human life.

There could be no grand illusions as to unforgivable acts. The group that killed the postmaster were on every wanted poster anywhere, they were thought to have vanished their human form in the blizzards of sand and snow into flurries of winds, sleet, and hail having fallen by misstep down steep ravines, compasses of no durable realization. In a series of photos the cop who led the postmaster through the brush alongside a vacuous creek to a small cement installation took his life and then emerged in his uniform, drove off in his sheriff patrol car, and rode the high road into the Sierra Mountains where he sent a handful of post office trucks and tow trucks off an even more treacherous incline. If any witnesses existed who saw him push drivers to their worst nightmare, they just as quickly slipped out of sight, left the road forever.

Lieutenant Avganes kept to his usual daily doctrine. The lab report on the teens in the van destroyed an even meager assumption of courage. They died by horrible dislocations, each vertebrae cracked by some immense crusher, each phalanx tightened beyond breath. He hoped death came fast but in his experience of survivors he might understand that whatever shattered bone and wreaked loss of musculature also robbed vocal volubility. It would have occurred in an instant, a micro neutron shrunk to a second. He thought also they were mostly unaware of the cost of life; that they didn't have the where withal to comprehend their own instantaneous dying when they were flung without response of natural defenses onto the ground in a collapsed state, unable to appreciate the extent of bodily failure.

JONES

8

US CUSTOMS denied entrance to all countries 1981 after it was discovered foreigners were pouring in for training in an illegal renegade army corp.

While there, the teen sons attended army camp for rifle range training, shooting firing pins, squashing through tire runs, bungee jumping off bridges, and cable zipping in a forest from high to low ground; traversing frozen lakes and ankle-deep marshes; hanging from traps in trees, living in survival camp with a Fortress blade and semi-automatic pistol. Practice consisted of ambush and abduction, roving patrols with savage Wildman types. Periodically these men went on wilderness tomes hiding out in the forests attacking towns for money in markets. When evaluated trained at base boot camp, they entered New York state flying out of a helicopter in the dead of night to reside in unapproved condemned skyscrapers and looted stores for cashier drawers depositing these thefts in private accounts which were later apprehended anyways by real stealth. They bombed sky scraper businesses plummeting floors, rooftops, and egress until all were uninhabitable, training new child recruits whom they took as hostages, almost never feeding them or providing adequate shelter. They copied

Intel, stole jeeps off parking lots, and searched for secure stations to vanquish stealing uniforms and weapons. In five brief days their acts were considered a national threat.

By the hour Lt. Avganes received the transmission of a row of removed photos from Scott Terrier Wade, he had placed the desert larceny of Rock Post Office in Independence at the colony in the mountains inside a science lab with ridiculous enlarged photos of flying shrapnel and windblown debris. His immediate concern was for the dead postmaster – where had he been killed? Tahoe was little more than winter resorts and spring and summer blue crystal lake, handsome glass houses worth a fortune. Incline Village at its best was several stone lodges with ski jump-offs. These kids looked like affluent widow's children and grandchildren who grew up six children to each family; thirty families to a church and youth minister. For many teens who never committed a crime with their training they were advantageously offered jobs in southern Florida's border ocean patrol.

The situation was a disaster. A posse of Wildman trained adventurers had stopped a line of vehicles entering the pass at the time of day the sun moved behind the range assuming too bright glare was the cause of a post office truck stacked with mail toppled off the road falling onto a steep gorge. It looked to have taken several hours to get a crane pulley to the road to bring the vehicle up topside. Another two hours to put boxes of mail onto smaller trucks. It was there the postmaster was shot as he slid down an embankment to see if the driver was alive. Obviously someone dragged his body into a creek cave. The wanted criminals had fled on foot, four men including the cop, and a blonde. Identifications gave them as boot camp experts who trained for cut and bait and desert hiking. The lieutenant circled each individual; then posted them to warrant status.

Meanwhile up in the Great Mammoth Mountains above hard yellow and mustard colored rock, just northeast of the national park service visitor center, a calamity was occurring. A dozen men wearing fake army garb had erected a mild Sting Gut and fired it over altitude. Its beacon honed in on a creek as it flew airborne into cloudy skies crashing a NPS airplane descending to a short runway. Airport personnel ran onto the strip and bailed out the pilot who murmured his scope became interspersed with soft shell shot. The incident was called to air traffic northeast on its selector. The event was ample to send in dozens of freshwater and group teams to apprehend the five. On retrospect a truck coming through the gate could not be visibly recorded due to its having a vesper enhancement used by the military. It was questioned days after its riders were determined to have conducted an illegal operation in northern Washington State.

In another walk of life in another agency known to local Intelligence a group of agents was trying to assert to a recurrent problem – people approved for research in destitute areas were adversely affected by unusual strains of psychosocial stress as they worked labs for paramilitary observation. The Rescue unit was trained for a hundred and sixty- seven hours under the ocean and sixty-three hours in a sailboat without a motor and the sail down, which gave every man working the shift the necessary endurance for predicting outcome since the area possessed both a major river and freshwater lakes. When the postmaster's grave was encountered and cop tracked down, the initial questioning made him out to be reticent, a thinking individual, as though he were weary of recounting an exhaustive autobiography, but having been found in a bad lie, scarcely aware realistically he was lying, gone to bed and awakened the same man, he made furtive attempts to explain his presence inside a natural lab which had undoubtedly fallen sixty feet in a sinkhole, a lab which floor and walls led through a descent of a cave, its fifty year purpose which had been to detect in underground water an extensive aquifer system, for which dye tracing to map water flow, fault lines and above ground collapses through limestone revealed open trenches of abundant rainwater, swift subsistence, fallen trees, a sub-soil cracking under severe back pressure of depth. In spite of the oddity of discovery of crystalline spires and igneous gran-ite stems, rushes and serpentine mica columns, a wealth of nature, the cop was released as having no discernible motive having been seen the better part of an afternoon tramping through a forested lake burdened by swamp trees, remnants of pinnacles, distant slopes of gravel mountains of snow and ice which left a flood fallen topography with the illusion of cities floating on the air of clouds.

So there had been extensive queries. Whatever was deter-mined remained unresolved, or perhaps if loose ends could now be reasonably understood, all witnesses were dead, endangered or no longer age appropriate mentality being too seriously regressed and having mental retardation preventing them from being credible as witnesses. If they could define an assailant, descriptions varied too greatly – the man was black, Hispanic, Caucasian, young, old, with moustache, or clean shaven. Intel had him on deposit film neglecting his duties sitting inside a stolen patrol vehicle, shooting at the desert or at the pointed toes of rawhide boots staggering, drugged, intoxicated teens; his motel sheet tied to a tree flapping in a wind. Still they lacked evidence on the postmaster which was the real item. The desert now had him on continuous surveillance, morning, noon and night, and no one could grab him. Could they tie the wife in – they had her scrambling up the pass from the lab; associate her to the cop further than staying a night in separate rooms at the Sleepy Owl, proof of illicit relations or anything more suggestive, they were looking in an interstate search off dusty roads and winter moorings. He had made it to two

Tahoe stations, checked in, recorded inventory, checked cash and taken mail for distribution; and then apparently headed back stopping somewhere near or at Fish Creek Canyon.

There had to be some connection to bring out of the mountains another cop seeking the death of a postmaster captain. Lt. Avganes thought he knew what that connection was most probably about – the taking hostage of ninety scientists off the El Centro to Mountain Springs railroad station and the Chicago to Denver hostage taking of seventy postmasters nearly forty-five years ago by movie stunt artists hopping freight. Accounting investigators who periodically appraised small towns for three builders, one foreman and one landscaper had come across an essential discrepancy in the lunacy-driven bureaucracy of crime and that was photos in high altitude desert of postmasters and scientists in mountain abandoned laboratories staffed by a foreign militia, such an oddity of convention that the very finding was considered a forsaking of order led by disturbed adults who were too constrained in rational thinking to invent honest livelihoods. Instead they made a play for value stamps throughout the States like inveterate casinos that had lost sense of capable life-tending, among these was whiskey stamps for Tennessee, bean stamps for Wyoming, overseas by *par avion*, mill stamps for the Dakotas, any situation that took crates off post office trucks and destined all to an unseeming destination off on a lone pike barrel rail dock.

This sort of thing took away one's confident faith in oneself when after twenty-one years one had settled one's score with mid-life and was finally beginning to enjoy oneself on the job. Crisis had a mean way of withdrawing one's acquired enjoyment with work associates. He hadn't talked to anyone about it, just sat in a room and tried to figure out the implications until his mind began to work out the sordid details of office staff politics, who was having an affair, where they shacked up, who knew; and on the far end of that spectrum who operated a venture and how their money profited. It didn't interest him to know where the start up funds originated but he thought it was easy enough to learn. The Winnebago discounts earned anyone moon-lighting a pretty meal. There was teaching ESL, and then very popular these days selling insurance. The not so polite tricks also, drugs from Rio Tijuana including Baghdad pipe, Mesa mescaline, and Tahoe heroin. A feel-good generation of hunted kids wanted for their secretive knowledge of the desert crannies and vagabond wayward groupies, hidden places and opportune transcendence.

What was it for?

Answers were anything but plentiful.

Avganes sent for the complete file. He hoped that out of any average grid of forensic-proof photo line-ups there would be at least five clearly convincing demonstrations of the assailant.

The photograph had moved five times on the file grid over three pages between numerous photo ranking of snowfall and mountain transportation.

The tamper proof photo was in the morgues, number eighteen, at the end of the middle of the third row, the first row showed the first four for time sequences on Missing Persons for the missing postmaster consisting of rescue aircraft combing the high desert range, a Doppler survey of a map of clouded terrain, a bicycle posse over the summit, and the entrance to an underground cave system of tunnels to a lab. When the finding photo was chronicled in the 127 to 134 numbers of the 170 photos in the complete file, he was lying in the Mitchell cave lab dead of a blow from a blunt instrument which as a result surrendered him to a slip and fatal fall. Sorted out of context, although the body was not discovered until that winter in mid December, hands mottled a grayish pink, feet rigid in dangerous heat. Because a second photo displayed the body mostly blue black, these being the signature hallmark he died twice, four months apart, it stood to reason that after he was clobbered, he awakened, went for a walk, and was killed again.

A photo of a rain shadow lay in the high resolution of a two hundred optical zoom device manufactured for armored van thefts. A Remote Program Watch for Cam Watch Dragnet, a closed circuit TV, monitored twenty-four hours during all weather, day and night and predawn, with visual alarm verification, and broadcast transmittals as far north as Medford, Oregon and due far west to Brothers Island lighthouse in the San Francisco-Petaluma Bay and to Kent Island in the Bolinas lagoons.

Even with a major disturbance brewing of blowing sand and high velocity winds of forty miles an hour chasers in which everything flies, trees, tumbling boulders, gusts of gritty rocks like a Tropics bender, the advent of flowing descending air, often opaque mist, made for a shroud with cascading air flung into the path of travelling traffic. Winding mountain roads in summer thunder storms in the grid for 22 to 35 gave fog and cloud height as loss of visibility designated as IFR 500 to 700 ceiling less than a mile. Cars not only small aircraft were blown into deadly collisions, which that winter became catapulting disasters involving a vehicle in which the alleged dead postmaster was a passenger.

Other pertinent photos for that grouping listed snowfall conditions for two shots of ponderosa trees covered by heavy, light bluish flock by night; dim visibility for a collision caused by an avalanche; frozen rain curtain due to freezing temperatures hanging from a grove of thin trees standing in a flooded pasture before they fell into a sinkhole that month; rock fall boulders careened onto a narrow road above a geode tunnel during the dominant second half of a raging storm that dumped four inches of icy snow in crackling lightning toppling two postal semis and a fatality car accident in which a red car smashed into oaks; and a washout of rainwater pouring down street gutters. Where the postmaster was seen fleeing the crowding avalanche from an overturned twelve wheeler postal truck and his wife desperately trying to flag down motorists on the pass, early photos taken by aircraft gave indicators of severe distress as evidenced by skin flagella, scored retina, probable mental confusion or disorientation as a result of being in one head-on collision on a twisting curve, unsteady gait and possibly cumbersome strident response.

Avganes re-arranged the photos in history chronology charting by place and date. This task took the better part of four days. Avganes began with summer photos starting with the day of the theft at Rock Station up at Big Pine. The first photo in the second row #8 was of the postmaster hurriedly leaving the vault at the distribution center along with the security cop. The subsequent photos #s 9 and 10 showed them at a rest stop on 395 at Bishop and seated to coffee at South Tahoe.

A series of pictures found the two entered a lab attached to a cave and extensive aquifer almost a week later beginning with #139 somewhere immediately above the Incline Village post office in northern Tahoe.

Bogged down by an excess of information that included additional files, it took him several adjournments to post a logical order. Over at Truckee there were packages waiting at the train station; in an ensuing melee about sending bulk stamps to Utah and Montana post offices by train the two men pulled off the road in Dorrance listening to 1440 KMED snow conditions for road closures to Klamath Falls where a half day was spent in approvals at the depot before looping back the next morning. The journey to death took three days. It took into account a package sitting in Klamath marked for the research lab at Mitchell Cave and sometime later the blur of a camera shot of the body. The final resting place however was in a dank river building in ten below surrounded by ice, six foot high snowfall; skin well blue blackened with post mortal bestowed clammy flesh.

Once the body was brought in, lab evidence revealed assault during heat, tips of fingers lost circulation, nasal passage was glutinous and final succumbed state was determined for freezing.

When he contacted the Mitchell lab he was transferred to the chief chemist who told him that the Klamath package contained films of a crashed train from Chicago to Denver, unconscious hostages tossed into a bus, a gunned down plane in Idyllwild, and a holdup and take-over of the evidence lab belonging to the post office in Washington State for use of its unpainted trucks. The crimes stretched across states of red bean over as many miles as track put between stage coach and destination might allow and as many moonless nights complicated by howling coyotes and chilled losses of salvation.

A final report filed on the desert bodies listed sudden subsistence of the ground giving way pulling a group of six students to instant death.

JONES

9

J ANUARY 2008
The file lay in a stack of recently opened files each
which required updating onto a new card index system.
It was a few inches thick jammed full with notarized dispositions, required obituaries and numerous billing inventories.
There were no photographs. The dead could be damn near
anyone. On the top page inside the first section on top of
handwritten entries that included sheriff dispatch calls lay the
reference for the photo post warrant declaration: 148 to 170.

Someone had taken considerable effort to put in a summary of pertinent historical facts. These began with billing statements and quarterly budgets for per five year
doctrine product funds for Foundation Grant, $82,000;
State Laboratory, $2,004; Building & Research Applications,
$4,579; Equipment Lease, $50, 600; Travel for Investigation,
$4, 680; Salary, $6, 000; and Vehicle, $680; approximately
seven expenditure categories were notated with the carried
balance of $1, 118 always the same. Billing gave five item
lines – evidence, beetle test listed by batch code and date,
berry color gradation, incidence graph, stain index, and causality by bar code; all determinations referenced on dictum

files numbers 57 through 60. Activity consisting of accounts receivable, collections and debt ratio were maintained inside a thick, worn, yellowing ledger.

The next section gave terse descriptive by date and time, climate conditions, applicable morgue and medical signature, and other references. Thus numerous asset preparations consisted of wake, one dead, five adults tingling and muscular absent; shotgun firing in range mountains, 0 dead, ten adults with joint occlusion for slipping and falling off heights; funnel, seven massive hematoma, all adults with trans-corresponding skeletal dislocation; overturned rig, blizzard rock slide, icy pavement, four adults, one driver hernia, other retina blackouts and chill ear; drastic combat with brown bear and cub, two adults dead, limbs intact, vomit herniated, rifles disposed; numerous small tow trucks into lakes, 0 dead, 1 fazed with mental confusion, some halted breath; lightning down, bolt struck petrified tree but ignited fast speeding car, 1 dead due to frontal collision with high boulder; a seemingly endless list of ten or more years.

The shell of the down weaponry-fired Trans World air disaster had long ago made the rounds by fragment to over a hundred research institutes, of which Mitchell Cave was one. Eighty dead had been renewed and restored to vitality; not one life required recomposed total skeletal abridgment. Despite a terse, seldom reclaimed storage of often tedious and meticulous search as to type, twenty airplanes drifted to near-extinction crashes, many littered throughout the eastern mountain ranges of high desert isolation.

But for the sequences of fatal scenes for references of numbers 47 to 56, the sections of the complete file delved into every verified document-proof evidence available. Two numbers, 47 and 48, cross-indexed all suspects on crime to each aggregate. Thus the photo for the postmaster's wife cropped up twice, once for opening a door that led into a two-floor building in the Spokane Mountains where three post office generals were tied to bed cells and another for leaving postal crates at a market in the outlying area above Dorance which her husband's security cop retrieved and took by post vehicle to a postal office in Billings.

Jones decided he'd have to conduct an intensive look for a previous relationship no matter how amorphous. It could mean thousands of photos before he came across a match; far easier to pull telephone contacts for fifty years off a parallel index computer if he could locate a seldom required listing database which he thought could wind up being a serious negative. For people who had managed to crawl into the woodwork, any retrieval of leads was likely to be followed. He went onto his usual database to access the network.

Bess stood in the snow, blonde hair cinched to the scalp, boots to the hips, buried in thermals and a sweater and jacket, working out the prinks, sawing off broken branches, shoveling a path to each front and back doors, having now spent over a day and night summarizing his work and filing information on index cards, not to mention sticking a pot roast with yellow potatoes in the slow cooker, shredding cabbage for tomato sauce stew, and baking six yam pies.

He walked outside to where she worked. "Need any help?"

"No, Sweetheart, I've got it all under control. How's the case?"

"Coming along. Can't say I'm needing."

"Good. I'll be in shortly. Lunch?"

"Sure. Sounds fine."

He had suffered when he first retired. He'd taken to his bed, slept for months on end. Was washed up; couldn't eat. Lacked interest in just about everything.

Forced himself to get out of bed, to get moving. Took a job as a night watchman for the better half of a year.

These days he preferred to share his thinking as seldom as

possible. He thought of the relationship as a live-in without the commitment to obligation. The alone time had become a much needed priority causing him to long for the separation of household characteristic of his island years. The frequent cohabitation got on his nerves and he took long hours of isolating himself inside his study. The fact that Bess was by nature self-sufficient content in solitary activity removed the brunt of blame and gave him a peaceful self-reflection so essential to his aging. Once when he locked the study door he reproached his defended need as erecting a barrier and opened the door leaving it barely ajar but as usual she gave no notice. She was herself too complacent to comment.

Perhaps she realized he would have preferred to live as neighbors, but the uncertainty of having a big place and depending on one income was risky, and she had pursued joint retirement because it made more sense to her and six years ago he chose a plan of least resistance wanting her to be happy. Work had been so demanding he had given up his personality in too many respects to count. The Islands were everything like crime detection was for these desert badges. Nothing counted except the job until the perpetrator was locked up; the longer one stayed the less conscious one was of having a lifestyle. A sheriff served twenty-four years active duty. When retirement arrived usually around fifty years of age, any conscientious man worth his salt purchased a case of whiskey and began a slow consumption into lessening of indoctrination. It was exceedingly difficult to shrug off instinctual concern even when drugged out of daily confrontation.

Certainly a big group of train jumpers of latch-key teens borrowing of every trouble possible out of Chicago became a long lens for repetitive crime into any isolated desert or forested jungle. Jones' own recalcitrant nature belied all sorts of instinct patterning for which his career had amply supplied him with fortified hours of keen deliberation. Thus although retired to a solitary confinement of landscapes, any resurgence demanding investigative prowess grew into a deeply perceived necessity to begin a foray of facts known. If he wound up working any major portion of a year on research he was likely to return to those years when he felt overworked, subjected to an endless tedium of little known facts, an almost stupor of outpouring of tired energy feeling he had far exceeded normal limitations, job burnout, each new day feeling overwhelmed by the extent of investigation each new crime consisted of, an abrupt abnegation of wanting to find a deserving analysis.

Photos of men lined the reference pages. Typical wanted poster photos had two to seven men in the ages of late forties to mid seventies, most were reddish blond, height unable to be known before going to a fingerprint base, all were Caucasian, one or two were photographed at bomb sites. Although the wife did not appear in any of these photos, Jones honed in on streets leading to or away from her usual residence, searched for her at her job, after- hours bars, libraries, markets, coffee houses, road stays. He pulled up parking lots, database centers, gymnasiums, blizzard fly-away zones. Finally he brought up her on a special sheriff broadband computer and tracked just her. The computer circled her image twice. It found her in a wedding photo in a Palm desert oasis with a tall strange man, both in white elegance, her one shoulder bare, blond curls topped on her head, together hand over hand cutting a five tier cake lavished in chocolate and lavender roses and then in the blink of a blizzard at three in the morning manning the high road at Donner with one of the photos. They may as well have been perched in a crashed car in a tree themselves, they weren't all that easily seen.

That high road lived in a perpetual airborne silence of which a crashing boulder was its only resonance. Jones was taken aback, all thought exigent extinguished. A whitened lightning crack struck off a cliff lane of solidified rock. It would take hours to calibrate the damage people were capable of. He hadn't considered her a renegade; she had seemed placed well in life as the wife of a postmaster at a weather station, not some hussy with treasonous loose morals; could be the wedding was a photo shot for a favor to a friend. It wasn't indicative in or of itself. Jones had visited them in their modern home at Shangri-La amidst a floor of red blooming wands, cacti and sand; had admired their ease and untroubled living inside a cube court of minimalist design, kitchen and living room and shower on a ground floor and two bedrooms and bath on a loft, lounging around a pool with dark shades in swimsuits under straw hats. Who was to say who made a good judge of character? Deceit gave off raw enviable tension. There were dozens of make-over artists in Palm Springs and no one wiser to detect polygamy. She could have been two-timing the guy all along; the idea of knowledge caused a judicious knot of treachery intersected against pride of friendship to emerge, protective anger for the station master, caustic antagonism at her, more at antipathy. He recalled his introduction to them, six years ago when he rented a five room desert home, all glass and lights, lit up green like a train compartment below a starry sky just prior to meeting Bess. Having the same Japanese architect, they whooped it up long into late nights and weekends on fifteen house retreats of all buyers. It was a discreet find, each house had different lights, blue, yellow, gallows, faint orange, sunrise, dusk. For their sense of intimate identification, ill feeling sprang up. To now have to add in the certain knowledge of her complicity, he felt dismal for each of them, querulous toward her; after all, who but her could have known post delivery schedules and destinations, as well as last minute arrangements; who could have anticipated staffing changes and size of trucks for transportation? Resentment turned to bitterness. It was a serious accusation to say a woman had killed her husband over malice.

He'd ask himself where had the design begun, probably over a desire to leave the marriage although she gave no indication of dissatisfaction, no hint at being abandoned; no inclination of necessity to want her own relief. They were a friendly couple, likable to one another, often to be found in each other's footsteps; akin to no great periods of separation. Despite this accommodation, couples split up all the time; impossible to see what lay behind opaque glass. It was one of those unreasoning situations, no way to predict.

He returned to his task, to her image on the monitor, searching for any incumbent dead give-away. The photos revealed piled high drifts congealed at doorways, buried trailer tractors, roads through fresh fields too congested for passage, branches like half hidden skeletons. Somewhat anticipatory, his heckles armed against what he might come across, he slowed the pace; an indiscreet photo still had to be here. He took a break, joined Bess for pea soup and grilled Swiss cheese on rye. She didn't inquire, but he talked it through anyways.

"Seems Lester's wife planned to leave him."

"I put her in a photo committing a rugged blast. Of course, I suppose she may have had to take down an avalanche herself, but these are boulders. Perhaps Mitchell was blocked. I guess that's realistic. It might depend if Lester is dead or sealed. It's a bit crazy because she's in a wedding while Lester is still living. It looks as though she led a double life."

Jones sipped his soup. He got up and poured himself a cup of coffee. "Here's the problem; Cindy has placed flares on the road, she's frantic but she's set off the detonators."

Bess eyed him over her bowl of soup. "My guess is the authorities let her go because she tried to save Les from lack of air. Mitchell Caves is known to take rumbles."

When he went back to his desk, he felt detached.

He looked at an endless group of snowfall and hapless road crashes, before it occurred to him to obtain the tape driving up the mountain.

Here she was, dashing out of the Caves, circling out of the gigantic lot, speeding to the cliff line, a map of cross sections above the caves. She ran a red light, turned on the alarm on her vehicle roof. At some point having identified the correct road she removed a tumbler box, and was halfway down the slope to set it off. On her radio, she contacted the Institute; then a half hour later called 911.

He was dead. It took Sheriff two days working around the clock to bring Lester to the morgue.

Nothing was likely to convict; but he thought someone out there had been damn careful.

He pulled phone conversations. The year prior to his death, Cindy had talked to Lester almost once a week over a data-com line, each call about three minutes. There were numerous discussions as to road obstacles, traffic problems, down trees, fog and dim visibility, minor chit chat as to staff, and activities planned for weekends. There was occasional discussion about staffing at the Institute and tests getting run for hikers and homeless, anyone injured in the wilds.

Cindy was an independent sort who like a willful child, stubbornly afflicted by an inability to learn something she did not tolerate nevertheless recuperated from the confines of a controlling marriage. Jones would tell himself the desert was full of rebellious minded adults.

Contrary to all ambiguities Cindy met her husband numerous occasions at the Institute to carry in evidence. Her most recent evidence was redirected to Washoe, Colorado at his request because the package scanned for scalp replacement as a result of stabbings.

Similar to vomit which had to stay with the deceased in case a persistent transfusion was required; in the event of sub zero damp caused by excessive chill. Indicated for tracheotomies was Boston Research Advanced Medicine for the primary receipt of sloughed off -rejected cells.

Minute skin tissue required an ERG and ERH antibody genes that permitted coagulants.

Cindy must have had nursing knowledge – length of career helping war victims endure against malaises. She would know time it took to waste away in cold. Her expertise probably bolstered Lester's diagnostic semblance for handling chemical nauseous gasses. Probably only time requirements that all nearly dead came to was a certain knowledge she instinctually took for granted.

Circumstances of dying varied, Lester was exhumed and returned by subhuman extension where he did not retain bogginess; many a chemist who dealt regularly with drowning victims self-indicted against the possibility for drowning also. Thus it became impossible to neglect the body to absent itself.

The more frequent watery graves were boating deaths – catching a motor blade while in the water, too much sun, sleeping, drunkenness, eating too much; all caught subdural chill.

The mine operated for waste disposal, much of which was blood.

It seemed to him the method of death rested in a consultant's medical proficiency. Although in the summer the man was rescued out of a pond, pronounced dead even though his body was revived not over twenty hours, by the month he succumbed to the chill of Mitchell Caves, he had certainly adhered for insufficient coagulants.

The kicker looked to be a note posted to a death certificate.

"After dark, come to my suite;" the note read to Cindy tucked into the visor of a windshield wiper, and she did, not in the least concerned she was photographed from across the road. She knocked on a motel door as though this was a last hurrah with an indiscreet jealousy, Number 29 of The Desert Inn off the Colorado River, a swath of her blond curls falling below her shoulders.

The notion of killing must have seemed quite easy, to secure a man into a cave and sight unseen take his life irrevocably. Despite the earlier episode of leaving him to a watery field that gave way under a subsistence of cracking rock and mud, he was persuaded to return to a cave laboratory most likely by the people who had previously set about to take his life.

Jones left the house to take a smoke in the acre yard. He lit a cigarette as he gazed about. Although Lester's death appeared to be personal, he didn't think it was that easily explained. The cold made his eyes smart with tears. It was damn chilly, bitterly so. The damp ground had iced, the snow piled in long drifts. The bulky fir trees stood weighted down by immense amounts of fallen snow. He didn't think he could comprehend motivation at all; if she wanted divorce, why hadn't she just left, so it made sense that if she went through with plans to separate, something sent her right back. Possible the cop wasn't reliable with his fast-acting condition of protein deficiency or he went off to settle a score and was too difficult to keep company with. Jones figured he'd bet money on the cop having acquired his malaise as a result of having become exposed or contaminated.

He'd look at the package idea. Someone had arranged gaseous rock matter and three hours later it killed him. He'd have to determine who packaged. It looked to be from the same cave as it was sent to with sodium chlorate. Standard add for packaging. The problem was when he placed the rock matter in a silver dish to look at it under the microscope the rock gems were solid gold shiny rock. He was not suited in his toxic waste protective wear when, too late, the rocks fumed and a cloud of fumes emanated. He stepped back immediately and left into a corridor to breathe.

Across town at the desert hospital lab the same rock matter was placed in a plastic white petri dish under decontamination procedure for which each of five chemists handled the same matter as a stream of heat filed into the lab.

Jones returned to the computer. The document read for adequate barium burial. His gaze looked at the initials. They were the postmaster's lab assistant who stayed over at his home on weekends. She wasn't permitted in his lab, she only evaluated drugs.

The test on rock matter revealed it was absorbed into trees and read for human wastes. There was also no umbrella; a match against blood sample.

The problem was that the billing didn't correlate to the correct lab; the initials read for the female lab analyst who took the note to the motel. Presumably she went to pick up new assignments, not to bring disposal.

The blood type was for a male with low red blood cell count 11. Blood looked a certain way for murder and not for disposal, that was the real issue, human blood disposal was usually found in rock.

There was pistol shot in the bodies in the desert when the bodies found. One didn't have to have a way to get rid of a body. The Post Office knew what evidence should be; the lab made it look like a transfer of human parts when it wasn't and shipped the specimen to the lab it originated at for an analysis of probable type of death. For unknown reasons they didn't want that specimen registered in as containing no human parts.

JONES

10

THE DAY began as it usually did; striations of clouds over a light blue sky, the parched beige desert floor damp with the first intake of rain. The sole house on the cliff overlooking the Joshua Tree National Monument let three teens out the back door for an afternoon grill, for which the hermit residing across the dirt path came down on his bicycle to join them. He was tall, tan with a roundish face, large eyes, and moustache, a mild looking non partisan male whose brother worked security at Rock Station. An imperceptible wind blew sand in all directions bringing with it erratic rain, too soon evaporated into air. Today the hermit carried a metal box which he opened for them to examine. Inside were at least a dozen gold trinkets, some pieces as big as fingers; a real killing as far as anyone would ever guess. From hour to hour he would laugh with the overconfidence of a cage man that the goods arrived periodically from the Klondike, pieces as long as a man's leg. Lunch came off the grill in healthy steaks of seared chicken, together with chunks of potato salad mixed with diced pickle and bled tomatoes, the feast would substantiate several days with cool methamphetamine keeping away hunger. The desert was a lone coyote's paradise,

shrieking contentment to the edge of civilization, the yellow meandering light of a cargo train attuned to nothing but
empty space, fauna, a sea of sage, yellow sandstone monu-
ments rising off the white sand soil at recessed embankments
below sea level. Into the night, music rock and roll blaring
off the stereo, a block of light seen in the darkest night, came
hysterical laughter, sound that traveled into distance, the four
of them on bedrolls beneath a long plank of glass fixed slightly
ajar above a screen, everything humorous and silly, the stupid-
est expressions taking on a crazy sort of living, each person a
star gazer, each set of stars iridescent and vivid.

JONES
11

T HE ANZA Borrego Range gave the eternal mountains of the federal deposit lands the bureau role of
watchdog for its more sinister chemical waste deposit.
Mud hills, high mountains scalloped by snow caps, gravel terrain of nothing but eroded gray rock matter, slot canyons with
waterfalls and then slanted sand covered rock wilderness in
all directions, only purple wildflowers, here and there yellow
and white, parched riddled cement, cracked sand, for miles
the world a barren landscape of ravines, canyons, and peaks,
shrunk foliage, by moonlight a wasteland of vanished living.
The air was suffocating hot, vamped, a closet of abstinence,
forbidding comfort, sticky and oppressive; at night far below
chill, trunks of trees ivory like bones.

On the vista overlooking the spaceship standing on its fins
stood the home of Michael Heavenly of Healdsburg, Germany,
co-manufacturer of Chevrolet, who in his youth married
Radcliffe flame, Mary Carnal, known to the world as carnal
desire for her silky bronze blond hair and soft feminine stature.

Alleged relation of Andrews Villikan and Roberta Bowman,
Carnal placed restrictions on physical science of astrophysi-
cists after the deadly incident in favor of a neuropsychology

philosophy to focus on the sickness of human anxiety in the quest for the stars despite her being an airplane pilot herself able to fly at five thousand feet without air chutes.

The two were out tooling about on Heavenly's Duisenberg motorcar with limited radio distance in the Southern California desert when the ground lifted like a heaven into the air flying them to scattering winds. As they flew to earth, bullets shot as if from a canon and took her in the back and rib cage. Prior to the moment she lost her wig, they were the celebrities of the eastern seaboard where Mrs. Heavenly had just opened the Institute at Princeton. The Heavenlys were an enactment of human liberties, socialites who traded in their poisonwood bibles for a new religion known to the world as the movie-era motorcar presented during the ribbon cutting ceremony of the first kitchen in a movie. On occasion they visited her teenage nephews on their ride back from Rialto Palms on the other side of the bridge off the Sultan train station and train yards. Michael himself was known to the gold industry for having invented cast clay which restricted fossil gravesites leaving any portion of burial intact. Invited to operate a lab company in Hollywood, he brought his carnal desire west to the inveterate cement riddled mountains which would one day become Joshua Tree laboratory base.

The situation probably wouldn't have gone far had the hermit who received dinner at the house where the teenagers lived not submitted several gold pieces for proof of gold value to the Heavenly lab. Heavenly was often in dry wit humored by the reality that the kids were distant relations of his ex-wife; he declared the few gold pieces were of rare value but had been removed from a dry bake lab and wanted to know the location. Confronted by the horror he might go to prison on a train line sentenced in the high Sierras, the hermit lied saying the gold originated at an abandoned mine at Searchlight. Heavenly entered the explanation on his coveted application to UCLA. Within a year the university built sites at both Coronado and Searchlight and sent detectives to look for gold adventurism. The gold tested for a group of people who rolled big post office trucks off steep mountain passes who stole the kits containing gold.

By the evening on the inland freeway when six bodies were discovered dead shot to death, one teenager left upright in a hole in the hard ground, news of the attempted murders of nearly all Heavenly's killed went live on radio stations nationwide. Heavenly suffered dislocation of the lumbar; her husband took shell cap blasting to his right ear. Another body was found, both arms twisted as though he were tied to a tree, approximately a half year later in the hills of Searchlight.

The saltwater sea at Trona toward dusk saw five aircraft lift in formation and fly over the beige snow flanked mountains most evenings into dispelled darkness when the metallic wings swooped down onto desert roads, clouds of sky closing in. If it could be said in the past before she lay severely injured that Mary Carnal marshaled in sights of apparitions across the desert floor leaving the painted hills fit with ponds, certainly it was acknowledged that a detachment flew only to dot the desert with new outcroppings of purple wildflower sprung to existence as tortured shrub broke loose with dew. The sight at the heights of salt was mesmerizing and no one knew how life grew.

The circumstances of removals of waste burial deposits could not be comprehended. It might not account for all the air space landing test sites or for a consuming fear of tracking down the last sexual partner who gave the murdering cop an irreversible fatal disease; probably not consensual sex, a rape at best assuming the female knew she had a contagious life threatening illness. The only oddity after stalking these people for years must have been that the coin stolen was virtually worthless, good only for the purchase of stamps.

THE DEAD

1

THE HOUSE had been in the family for years. While we were growing up, it was a gigantic four room cottage on a dock off a narrow river on the Great Lakes which froze each winter; in snow a ranch house with a side of glass; in summer it sat on a breath of lawn amidst a focus of elm. At one point all exterior was replaced. From the front surrounding the door was dark green wood panel laid horizontally; on both sides red brick around three windows, an all wood porch with five stairs on which sat four broad rocking chairs; on one side a wide window overlooked the river, at the back nothing but mowed grass to sand and a pier with a light on the end, no boat; the other side looked onto dappled shade of elms, shaded dry dark dirt and a ground cover of cotton candy and a hammock.

Voices out of memory give me a start.

"Oh, Benny, are you about?"

"Here, Karolina, come find me."

"Hey, hey, Benny. Oh, Ben-nee."

Our voices from the past call out as though it were yesterday, resonant, distinct, and disappear as if in ghosts.

Or perhaps I will say that years long gone make for

fruitless distractions.

I have never been one to be maligning or hurtful but on that particular day I said remarks I would live to regret. I can still hear myself, angry not to have been invited onto the lake.

"Come here." I can hear Ben calling me far off from the glade.

"I'm coming." I ran toward the sound of his voice.

And then the sharp words, harsh and unforgiving, light of day dying. Would I ever forget them? I remember because I have no choice not to.

I awoke with a start. The jagged cry of a buzzard penetrated my dream state. I donned my white worn robe and hurried down the hall to the yard for a look. Nothing, no one was there, just the mist rising off the water. In the distance through the shroud of mist was a figure in black casting a net off a small boat.

Life worries us all. It compromises our comforts, scorns our wizened senses. Who is there to see us, to guard us if we fail? It's just intended to be a question, not necessarily a reality. Reality, of course, offers no explanations as to disturbing trifles.

I was living in upstate New York when my mother passed. I hadn't seen her in a year. I was hard at work in the morgue on the shipping docks. My brother Adam boarded the house and contacted a solicitor who read me the will over the phone. I was to inherit the house and Adam the lake side summer hall. The house had a musty dank odor throughout; the maid cabin was lived in, a scaling down at ninety-five when my mother had stopped walking and getting about.

We were surrounded by dismal brokers, each one more person in an endless list of nobody's who had the tolerance of a thimble; just a stream of low grade humpty dumpty's whose idea of intelligence got engraved in mud. The exactness of crime and criminal intent revealed a shorn lifestyle of repeated mid day thefts that could stymie any an uninvolved individual.

We lived a closeted life. Winters were kept in a sand-stone balcony townhouse in New Rochester; summers at the house were given on rafts sailing downstream. The house stood through lesser enticements, four of us sitting on the lawn under the elms watching speedboats jettison in wake. Ben Charly lived on the opposite bank. He was a strapping boy, a presidential college lifeguard whose sturdy air never released minor confidence. Despite popularity, he exuded sadness, an erstwhile longing of inquiring gazes as if waiting to be accepted and not sure he would be.

The recast of fifteen burglaries on the eastern embankment left a cowling howl. A bounty of police arrived, measured break-ins through the treasured lawns and Victorian gardens, red tape across grounds and a watch-guard posted round twenty-four hours. Dubious penitence made for ongoing distress calls until one by one few properties were boarded up and remained empty. Not the least was the couple removed by boat patrol to an awaiting ice cutter on the marsh. We convened on stories made up to explain the night raid by police bearing rifles upon mounted crannies.

"Come quick, John. The old Gardener lady's dead in the dirt." An officer's horror was palpable.

Another voice was slightly querulous. "It doesn't make sense. There's not even a cent in the house."

"I found the drapes opened. Maybe she enjoyed watching lightning strike the bay."

"The Lighthouse reported a yacht downwind keening to the Mitt."

"Who knows if the assailants knew these home-owners personally?"

We strained to hear other pronouncements like soft waves breaking against pilings.

From across the bay the vessel remained break lights bright red for hours.

The up-welling sorrow is so vividly perceived it feels as though I might sob uncontrollably; where it springs from I have no idea. It's an idea of someone's, I suppose; who is seeking an anchor in living.

"Jesus, will you look at this?"

No one knew we were there within listening distance. Thus, there was no need to have explanations. The wind breeze breathes and abates; on a high course it whistles a bit, at length it dies altogether. Even now it holds me in a peculiar possession as if heard, it enters one's dreams.

Might I be excused from its fleeting terror? Working the Plains cargo shipyards, I'd met tens of detectives, each their own desk of expertise. It wouldn't be me to pry; although I have no worries to pursue, that memory of the break lights flood in with recurrent tides, a red alarm shining in thick rising mist.

The schooners lined up by barge tow at the western coast wharf of the Great Lakes beside the turnstile lit lighthouse, plenty of ice floating freely. The wind sharpened a captain's ears, blew drifts in for a mile. The horn blowers recapitulated a good blast of ear-piercing sound as their ships steadied on choppy waves. Every so often a body was pulled in, having been blown to sea under conditions of slipping ice. The twilight of day returned seldom visited views of oppressive past memories. I thought I would escape altogether the haunting debut of lives removed. The fact was I had abandoned studies of psychology by trading them in for a chance to row asphalt on coastal shoreline. In those days I believed myself adventurous struck by the calling ocean roar. Today I am placidly retained, worn to the joints with everlasting thick coil rope burns, willing merely to wait for a boat to steer in dockside.

What could anyone express had the same crime to repeat?

As if Life doesn't come often with complications and hazardous revelations. The jagged sound of an owl alighting became
once again a sordid flight, I ran through the hall into the trees,
caught sight of an ambulance on the opposite launch green,
and grasping my shawl stood in stark terror as the bodies of an
entire household were loaded up. It takes any person another
series of thoughts to question why.

This hour I walked onto the dock and waited. The ambulance had loaded four dead bodies and one injured. That was
the biggest indicator they were murdered, because people don't
as a rule die at the same instant. The driver waved upon seeing
me, and I waved in return. As he proceeded up the knoll out of
sight, I asked myself, how common was that, a Tudor mansion
filled with nothing but the dead? The eventide of nightfall left
a stigma of uncommon category over that estate.

I stepped down onto the small boat and sat on the even of
the bench and rowed across the river to the opposite embankment, got out and lugged the row boat onto finite ground and
walked up the bend some mild kilometer to the four gabled massive brick house. It stood on a parcel surrounded by seven standing stone nymphs with arrows in their hands and a drive made of
bronze cobblestone. The green copper front door was ajar.

I entered fascinated by dark pink stone high arches, leaded
pink and green stained glass windows and a fluted mantel-
piece over a quick hearth without ember. Sheets lay over the
furniture; beneath them were high backed, black ivory sided
damask sofas of blue needlework depicting lovers' trysts. The
handsome ash pine floorboards lay cold, apparently unused.
That great room descended down a small handrail of five
broad stairs into a cool kitchen and sitting room outside where
the ambulance had parked near a grove of manicured rose
trees. A table was set for five; half eaten food of cubed shellfish
and stewed carrots, ham hock, green beans and noodles sat
in a large baking dish, a used spatula beside it. I smelled the

profuse scent of fresh blood from the first flight of stairs which led behind the dining hall to a higher floor and separate wing overlooking the marsh in five bedrooms, movie studio, bar with kitchen, supper chamber, and five long baths. Here in the bedrooms lay a blood bath, light yellowish streaks of bloody slashes, telltale signs of having consumed a quart each of wine, as if a jealous lover had quit sanity. Up close the bodies reeked of sweetness seconds prior to a sour odor. The shades were raised; through the marsh the fog rose, ominous, on cat paws. Banging shutters offered no respite. Wind rattled the roof and window panes and occasionally ceased and then started again.

The astounding signature of death gave me a reminiscent pause. Often boat deaths saw thinned blood over tablecloths and cabin bed sheets. The slashed blood looped upward suggesting an early meal, some sort of additive but probably not poison, and swift sleep. No one would know why no one ran to a window to scream for help. No one yet would learn who called an ambulance. I backed away from the violence, made my way down the stairs, breathed in fresh air outside, edged the boat onto the water, got in and rowed to my pier.

Nerve gas was used. The morgue lab thought it came from a device used to restore gas lamps or a remote possibility, a tiny device off a vessel used to breathe life into a very drowsy older person. Nerve gas produced the same faint liquid blood splatter. Usually this type of death occurred in gardens; rarely along a river, but on the lakes nerve gas was utilized for all different purposes: to reduce sidewalk ice in winter, to split apart icicles on vessels before sailing, and as breathalyzers prior to a dive under ice. The finding was popular rumor by the day my maid arrived to clean. An incoming phone call had gone unanswered from a nearby mansion whose upstairs studio looked onto a gabled bedroom and movie studio. The dormer lights had flickered and doused repeatedly giving rise to suspicions of burglary. Since all were dead inside, it was unlikely one of them had flooded the upstairs wing with the chemical; much more likely that a person who brought it in took it with them.

The coroner who had to be on site for a blood death had been there. He took twelve vials of blood and weighted the bodies prior to transportation in the event if any came to, there wouldn't be a convulsion.

2

I T WAS a complacent warm day, nothing to do except watch a little television weather, sip coffee, and work the crossword puzzle. Wood was stacked against the side of the house; the lawn had just been mowed. The windows were opened to air out the house. I was reading the newspaper first thing, still dressed in my woolen whites, gradually becoming alert, when my brother pulled his tan station wagon into the carport. Adam wore his usual red and black plaid trousers, black nylon shirt and red vest and matching gloves and woolen hat. I poured coffee in a Spode cup and saucer and handed him the news section.

"When do you suppose we'll see some rain?" He made light conversation.

"We've had snow; it'll be along shortly." I held the entertainment section in my hand. "Who have you booked for the lodge?"

"A comedy routine, nice couple. I saw them perform in upstate Yonkers."

"Early or late night weekend?"

"Late. Nine to midnight."

Since Mom passed, the lodge had become his life and he

gave to it faithfully morning and night. I'd discovered he even slept there forsaking the long trip home across the bridge.

"Any likelihood you might consent to a spring event here on the green?"

"Not a chance after what happened. It would wind up being a bunch of thrill seekers."

"I could staff."

"Won't."

"Has anyone come out since?"

"Not a soul. My guess is the matter was open and shut."

"My guess is the property will go to Ben Charly."

"What's it have to do with Ben? Isn't he up at Green Bay manning the ships?"

"I think so. It's technically his family's property. He's the remaining inheritor."

"He probably won't possess. Every last person has died there."

"Maybe he'll sell."

I couldn't see it either way. We sipped our respective coffee, thoughtful. "What's the word?" I inquired.

"His wife's driving down to inspect the estate."

"What's she like? Have you met her?"

"The non worldly type. Petite, small-chested, cropped hair, a sailing mug herself."

"What's her name?"

"March Rouw. Suits her, I'd say."

"I'd like to meet her if she comes."

We took a stroll on the gardens, most covered still in irregular clumps of snow. I paused to run the hose to melt off the ice exposing the inlaid cobble walk. Then I coiled it and we resumed our walk to the dock. We sat at the end side by side feet dangling over the plank.

"I've put in for an addition for another lounge."

"That's money well spent."

"I'd like lots of windows looking onto the harbor."

"Will the city grant you a permit?"

"They said it'd be a month."

"Then we'll celebrate."

"What were you told occurred?"

"Looked to me they were viciously slain, although the Coroner gave cause of death as nerve gas."

"Thin blood?"

"Plenty of that. I gave myself a walk-through. It's an immense house."

"Is there any indication of what took place?"

"Nothing."

"When did the police call an ambulance?"

"I didn't see any police, only the departing ambulance."

"Maybe one of the family rang for security."

"Could be. No way to know."

"It probably looks bad for Ben as sole survivor."

I was appreciative of the fact. The detectives routinely focused on whoever wasn't killed. Of course, he hadn't resided there. He worked three hundred miles away in a forested frozen lake salting lanes, tying up tugs, watering decks of ships, storing fifty warehouses, accompanying ferries to isolated fishing bays. The way I'd heard it was that Ben's parents had died in an automobile crash on the Mile leaving an aunt and her husband whose bodies were hauled out when we were children. His aunt's next of kin had been removed yesterday. That left Ben – sure, I could understand what any simpleton might assess.

"Who had nerve gas?" Reality had finally caught up to Adam who had always been the slow one to appraise anything.

"Oh, yes, I asked myself the same question. I think the gas lamps were deliberately cracked. Airborne, the fumes turn noxious. It's the same on a ship's wheel."

"I see," he said, as though he were staring right at the

assailant. "I doubt Ben will want to deal with any of this."

"He probably won't have to."

"Unless he is somehow implicated."

"I don't know how that would be." We were going in circles, each smaller. "He'd have no reason to want their demise. It'd be easier to take them to court if he suspected problems."

Our deductions fell to a lull. We sat broodingly, obsequious of fact. It was a detriment to suspect the worse because we knew him, an outer range sort of proposition to view the secrets of their dying; while joined to living they hadn't stepped past their own yard. It seemed only that they lived sight unseen without dependency on anyone in the tiny community.

Then the amorphous quality of the unreal struck me. "I didn't see a phone anywhere inside the house."

"Oh, that is a consternation."

"Yes, perhaps there's one at their pier to send for a boat."

"Hideous to wonder such a hypothesis. Maybe the ambulance driver murdered them."

"I saw him."

"Well, you could always say you didn't get a good look."

"He saw me."

"Shall I hire a guard?"

"You might. The assailant probably arrived to the dock. Maybe it's a neighbor. Do you remember the first deaths?"

"Yes. They had an outlandish argument. I heard it from our side of the river."

"What did they argue about that night?"

"He found her with another man."

"Who was he?"

"I don't know. I don't think he said. He'd come home late and discovered them in the garden."

"Where is that man? He must have survived, don't you imagine?"

Adam thought it over. "It could be that was his body."

"Odd, if no one's asked."

"Ben was here in those days. He may know."

The water swirled beneath us in a sudden breeze. Our reflections snagged us like falling disjointed bodies.

"Weren't there police?"

"Everywhere for days."

"Did Mother ever speak of the crime?"

"She said Dibs was not the nicest of people. Dibs was a man-catcher."

"She stole another woman's husband?"

"I'm not sure he was a husband."

"I bet it happens all the time. Look at what Dibs owned. The man was probably easy."

"It's primitive thinking," Adam said. "I think Mom thought Dibs wanted a life of no obligation."

"And he gave her five offspring?"

"I'm not defending her."

I see myself at age seven; across the river wandering through the lean trees a naked female walks. She looks young, possibly in her late twenties. Her hair falls down her back, it is cool blond, her legs are spindly, her gaze doesn't light on me.

"Maybe she was a bit crazy," I remarked.

Adam glanced into my face with sincere honesty. "I used to watch her. I thought she was beautiful."

"Was she naked?"

"Sometimes."

"Did you ever find Ben watching?"

"I saw him seated inside a boat."

"Maybe he was crazy too." I was being withholding, a bit jealous of her.

"He used to row her in nothing but a jacket that came down to her knees into the bay in the middle of the night."

"Did they mean anything to each other?"

March Rouw stood on the opposite dock looking every inch the self-possessed wife. She cut a tall lanky figure, wore her dark hair short to the nape, and had curious blue eyes; she was dressed in dark green breached louts and a pale green cashmere sweater, a grey shawl and black leather gloves. She was extremely young, maybe twice Ben's junior, not quite thirty-six.

She waved. "Oh, hello, might you be Karolina, by any chance?"

I was coming down the lawn, sipping a cup of strong China tea. "Yes," I shouted. "Are you March, Ben's wife?"

"Yes, yes. Should you like to attend dinner tonight at, say, five?"

"Oh, absolutely, thanks."

"Bring your friend."

"My brother. I'll ask him. Is Ben with you?"

"No, he's not free until summer. I'm sorry."

"It's alright. We haven't seen him in thirty years."

"It's seasonal here."

"Yes, six seasons, autumn, fall, Indian summer, winter, spring, and the oppressive heat."

"We have thaw on the Mitt."

"Does that exceed winter?"

"Yes, spring arrives late in May. Well, I shall look forward to seeing you."

"Thank you for the invitation."

It would be hours before I arrived to an awareness that she had visited one summer at age fourteen just after the murders. I had a vague recollection of her. It was entirely possible I confused her with Ben's cousin as she meandered on the lawn wearing a see-through sheath over a white sharkskin bikini, her long hair tied loosely falling about her shoulders. I confirmed this sixth sense when she greeted me at her door dressed in a pastel blue sheath with a blue slip beneath and a lacy silver cloth belt. She was painted in enough make-up to give her a delicate appearance with frosted blue eye shadow. She was the king returned after neglectful years to claim her man.

"I understand it was a tragic episode," she stated, as we sat holding dry martinis inside the dining hall, its walls pampered in evensong dark tan with gold swirls and a lavish chandelier.

"Four deaths. They were brutally knifed, blood streaked the bedroom walls. I heard they breathed nerve gas."

"I was told that too."

"I can't imagine that one person killed them each."

"Maybe there were several killers."

The liquor went straight to my head. "Was there a police report?"

"I am not permitted any discretion."

"You haven't been told anything? The bedrooms are in shocking condition."

"I can see that. Ben was told they had dinner and went to bed after consuming a good deal of wine."

"Nothing more?"

"No."

"Where were these children when their parents died twenty-two years ago?"

"They were attending a board and care private school in Rochester. That's where they were born and raised."

"What were you told about Ben's aunt and husband?"

"That they were discovered strangled on the premises in the woods. Their bodies were nowhere near each other. Apparently he ran for help."

"I heard she had a lover."

March mused it over tasting the sugar coated rim of her martini. "Maybe it was taken out of context. She sometimes took off her clothing."

"Did you know either?"

"I knew Seamus by reputation and had met Dibs on a handful of occasions. Dibs was one of these free love females.

She herself married young while attending nursing college at Dartmouth in Plymouth, Rhode Island."

"Is it true she stole Seamus from another female?"

"It may be; I haven't heard it. He was a physician for the shipping yards in Minnesota. He worked hard ice fall winters. I doubt he was home much. Perhaps she was lonely and that's how she got a reputation."

"What did Ben say about her then?"

"First his parents, then his aunt died. He thought she fell."

"Did he talk to you about her?"

"He claimed she was eccentric and flighty. He'd come across her and Seamus asleep in the grove naked on a blanket. Ben said Seamus was handsome and Dibs was beautiful. He said he almost stumbled onto them making love one afternoon. He didn't think she ever saw another man as she did Seamus."

March went into the kitchen and returned with two hot plates of sand dabs in butter and white wine, sides of mashed sweet potato with a dab each of Japanese green mustard and a small portion of pink sauerkraut, and a glazed cinnamon roll.

"This looks fabulous, March."

"Great. Let's start in, shall we?"

"Where are you from?"

"I grew up on the Lakes out on the peninsula of Sandia. I became accustomed at an early age of twelve to shoveling coal for ship fuel. My own family operates the steamers on Lake Michigan."

"Are you glad to be here?"

"Anything I can do to help Ben brace up gives me a certain worthy contentment. I'm most familiar with billing for county uses of his fleet. There's unclogging the sewers, catching the grain, taking cows across the channel for butchery, bringing in small tugboats; it's an operation that runs fairly constant. During the off season when I'm not sailing a ship myself, I sit the station on the wharf."

"What does Ben intend to do with the house here?"

"He wants me to throw on some fresh paint and plant a new grove and prepare for move-in."

"You've seen a good number of people in your life. What do you make of the acts?"

She ate a bite. "It's impossible to comprehend sick people, but I'd guess the five kids made enemies in their lives. Who else would dream up such an act of madness?"

"The crime was made to seem as though the house itself is the complaint."

"Ben said the same thing."

"Did he?"

"Well, they were his cousins. It's natural he would be sympathetic. He thought the killer may have worked rope tying ships and long boats to the fix, since it's not all that uncommon for rope to also have to shrift to set a boat free especially on a buoyant wake. But then you get the implication, don't you? This would be someone tremendously skilled at using a blade handle. Ben thought that this person was most likely male but his ideas don't eliminate a female particularly where history is concerned. Any onlooker could have thought Dibs might fare best without Seamus."

"Perhaps someone thought he'd do better without her."

"Yes, we've talked about that often, but they're all dead, so what does it matter? Talking won't bring them back." She broke the roll in half. "Initially the four girls were unwilling to inhabit. Their brother was not much better. It takes a certain conviction not to be queasy after a parents' murder. There's the town to consider, gossip, people are anything but polite; most are total sharpeners."

"I know what you mean, offensive in a confrontational manner as though one ought to have prevented the bloodshed."

"Quite."

"Did you know any of Dibs' children well?"

"Tennyson. She resembled her mother the closest. She was blond like her mother, willowy, delicate in the face, a spring nymph at nineteen; somewhat possessed of mind in her desires. Ben asked her to run the wharf tuxedo, the expensive monthly shipments."

"What about her siblings?"

"They stayed primarily at Dartmouth until five summers ago and then I didn't come down. I rarely saw them."

"Were you cognizant of any rumors?"

"Cog, what?" she asked, her eyes drunk, and poured me a refill martini. "Plenty of rumors exist when each child is named for a poet. Tennyson was said to be in love with her older sister Dante, also a stunning blond, tall, coveted for her thin shoulders and slender waist. I doubt though they would have said their affection was wicked."

"Were there betraying gestures?"

"Probably not many. Dante was seen from the pier post kissing Tenny. They were hauled into therapy on the straight away where they each denied the allegation. I'm not certain the warning stopped the nightly goings-on at least until I put my foot down and sent Dante back to Plymouth."

I had tensed internally. I wondered whether Dibs could have seduced her own children asserting to an unnatural disposition of experimentation. "How do you suppose they learned this behavior?"

"Anything's possible, I'll grant that. I think if a child views enough deranged acts, he or she eventually imitates it. Dibs was seductive. Anyone seeing her on those sojourns became fascinated by her body, although I'm sure nothing sexual transpired."

"Well, such matters are difficult to observe even when they may exist."

"Probable you are right. The first time I came to visit Ben was after the deaths and not much was said. The children were in their youthful adolescence."

"Ben is fairly reticent about most matters of family. At least he's had you to talk to."

"One has to read into what he means. He's reserved that way with me too usually. I try to cajole him, get him to say what he thinks."

"Well, of course, I was much younger than Ben when we were growing up. Had he to have told me anything of significance I doubt I could have understood him then or now."

"Dibs was found lying dead in damp earth. Seamus was found beneath piled leaves. Both were fully dressed. No one knew what had occurred. It was as if Seamus went about seeking her before he was struck dead."

I carried the distant limitation home. March would likely fit in with her newest liberty far easier than anyone could reasonably adapt. The floor was warm with the embers in the hearth; Adam sat on a couch in front of the fireplace deep in concentration reading when at my presence he glanced up at me.

"How did dinner with March go?"

"She was friendly, moderate in the way Inland wives are." I sat beside him. "She worked barge and stream."

"Did she have any opinions?"

"Only that the mad smasher may be a rope and handle on the wharf."

"So you two girls talked seriously."

"Hard not to."

"Would I like her?"

"Oh, probably; she is after all Ben's love."

"She has been since Dibs was killed."

"She talked about Dante and Tennyson."

"I've always thought they were fairly misunderstood. Their attentions were simply child play, and then it isn't what it was made to be. Dante was adopted at nine years old. The other children were of course the family entity."

"What were their sibs named?"

"The boy Emerson was a gifted physician on outbound ships. The other two girls were Donne, a mermaid of divers, and Merwin, a beachcomber of sunken ships."

"What did the poet Merwin write?"

"No one who watches sand banks form knows why sand nudges into shapes," he paraphrased.

"Their parents must have had a love of imagery of the lakes."

"To be kind. The sad fact is they were hooked on the heroin."

"Heroin causes blood to be pronounced in the height of streaks and light pink at the dripping end. It's not heroin these kids went to the grave with."

"That was the parents' goodbye charm. Dibs didn't function without it. Seamus did whatever Dibs did."

"Did Ben ever talk about that night?"

"Not in so many words."

"I think it's possible he had an affair with his aunt Dibs on one of those excursions on his boat."

"You are dreaming, Karolina."

"Am I?"

"Yes, Honey, you are. There's no way in hell Ben could have been lured by her. None. He is a good man with honest desires."

So there it was; proof of Ben's character. I had never had a chance at him. He had escaped a clandestine illegitimacy early. "Were the girls close as a group?"

Adam gave it some small consideration. "Emerson, Donne and Merwin lived within blocks of one another for years before moving down, although I tend to imagine they didn't want to reside with either parent which is understandable. Their careers were taking off; they had places to go. Donne was married for a few years to a surgeon who died.

3

I T HAD reminded me of the day on the beach in upstate New York where I was in the waves along with a hundred people when the sky began to snow and did not stop until the boardwalk reached blizzard proportions.

He was already ten steps ahead of Geraldine in the snow. His arduous back muscles worked off a tension in a rigorous stride. So accustomed to taking charge he was without notice of her. From a distance he seemed purposeful, and possibly upset. He threw open the barn door and disappeared into it. March followed equally intent. She felt she was on the verge of a decent recipient cattle run. She wanted to know why he continued to refuse marriage. She was the only one who did the things the way he had liked.

On the long peninsula, the pope Sir Thomas Sarhoyan Aquinas' body was found at the bottom of Candel Lake, which when it was renamed Superior Lake bloomed in summer houses. He was minister of hardship who understood the shrinking lakes for Chelsea, Marra, and Huron.

Sir Pope Bethelesmy was found on a yacht stone cold dead due to being knocked off by boom. Catholic Charity, Champlain Lake, college camps – Sir Thomas Aquinas, priest parishioner celibate, 95 footer, swinging boom driven by older brother, kills him; he lay dead dished out on deck.

Up at Tuoleme Lake, a fast speeding roadster had had a first accident with a tractor pulling out into bend of road. He was Peter Proust known to the world for being from Wind Daum, Great Britain and his carefree wife with four nieces in the cabin in a brown Rolls Royce car with chassis were unaffected physically, wind factor 2, speeding back onto the road he took another wall stile at the channel, mud congealing up to the stirwall at 90 mph. ramming a wall so hard his body and his wife's sank. He was the expert testing of the Brentwood car he drove for sturdiness of the entire car against frame rattling windows.

The report alleged he was going to a physician in the wooded lake private sanitarium; there was every possibility he had to locate an illegal deed for pond and property for illegal runoff from Death Camp Lake which was four miles down road when he either swerved to clear a tractor moving at 1 mph or a tree, then backed out, landed in a cow trail bridge stile which was almost totally consumed by mud and was killed due to the influence of partiality for those only in the car.

When they were revived spitting up water, there was an awareness of having gone under.

This was Birchwood, Canada where entertainment at unauthorized mills off the train; all since were shut down left to weeds; dark painted fences were exteriors of gardens inside which prison families lived for reckless sex parties. Houses on coves of Chicago were given for the insane only; one could never have invented the very thing that should have saved lives if to do so meant killing endless numbers of innocent people.

The manufacturers were Peter Ductford, manufacturer of car as a bomb to buildings and Charles Iffy, inventor, had formed an illegal religion, for which the symbol of a red cross bleeding blue was the essence. How bloodshot, Ductford often remarked.

Emerson stood on the stool to pull the light as his nemesis opened the door.

Barely audible voices intruded crashing in around his ears.

Word of advice, if in any desert don't eat the asparagus if it flowers. If in the Fez walk around in small circles, if you must. This will bring rain. Rain in the Fez is limited to two downpours per eighty years because of her five suns. There are limitations.

In a class somewhere, he heard, distinct and soft, Can you speak up; I can barely hear you;

Oh? What just happened? It's utterly still.

In the beautiful stone house on the glove, a man had entered the Peter home, tied a bulb to the kitchen ceiling, walked up the stairs, removed a scaffold blade and upon entry to the first bedroom swung the blade once sending five thin strips of blood onto the walls, then repeated the act each bedroom. In the last bedroom of the son, sensing foreboding danger he turned on the ceiling light whereupon it lit up like uninterrupted lightning as it had once while he was overseas.

An ambulance was dispatched immediately and arrived in fifteen minutes.

Who wanted them dead? The unauthorized mill owners? The unapproved house gardeners, or the hundreds of illicit sex clubs?

Who taught him to tie a knot to the brutal bulb in the dark?

Always the dark was going off like a light; four bodies in their beds.

In an original situation, they were training each other to dig graves in green hills.

In the new country Peter and the Menshien family are stuck, the car needs a lighter weight mechanism for the hills that are steeper than where car design is made, where mud grips;

Getting ships in and out of harbor with a craggy rocks underwater is solved.

It's a whole different world out there, big disturbance of living. Mother's ship; Hyperion, does not survive. Shipper's license left to eldest daughter, telescope Aquinas, fleet name Bethel, first major ship problem rope travel line slung under ship, wants ship to sink. Suffocation of air is what kills. What were friends involved in? These were parties for the rich who ate their catch. Massive death collected moss filled soft clam shells. The softest earth prior to running water that fills a basement was no trenched earth at all. They were buried with cotton and shovel. The owner was cramped full with soggy blood waste. The first lab sifted through blood and skin until they had fingerprints. No one touched the parents; they were dead of ether. The people who tied the float hub of ships wanted the ships.

4

ONE HAD to be aware.

The end of Life was a smurgeon of gushing blood depleting the body of its restorative properties. The water was stagnant, all hope sunk beneath sand in trenches of barely settled clay. Grey skies, scuttled breezes, errant drifts, the wind carried among its trestles a high shriek of giddy laughter as the soft sun sank to its meadows. Ships moored along empty banks, their ribbed beds awaiting a descent of chorus angels. The entire shippers fleet scurried over a gradual freezing between New York and Canada, each of three lakes filling their basins with spent effluent to the frozen stack. All time rushed in bitter wind to the clog and stim of ferries which shuttled office workers to accountant companies each of sixty professionals in buildings at the water's edge. Blim and blah wood carved painted ponies for the calliope, music repeating by fifteen minutes, popcorn overflowing in its stackers, parents standing beyond the circle on the grass, their children on the carved painted ponies laughed with glee. The summers shrank under the convoluted acquisitions of marked bench placed like docks in the water; from a distance the port gained admittance of bridge dockers as progressively larger ships were built with an idea of carting suburbs across a measured sea. The Amsterdam Holstein Company took tugs into the fifty-eight channels to erect Thompson buoys at mile marks until a string of red lights flashed periodic songs to which ships in the night gave searching lights by tall deck bridges. An extent of exigent taxing courses opened and closed as on each separation of coastline a blue light beckoned arrival. Just slightly beyond the bayonet stood a cargo train at the ready, its eventual passage would depart for iced groves and smelt bait.

I sat on the stile with Ben, all time ushered to a dark stillness.

"Tell me I can be as decent as you," he whispered.

I turned my face to kiss him, and he held me fiercely as if he were about to take leave of his senses. His hand cupped my breast and I breathed in his essence.

"Are you not decent?"

"Adam and I took a girl to the calliope and undressed her."

"Was she pretty?"

"Yes, she was."

"Did she like you?"

"She cried."

He felt beneath my skirt and I let him. "Give me your love, Karolina; please, sugar."

I gave him my virginity that night. Do you love me? Can I possess you?

"Oh, Karolina, I do so long to be yours."

We tumbled about on the grass beneath the stars. Later, I asked him, "What's the matter at your house? Your mother behaves strangely."

"She's actually my aunt. I'm born a Stelly."

"That was your dad found in the lake?"

"My uncle."

"Mrs. Gardener is your dad's sister?"

He gave an assent. "She is a drug addict. Raw bone."

It meant she injected human blood into her veins.

"She's given to her passions of ruminations."

One degree cooler than it should be, stars rushing about in diamond strands, he came for me nightly for years with the exception of one night when I happened to come home later than usual from choir and overheard him inside Dibs' studio.

"I've tried to forgive myself but you are my undoing. I just cannot stay away."

The ships left without their grain all year long. The days wended through hardship and relief of sailors going on shore for durst. My ear trained to a yet newer harness of misgivings and betrayals sought sounds far off in the distance. By the time I finally attended university at Canada's South Farm for morgue in distraught fevers for all occupations, I had long forgotten the jealousies of youth.

"Can you love me, Karolina?" Ben would implore in a coo.

"Oh, I do Ben. Everything of me is yours."

And so on it would go, backseats of Stetsons, on board boats, in barns, in meadows, loose or restrained. Until one afternoon at the Packard Club he said he had met a girl who he agreed to marry.

The typical ship contract came with a board wishing well for bass on the half mart. Ben worked trowel line at night. It would become known he was the last person to wave the boom yacht off at north bay on which the priest was killed by an unknown person.

The winds blew a catastrophe of disaster over refrigeration in meat lockers. Meat was dragged out of storage lockers attacked by salamanders that came from underwater excavation and retracted in large G-Aladdin bags and set in garden storage. A disgusting entrapment that photographs showed a Gardener look alike of, but not Dibs who at that moment had taken my brother Adam to her bed in constant adoration.

There was a sort of non-completion about their embraces that fell short of playing fields, that looked into a blow pipe of acrimony, love to distraction, rankling, a discourtesy that was at once rapturous and begrudging. Obliging celibacy subtracted tender endearments that would one day leave her dead in her widowhood, or cancelled by immaturity, modest yearning.

Freedom, immunity, reverential, as though in going to sea he had turned his back on her and then fled home to her to save her from a scorned derision, slander, alleged tiny transgressions. Whether she broke her word to him or momentarily caused him presumed hardness of heart her husband forgave her as certain as that bootleg that surrendered her in fortified dementia, and as usual like a shepherd to his flock, until his father's return, her son stood like an armored sentinel standing watch at the roof window holding his breath, fearful.

Perhaps he thought his frequent observance of her courtesies, inculcating as a steerage brought on by loathsome veins, sailed on the stillness of lake surfaces into a seldom visited embrasure, visible from his smaller window gave her over to selfless marriages of mind to soul for a pittance of vigilance, for which she took to herself, wayward and unmindful of danger, emotion cut up rough on a rouge plate, a distraction of sorbet, left her sulky, knowledge surrendered in kind entreaties; good nature flowing, life killed with kindness, philanthropic charities like rowed mercies in the wind.

The channel boat crew tossed both bodies into the sailing river in view of the vessel they had stolen, an utterly repugnant act for a hospital ambulance; which left the murder of Dibs' dad Priest Stelly all the more suspect, uncommonly virulent succulents attached to his skin thirsting his pores in mud like harvest ingratitude, only his wife's stencil knife packed into the lining of his lambskin jacket, limbs unbound, face cherubic, curly silver blond hair wild with tussled course. A vulgarity of uncommon quest had kept him off shore to take samples of downwind mud seeking sewer effluent to answer a concern over a barge tow sinking at that very position midway across the Candel. These crews were not ex-convicts; no one would put an ex-convict even on a yard line and thus the question was, what was the issue, where did faithless impudence begin.

I began with search and find for Stelly's trip to supervise building a new dock for grain, a photo of two sails with cabin; when his boat pitched, it was a three sail small sailboat, he must have taken down a sail causing his boat to fall over. He was carrying five cases of pipestone quarry which clunked him in the head, his feet were pulled by catapult into the map room, he wound up caught on coiled rope in the bad weather gale winds, another sailboat crashed into his, the sail mast he had taken down fell into the high gusting wind, bloomed and drifted, covering his head and he couldn't breathe, a freak accident before there was a flurry of ocean, suddenly choppy waves rising, a portent of no good, diver fins rising, maybe ten of them.

The trouble probably came with the advent of Packard sales. Highhanded, automotive transport handlers, whose engagement to heresy, amidst the shrill whine of the cargo train bringing ten cars to Colorado and California each month started at the wharf of a high-strung dimpled trowel, once only for pike staunch chore; a garden display on the bay of the car netted seven sales monthly; the knap of liberty and behest of grandeur, many six purchasers per vehicle each who resided in cabin orchestra gardens camps; that's what sold the society.

Drivers drove ditch fallen, wallowed by intent in watery marshes, netting the newest industry a red-faced humiliation to many a degraded householder; ships were instructed down the pipe to go by train to Boston Harbor; from there smaller ships transported to the islands, to Havana for movies, to Santiago for captains and through the canal to Hawaii and Alameda. Through chilly sea passages fleets of vehicles made the journey halfway around the new world to equestrian owners, prison estrangements, a hundred models to sell small houses at each plot section; eventually control accountants were given a vehicle to make collections for each major city. Provincialism defined the number of cars; refrigeration followed some fifty years later. Then the department store, mass produced products, fishing vessels to sea by two and catch to bakeries by six weekly.

Stelly lay in linens at an undisclosed cemetery for four weeks during which the world looked for him. I would wonder why the carnival played raucous bandstand until after midnight; why churches permitted year round Sabbaths.

"They'll find him, Karolina," Ben said, because he was given to certainties. "We're conducting an active search."

"Who is this female? I heard you say that you can't keep away, you're bound in your existence?" I asked.

"Where did you hear that?"

"In the garden dock house. Who is she?"

He lied, I caught it on his breath. With scarce uncertainty, he pulled apart, cast me a sobering gaze, left me in an abandonment of cold implication. "I do have feelings for you. I was hoping you would in time live at my house."

"I can't. I'm off to college in the spring."

It was an ignited strange futility, a wretched immorality to have to watch and come to terms with, his sisters provocative in their leanings, an entire household bent for compelled underdeveloped satiety; liaisons of tempest marshaled incarceration, tempestuous in their psychological flight, unguarded provision, a perfidy of duplicity, a conveyance of infrequent personhood, individuality, and possibly of creative injunction. Whatever reformation the emergence of institutions brought a revived teenager from the wharfs, there was no governance for the fitful of mental detraction.

5

THE UPSTATE New York mansion kept no displacements. It was a stately two story blue colonial mansion tucked away on a river shrouded entirely by old weeping elm trees. A portico beneath a soft blue light sat in full view of a semi circular paved drive around a large circle of mowed grass.

My second husband was a slender, tall, reddish blond, stultifying looking southern officer born in New Frampton, Baltimore. He was a physician expert in dementia due to sedatives, intoxication, domestic violence, severe depression, and mental deprivation. Often we sat in the dining hall sipping tea from India, sampling nutmeg bread with plum marmalade, eating an egg cup, and reviewing an unnatural ream of testimony, conversing back and forth as the morning permitted to the changes of interpretive laws. He oversaw a handful of mansions which housed about ten demented legal physicians in dull unimproved New Bedford, southern poverty row in Virginia, Next Camp Rhode Island, Junior River New Orleans, and Mitchell Texas; all sanitariums had a dozen large houses for the afflicted, all hospitalized men wrote long dissertations and drank to excess and said filthy things like I fucked my mother and it was fun meaning their wife, their intended words never came out right and they displayed extreme upset. Since none were physicians, Ben's family wasn't qualified to enter these residential treatment centers where minimum age requirement was fifty-six years old; had they been even ship board doctors, I suspect their fragile existences would have been assured. Physicians are regarded as denizens of society, bearers of integrity, responsible for life-saving honor. The law differentiates between malpractice and poor judgment, the former being a disgraceful act of maligning blame, often of dementia. Flamboyant schizophrenia on the other hand weighs against reasoning and mood syndromes against depression. Such as they acted completely oblivious of their surroundings they were not granted a diagnosis of dementia with an entry to the corridors of pathological study. Rather their etiology was known, the course of delusion rigid; behaviors non-symptomatic.

We drifted river to river, the doctor at late night rounds, personalities in abstention. John was meticulous in diagnoses; I a copious reader who provided narratives for the constable gave the similar attention to summaries for his index card descriptions. Nature existed in ample groves; strolls through gardens gave me no indication to state of mind nor to deterioration of once excellent intelligence. We slept locked in an embrace tangled in our sensibilities. Gradual complacency sent me home to my mother and her overly critical misunderstandings. Ben had stayed over that entire summer creating an impasse between her and me, a deep regret on my part that she could have played to Adam's cause célèbre requirement for close friendship.

"I've missed you, Karolina," Ben said, as I sipped steamed milk on the veranda overlooking the river and newly remade dock and dock house with porch light.

He stood blocking the sun, aged as his uncle Stelly had

been, still handsome in his brash wild thrown appearance.

"How have you been?"

He sat at the lawn, round glass table beneath the green slightly tilted parasol. "Can't complain. Your mother of course keeps me at the dinner table all hours as a polite inducement to your brother's visits. We play cribbage; I keep her hearth warm. And you?"

"I'm more or less fine. I travel at my husband's bedside to winter mansions to view dementia and amnesiacs."

"Does his work keep you busy?"

"Much more than I'd prefer. Sometimes it's all I can do to grab a late night bite."

He took my hand into his. "March is at home on Long Island."

"Will you have children?"

"No, I'm crystal clear on that score. March agrees."

"We've turned out fairly similar. John doesn't want children either."

"No similarity is there. I have no illusions as to my unfortunate keep-holds."

"Does your wife understand your life?"

"She gives it every try, but I'm locked in in my privacies where no one can get me."

"She must consider it lonely."

He leaned forward to kiss me. "I need you too badly to say."

The evening was a deluge to surrender. I perceived him differently as a full grown man who brought errant chivalrous adult men to his Mardi Gras for the disgraces of impugned civilities.

"I've missed you in my affections," he said, kissing me in passionate avowal.

"Why did you marry her? I can never keep you."

"Sweetheart, I will always keep you, but you don't know

me the way I know myself. I've fallen in my aunt's garden, I've kept to affairs, I've known illicit loves; even Dante who loved her Tennyson made me her sought-after appraisal. You can't know these trysts; they precede you. I've never loved. I am forever vanished. My soul was lost in another country. Even I don't know who I am."

"But why did you leave me? Marry? Why didn't you stay for me?"

"Because you were very young. I didn't want you to be affected. March was spoiled by Dante, she herself isn't aware. Please don't put me aside, it only breaks my heart." He wrapped his arms about me and I shivered in his reduction. "Take me, Karolina; make me over; at least complete my sad self."

As I gave in willingly, I knew I was damned; my faithless marriage vows released to no one except myself. I closed my eyes, let him steal every affection, turned my being over to his, went slack against him, promised myself no one would ever know, told myself I was now lost to him.

"I'm sworn to you, Ben. I can't love with my entity without any man who is not you. I am yours."

"I've confessed. Say you can't love me, say I'm a foolish affection."

"Never, Ben; never."

I will say nothing very honest to March until I look upon Ben face to face.

I see them through the trestle glen as he strides ahead of her leaving her hurt and very possibly rejected. Married couples make love, so I know he has held her, his wife. He has traded his life for her. At fourteen she was his aunt's selection for him. She still exudes attractive beguiling artifice.

I have left my second husband for no rational sanity. I left him when my mother died. I was content to end that chapter knowing I was returning home.

I watched them sensing their argument was more his doing than hers. He inherited his uncle's home and possibly wants to remain, but he seems to want to chide her for her presence. March is an obstacle. Maybe he didn't need her any longer.

"I have nothing to offer you but my eventual death," he explained one afternoon.

We sat in a secluded parlor, his lips pressed to my neck when there was a knock at the door. I went to see who it was and opened the door to March.

"Is Emerson about?" she solicited. "I can't find him."

I stepped outside with her. "No, I haven't seen him."

She placed her hand on my chest, nudged up to me. She held me by the neck and pressed her mouth on mine. "I thought I saw him come in."

"You're drunk, March. Please don't." I took her hands away.

"I know you want him. He won't stay. He's like a boy who has to be amused." She crushed my lips with hers. "I myself am always able."

I escaped her. I walked through the hall to the sitting room whereupon he seized me and smothered me with treacherous intimacy. "Come back with me later tonight, we'll make love while March sleeps, I will rob you of your decency."

"Oh, my darling, I spied you through the blinds," he said to her in the kitchen.

"How could you? You've no right to put me off."

"There, there, be a good girl and be kind to your guest in the arbor room."

She entered a bit miffed. She exuded a pretension of friendship. "So tell me, how's Adam?"

We were the most of conversation as to Adam's summer cottage in Chicago on the teems. She stroked my arm and I hers for an hour until Ben served drinks and we walked about the evening talking about my mother.

At length she came to kiss me goodnight, her silk gown clung like withdrawn reserve.

It was after two when he aroused me from sleep. "I so desire you," he said.

"Won't she awaken?"

"She's passed put. You are my steadfast worn ideal. I hunger for you, my darling."

"I'm afraid."

"Don't be, there's nothing to intervene. I adore you, be my Dante, honey."

"Seduce me, Ben."

"I'm all yours."

In the morning March was gone. He had chased her away. Her fourteen year old magnetism had finally lost its power to control him. There was nothing to discuss, nothing to learn. While I set the incident far in a past of no requite, I told myself the others had euphoria, Ben alternated among euphoria and abject apathy. He had enjoyed a release from life but he came back occasionally to that dreaded place where he brooded over some unnamed fear that he would die young of age. Whatever he thought I needed to understand he tried to shed insight. He had joined the family in Great Britain along with Peter's cousin Dante whom he let her make love to him often, she dressed all of them each day patiently; she home schooled the girls in patent law, prepared the dinner meal and gave discourse in the music room; for her efforts he thought she was a most desired subject even if she loved Tennyson more.

There were other serious failings. Twenty miles away a ship had exploded on the lake capsizing his uncle Stelly causing him to sense the tragic loss as eventual doom. That autumn he had taken a lover about, an unequivocal ejaculation, no one was less perfect than he, no matter how he extended himself he was void of bonding, he couldn't save Dibs, he had no way to keep her free from musings, if he was his best at love making that limited him too as it had his father; he couldn't shake loose his belief that she would never feel he was completely hers.

I heard these confessions as one who hears an incoming petulant storm as patter in every direction scattering leaves and brewing into a maelstrom of preoccupations. I sent for a divorce, secured of no longer giving weekend parties by lamplight at night, inviting faculty down for week stays, although daily I advised a chef and on summer weekends brought the patent ship experts from New Bethesda and Chicago to him. I languished in his spill-easy's of affection; frequent borrowed semblances of loving in the garden and meadow, rowing to the coves, spending a night at a hotel, keeping to the passions of new requited love.

"I ought never to have won you," he said awakening in a strong sunlight, the breeze calculated in through the open window of my house in my bedroom, a gabled narrow rooftop room that overlooked the spent marsh. "You deserved to keep your youth."

"Why? I've loved you since that day Adam brought you here."

"Do you find me very vain?"

He was getting pulled back into the tide. "Am I very vain?"

"I see no evidence of it, Karolina."

"Are you plagued?"

6

W E WERE in our forties. Life had been precious. I could recount much of the strident night- mares. Ben had had unsettling distressing night- mares. The Tuolumne River above Sacramento overflowed plunging the lake high above its grazing country and in his mind's vision he kept seeing Peter and his wife sinking below the cement stile and bog unable to crawl out, their deaths blamed on a mishap aboard the Stammerer ship when five cars fell off the plank in 1919. Ben said he heard their voices calling him. This delusional syndrome made him take the boat into the bay far from the cove for which his doctor said he thought Ben was attempting to cope with powerful insidi- ous hallucinations. He returned each and every evening dis- traught unwilling to be consoled. Finally convinced his house contained demons, I boarded it and we resided permanently in my house.

Afternoons we sat on the patio at the outdoor glass table served with olive paste sandwich halves, fresh fruit or asparagus tips or a dinner salad, broiled cut potatoes, fried plantains and a small custard, together with a book of psalms or a weekly. A breeze might stir off the river; every so often a tour boat wet the thralls. He was making a comeback; I was learning endurance.

It was on one evening that Adam had traveled down from the North Bay dock on the lake I was making my way home from a sojourn boat ride I passed the small cottage house feeling energetic and hopeful I overheard a long ago remembered tryst. I paused along the walk between the rose bushes and lawn and peered inside to glimpse my brother and Ben in the throes of husband adulterations. I withdrew instinctively, repressed shock, ignored a rising tide of alarm as I imagined March must have done once, and returned furtively to the enormous house. I suppressed tears, convinced Ben had warned me, sat down to an early supper; instated to a keen awareness of the man I had married. In many ways I was naïve, unquestioned as to the disquieting repugnancies of which a youth governs his sanctions.

When I had enough strength of self-possession, some few days after Adam returned to his post for another seven months, I asked Ben, "Why Adam of all people?"

We were in bed, the morning having been consumed of wanton desire.

"My darling, it's of seldom duration. Once yearly is a sparkling wine. He maintains the barge tow."

"But what of it?"

"The other man tosses the deceased into the lake. It's all I've ever talked to Adam about since Peter."

"I am stultified. You have cancelled me."

"I am not able to see to an ending if the other man has to cart my body to plow. I do love you as much as I may."

"I foreswore myself to you."

"My sweetest, it's only I who detests living. I told you I can't employ against my fate. I've given as much as I can yield."

"But I needed to possess your soul."

"It's a mere accoutrement. Make love to me, honey, only to me. I am for all eternity bestowed with you," Ben said, catching me to him.

We were in a wave. I took him wherever he was bound for.

"I worship you; you are my soul," he said. "Take me to your grave."

"I must possess you, Ben, in your entity. I have wanted no one except you."

"You are my longest endured. Never leave. Give up your pride."

"I give you all the foolish pride I am capable of."

"I will never leave you; I am come home. You bear every secret I have ever lived."

"Make me yours. "

"You are mine, my sweetest, sweetest love. I didn't allow March to see through me the way I have been close with you. Could I have been able to determine shipping, I wouldn't be in this situation but no one improves shipping. I've taken every chance I can with you. If I'm new to this, please forgive me."

"What have you told Adam?"

"I said I'm just residing here. I haven't told him about us."

Not that my admissions could do any good. I fought against every instinct to be bitter. He couldn't move past the bind he was in. It was true of every Charly; they were the shippers. That was the extent of life. In time I learned to forget the observation.

Ben took nine years into the battle night of forest snows, tent, lantern and dried meat, ten pounds of pack on his back. He began on the isolated Isle Royale of Michigan where he walked for five weeks beneath the Windigo spruce in damp shade, a love-sick man sampling mustard greens on dumping grounds, pink spinach, avoiding knapweed and the vegetable love-lies-bleeding; walked a month to the precipices of the Acadia rugged mountains of evergreen spruce and fir and days to the stages of pink granite where food grew in dark red roots, as many as he could unearth. Like a wounded soldier in deep grief he entered the Ipomea white morning glory that sprang up in ivy draped woodlands of mostly an edible jungle, a climbing habit which eaten caused him swift overwhelming nausea; during a week of aggressive mountain hiking, his pertinent eye spied out dangerous lowly white bindweed, Pulchella blue lettuce, evil radish and poison hemlock in the Saskatchewan hills, these poison weeds growing in shade acclimated coolness beneath coasts of vociferous pine; he would return one day to say only he tried to kill himself repeatedly any way he could and still had cheated death where lots of people succeeded.

Four long months later, a month into Spring, he climbed the Kenai fjords, blizzard driven winds of time as remote as the beginning of life. He went further into the non salvation of Denali over the remaining year to the highest peak at nearly twenty thousand feet high above sea level over the subarctic boreal forests of white and black shrunk, gnarled trees, fighting the almost non-breathable frigid air through shaded spruce, aspen and poplar sunk into glacial snow hiking to the gates of the arctic into a half million acres of black spruce taiga over inhospitable permafrost through a subzero lengthy dark winter; riled with tansy ragwort he ate several plants and lay cold nearly two years; and garlic mustard that caused instant vomiting and left him abandoned to spellbound dementia until air condensed snowflakes restored him.

Eventually slept tired, a durst of wind battled fatigue he stepped onto the Grand Tetons of Montana some three years later and made camp more rejuvenated next to age old bristlecone pines that stood like war survived sentinels flocked by snow. He sought contemplation in a series of pink sandstone amphitheaters the color of sunrise in narrows of tall spires of ponderosa pines and red leafy trees cropping up from red rock; bathed at the sole resort he'd ever be granted in forests of crimson and rust trees in Guadalupe, Texas; far from the poison weed pastures of spiny Cholula, tansy, pigweed, thistle and the black henbane prickly dandelion leaves that he consumed with fair success; into the Tennessee blue mountains of evergreen forests, relieved to salt tears at last to finally be headed home, his senses given over to the suicides of greater rustic tomfoolery. The decision to not be able to be found was over far too quickly causing him to sink to major bouts of defeatism.

We talked for weeks, each trek detailed for its bouts of platitude. We were close in an unusual reckoning, at divination for the tracks he laid, living in the mist. He was of a mind that life was for the sensation of pleasure. The agony of hiking such as it produced ribbed leanness lent itself to the survival of the body. On occasion he lost all awareness, he was a pioneer learning natural living. Remorse was essential to undigested recovery. Ben grieved, despite ravishes of misunderstanding over the loss of his family particularly his parents and Stelly. He had traded in despair for a howling existence of destitute wilderness internal to the belief they died without cause, gone to final resting places unfit for having lived.

I had once decided no matter how I lived I should remain faithful to living. I was a child when I came across Ben; I would be in my end seventies should I survive him.

He packed his arms about me. "The trees are dying."

Sunlight waned a beautiful amber glint. "They'll be back."

Prior to marriage I studied three years in the realm of Czechoslovakian Camden in a high mountain town on the study of dis-correlation for adults whose lives consisted of cabins in year round snowfall. The similarities came back hauntingly, the sense of a completely different world, minor comforts, snow a continuous reality.

Of due encumbrance I told myself no one really knows

another person well. To see to their soul one must be able to sleep awake.

"I exist for you," I said one night.

He awakened. "Yes, sweetheart, I know."

"Please don't lose me."

"My darling, have no fear. I worship you."

I took him circling my arms around his neck.

"Oh, Dante, why did he do it?" he cried out.

"Ben, I'm here. I'm here."

I fell into urgent slumber cradled by him.

7

BEN WANTED to achieve some great significance. To stand out over his fellow fleet masters. Life was brief, a whimsy of earnestness in a sole reduction of a penny whistle of endearments. He had studied his mother's invention for steering the wind by a rudder turn system and thought he could lift the hub higher by tightening an already complex system of reeds which harnessed by a leader rein would add as much as forty miles grip steerage. She made a ship that wouldn't sink, his dad improved its glide mechanism to a hundred and forty miles an hour. He would be remembered for determining how much poison an herb could be ingested; long into the era he would be credited with a glass plastic hull side that could be interchanged with a load bearing ship on skates for when the lake froze; hearing was everything, the scantily perceived wave cracking deep ice, rifts freezing under stunned crevices, tympanic ruptures, sodden breathers, disoriented chatter, glimmering condensation, acoustic wings quavering; hollow twangs for a measure of fathom, a death-like silence, an illumination, more at humiliation, low strums that produced frost, cracked clutched hums, became visible as beams, then a flood of light, in the distance a lightning fork at the horizon. In the forests he could hear the bark expand in the darkest hour before dawn when the air was exceptionally quiet, when nothing moved, not even snow. Whatever killed his parents would have pulled on their larynx surrendering each to suffocated pleas disabling speech had they lived; to this, the trees spoke to him; he developed a keen instinct for herbivore and crystallizing air, even for invigorating calm.

The worst disinclination was of being insensible; a sort of numbness during which touch that should have seemed pleasurable or at least interesting was indifferent; too faintly accentuated, nearly invisible but sensed, intangible to the awareness, not actually taste, sensation or emotion; nor a specific color, perhaps neutral, as a bystander witness might come upon a sight; something transparent, evident, aerial and fresh but not a capacity nor keeping with order, honest, holding nothing back in the experience.

He had avoided any indulgence because temperature as well as darkness gave way to stark realism, after weeks, greenness all around pricked one's discernible vision causing him to rely on varying degrees of listening with strained perception, on unlearned intuition; snow blindness subtracted every landscape often for days while the pressure of refrigerator cold abandoned, and shade convened; seldom had he heard a harmony of nature in an unadulterated obsequiousness, in absence of thought – what he termed observed mysticism.

Sporadic ventriloquist apparitions called at him; judgment and wisdom called to him, there was no lack of concentration or meditation, no fleeing discrimination, only unheeded neglect.

He said there were ways to intone vitality or to conduct intellect, and I agreed.

"I returned to see you once more," he said, a few months later.

"You left for a long time. It was hard for me."

He held me. "You don't seem to realize my problem. The

killer of my sisters is known to me. He operates the bag floating dock to North Bay."

"You had your back to the man. It's possible he's not Tenny's husband, but a stranger."

"He pulled the cord after he entered the kitchen. That's his chore on deck."

"It isn't conclusive."

"They were asleep; I was awake, that's why I am alive."

The moment I fell asleep, he was gone. He had left; if danger was imminent he had eluded his tormentor finally, shut the kitchen door, given me no note. I waited for him for days hoping I was mistaken although I realized he wasn't returning.

I am pulled in favor of abstinences of embittered leanings. From time to time I console myself he's in a better existence. He's hiking Denali through the petrified black pine taiga in spring nothing in his possession except the bulky pack on his back.

8

1⁹²⁴

The years went by quickly. No one who knew the family could have denied that Tennyson's husband had murdered her and her siblings by inviting a killer in at night. The man himself operated New York's barge tow. He was sent up on criminal charges and served time at New York State Prison. In the year when the Prousts traveled across the country in their Curtis Duisenberg and they crashed into the Tuolumne Lake and sank in animal excrement, the man was transferred to solitary confinement on a mental incapacity unit.

That year the State of Wisconsin erected its county hospital system on Michigan Lake. Ten miles away The Apostle Islands ice caves took their ice bursts which resembled an oak harbor mast rig ship, a hole in its side through which sunlight poured, light aqua water floating inside the hull, its cargo taking blood wastes from North Bay to a new filtration pond off Wisconsin's coast of her Upper Dells and Witches Gulch down her river of dark grey slate mountain slabs alive with sapling spruce leafy trees barely adhered to the slippery rock where placid waters drifted to vibrant orange and pink sandstone strata. Stuck between two passages the ice caves arose with spectacular majesty, the overlooking omniscience of all time breathing through passageways of spellbinding frozen pinnacles bedazzled light weaning into narrow drifts at forty-seven north by ninety-one west off Sand Island beneath the northern lights of lilac sheets and light citrine and pink at Little Sturgeon Bay. In the density of grey colorless winter a solid block of light spoke to the dismal confluence while on the roof a snow-blower released a mantle of snow and ice. Up river in summer there would be a half mile of red cranberries pushed upstream past the hospitals that stood like white house Parthenon mansions before it was ready for production. Extending almost to Cornucopia, ice caves stood like fully anchored train stations, a ghost train held in thick red strata between layers of crystalline gray opaque ice; churches with light flooding through, a phantom suburb of white ice row houses, ships on the sea, a church on a jumble of rocks, three church museums held transfixed in blood red stone as in Jericho. The tourist tour trade was about to go berserk.

The first problems of arson never went away; then there was prostitution and it never went away; and then the investigators' offices became established and with them the social halls providing coffee and meal dishes. This brought in coffee, potatoes and yams, fish and oysters, and a barrel full of additional crops, and odd music emanating from small radios such as the oriental geisha girls who pushed carts for the murders on Country Lane in New York Brisbane quarter off the squares of Rochester City. Between 18th Streets to 27th Street along Taraval one had the opium dens, any Victorian house that sat near Golden Gate Park, its shady tree lined sanctuaries of churches and porridge oyster and shrimp eateries; could be over fifty houses at a time before the government busted them for illegal use of heroin, opiate or morphine by injection. Drug trade consisted of: Opium desiccation, scent inebriates came through ventilation in apartment buildings of ten to forty flats each; these rentals took large amounts of money for this, often $10 a day; clear morphine IV hooked up to patient in outpatient setting for $5 an hour accompanied by sweat blankets; seedy premises, mattress without sheets and blanket; restaurant room accommodations including Chinese herbalist, and restaurant and market upstairs office rentals as live-in residences, each $90 per month during era when house rentals were $180 per month and upstairs studio flats were approximately $75 per week.

It was all over the place. There were as many as three hundred and eighty-five addicted occupants. San Francisco was the only city where people could go to be addicts, and the city itself didn't like it. The Japanese tea gardens provided tea; the Buddhist church gave meals once a day. What happened to two ships on October Island in 1899? Was it to prevent transportation to emergency wards of hospitals? Gardener made a mast sail ship that could not sink below oar windows of the ship. If it sank by too much water lapping in the hull like a swan in love held captive, it did not sink with a bomb. They had all begun as grapplers of the ice caverns of Denmark. In that year William Proust and his cousin John Whisker were making whisker cars in Steel town for yachts. Whiskers on boats were dock curb mechanisms meant to help the boat determine its course by leaning into the wind.

I came by my adulterations honestly. That winter I had climbed Tamalpais in earnest on a deserving backpack of spice, powdered milk and abalone. I sat at the mountain top surrounded by mist acquired of stupendous wilderness ardor leading a life of normative ideas and sometimes purchased resort accommodations. The problems of the past seemed far away; as luck would have it, the forest dripped greenery and the chilly night air gave off a whitish tinge to stars and galaxies. By tent light I read amnesia and phobia neuroses and a host of resistances adapted by sociopathic disorders. In the predawn dissension I dressed and walked the summit to discover the best view of the ocean. Up there I decided I could overlook my infatuation with Ben, adhere to the belief that he had gone in search of a best leaf tree for ships, taken his grief of his parents to a grave. Milk product made in Saint Helena brought to San Francisco for monastery schools gave heroin its claim, storage of medicinal use popped up in many an apartment to augment the opium alley where cheap cafes served bowls of porridge with diced shellfish. Best nine lives ever. A loss of ego boundaries, inability to follow a course of action, loss of interest, tactile hallucinations, loosening of associations were common. I thought perhaps I might look for personal estrangement in churches.

"Hey, you want to have dinner?" I asked the new neighbor when I next saw him emerge from the basement door.

"Oh, sure, could do it. Next Wednesday I'm off shift."

Wednesday we met on the beach in the castle at the Café Lounge overlooking the bay and sand. An old Balclutha mast pole ship sat beached across the street in its pier. We received almond light blue sashes for our wrists and were seated in dark red leather booths by the windows. Pale candlelight dimmed the room. On the massive stairs nymphs clad in swimsuits sat on the stone Sutro baths in orange and yellow lights. We ordered toast and anchovy with cilantro. The bistro clam tomato drink arrived with a celery stalk. A tiny garden salad, a shrimp cocktail, a side of bisque with potato stick biscuit, prawn in wine butter and a stiff whip of lemon and cranberries poule. Last a marijuana cigarette. We talked about our jobs, hectic living, court documents, rush to a store, queasy ships, ditch and run dictation. I would learn to be impressed by him despite the drug traffic contraband he had to look for; the countless hours and thankless court orders. Not without rum sugar; stored in every whiskey parlor, $9 a pour. Each death to slab town, each death certificate on file in the conundrum in Hawaii. When I received the info the man's prints tested for a Killer, not the father whose body apparently was tossed into a meat locker on Lake Michigan and left for dead. It was a distinguishment that left me with a realization that many had flocked to the beach to see what they could gain for three mast ships that sailed each lake – Erie, Superior and Michigan. He was someone who had turned a corner. He had made a tragic error.

UNDIFFEREN-TIATED

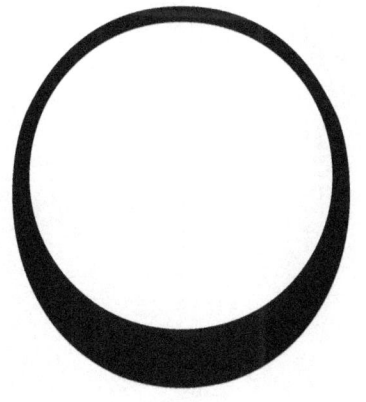

1

FREYA Mientras

Freya reluctantly pulled out of the drive. In her capacity as state tracker for the Canadian border at New York, an attractive leggy shoulder length bronze blonde, she had followed a man defined on a warrant through the county dell in which he drove a beat up grey truck with dislodged bumper; he had made a beeline down the hill to a small glass house on the crater lake beach of Minnesota where another darker grey pickup sat on a portion of bright white cement. He looked to be mildly Filipino and Caucasian, dark hair, fair skin complexion, a construction drill worker from the Illinois Crane company on the west side opposite Green Bay. The new plaza foundation preparation had come to an abrupt halt when the gigantic drill extractor had uncovered a hive of buried bodies in a mine in casual wear all tangled up with and lying on top of each other. It was a standard job, lime extraction – whether lime was actually removed; it was a way to get a big area sufficiently deep. The exposed earth lay twenty feet below red sand and was rich shale in composition and color, damp and a rich dirt odor. The resulting recovery was a rare type of death. The dead resembled teens, sixteen of them, could be Cambodian or Rhodesian whites, small semi round faces, child thin, average four feet nine, all dressed in plaid swimsuits and tennis shoes. The state board of death statistics was called to identify each person.

She thought it more than likely people watched them kill dozens of people at random although so far no one saw bodies getting piled in. When she saw the photos, her instinctual question was, Were they thrown off a hillside and covered over in tons of dirt? But the precinct captain assured her the acts had to have occurred in usual circumstances; such as erecting an office building along a narrow escarpment in a residential sector, there was ninety feet to scale and under twenty before construction went under hills with houses. The other hypothesis was a possibility they were on an airplane that crashed and got buried as cleanup and was explained inappropriately; that they burned up in a burning airplane, but there was no indication that insurance paid out. There was no way to explain the size of the cavernous pit in which they were found; and it was unthinkable some burrowed their way out. The real question was how did they get into their grave? All had masticated earth permanently stuck to their teeth and their light reddish skin was lightly dusted.

She walked around for hours with the awful upsetting knowledge that the scene was a shocking criminal foray. Many team profilers thought a first inquiry should compare where farming was done in hilly areas that had truncated roads on a quarter slope road across three hills with steep cliff lines.

She guessed a landslide for a haulage truck to have put a bunch of teens inside and upended them from at least a hundred feet into ravines to their deaths.

While their photos looked Chinese, hair texture, height, skeletal structure were atypical. Wrong in the face for India, too tall for pygmy, too short for Micmac. Laotian suspected, population largely in Indiana, jewelry cutters; entire country of Laos had fought ongoing sectional wars, lived in thatch houses, were migratory, without climbing skills. Dull blue black hair suggestive of Norwegian but wide face ear to ear. They were believed to dig graves for unsung American soldiers; some metal dissolution off cars parts but didn't work salvage.

She checked into a hotel at the base of the road where she took a room on the first floor that overlooked traffic coming down the hill and propped a camera in the window on a camcorder fix. Then she went to shower off the grime and tedium of her seventeen hour tracking day. With a towel around her neck length bronze mildly wavy hair she slipped into a white terrycloth ankle length robe, made herself a tall cup of coffee and unpacked a neat navy blue dress, white scarf, gloves, Stetson shoes and navy tailored jacket with hat and shades. In the past two years she lived out of a suitcase while obtaining addresses for residence, work, church and friends on suspected non-apprehended felons, neglecting both husband and son and a remodeled Chicago brownstone on the lakes and cross country ski trips. At forty-five, she was a two time graduate of anthropomorphic face changes and absolute abundance detection from Sutcliffe measuring the cranium to the neck for disposed of dead. While the study was very modern, no morgue analyzed without them. She spotted him in an instant, chiseled chin, abrupt neckline, slumped back, mild scoliosis, Downs syndrome gait, despite him being mid fifty. Her work gave her an untidy look at people. A knife in the flesh description of a man who did cemetery; as this sort of man got older, the hulk bodily physiogamy was tortuous to cloak due to operating power lift pile, maneuvering shovels, moving huge amounts of sledge and dirt, and grouping a few or more bodies, all taken by surprise, tomahawk, war club, or spray poison. Her job was essential in foreign countries where dictatorships would rise and fall in forty years.

He was an easy man to find, secured to a fastidious job, the appearance of nothing creative in his weathered mien. He strode in an ambled walk, a man swift on his haunches. The task was to find out if he visited the gravesite; did it start at a mine head, had he acquired curious onlookers or were they part of the original site task?

These days there were a handful of new profilers, sod burial extractors, city enclave dusters, primitive cave finders, lucrative destiny looter analysts, saltwater dredge scouts, each who oppined for human piracy out in any wilderness where a team discovered dead groups.

Late at night he barreled downhill in his pickup, charged across city streets past Barry Goldwater Hills to an underground entrance at the backside of the slip harbor where for three hours like a mad man he dragged out coffins, nailing each after he confirmed its peculiar contents, and hauled them onto his truck; then he returned to knock up a wood door and slab it over in stucco and plaster construction linen over it to conceal the entrance from sight. She shot photos, followed with headlights doused, to a clinic where he unloaded the coffins on a patio.

She thought she had sufficient evidence to begin prosecutorial proceedings until twenty minutes later when she entered her hotel room and found it thrashed, sofa overturned, bed gutted, clothes cut up, calendar pages torn out, camera wrecked. She sat down, nerves shaken, and smoked a cigarette and debated whether to alert the police. It would be a calculated risk to involve an outside agency, but the room was an appalling mess.

An hour later, head clear, without mention of her case, she called them from the lobby.

The narrative interview took all of a half hour once the gentlemanly officer arrived.

Once it was over she called the after-hours dispatch. The

switchboard rang for Tommy Siren, voice and sound van peep for a walk drive print.

Tommy Siren

A palaver of chatter, Thomas worked for Maelstrom, a closed house source which investigated live recorded chitchat that persuasively identified the Chicago syndicate. He was in his late sixties staffing a bulletin desk when he took his major hit on a drowning of seven college students trapped in brine congealed quicksand on Lake Superior. He had split his office in seconds and driven to the site where two homicide units bagged bodies. Officers in twos dragged each body onto dry ground, a photographer took photos, a sketch artist jotted three resemblance pictures of each victim and a coroner conducted prelim post mortems, before they were zipped up in white plastic human body corpse bags. He had summarized the case prior to the morgue examinations which conclusively assessed the victims killed in a gang plank bizarre ritual.

Like any of the police there Tommy kept his dark brown hair graying at his thin forehead cut scalp short, wore a dark green uniform and heavy lamb jacket and trench boots, and had on his person a five way radio that allowed a dispatch to stay in continual wire contact with him. A boat excursion gone awry that left each male entangled in tree roots, he would have guessed. The staid rationality that governed his ear's sense came over years of seeing the dead pulled from watery death scenes. The problems of the underclass were that they knew killers. Here it was again, bodies in caskets deposited on clinic property. Fingers intact. Soil in every orifice. Uncommon dirt for the area. Spoken on a cell phone,

Let them hang by their roots. Garbled from a pay phone at a lakeside resort several miles east of the border. He indexed the receiver to a cell phone no longer operative. Call phone came in as Ramona Luchesi, a mother of a missing teen. He listened to every call made by her phone, none other produced the man.

He sought any unusual environmental sounds; found trucks plowing earth on a mountainside presumably putting in one or more roads at night identified by rush hour traffic nearby. He situated each word of the truckers to nine distillers, far distributed wind, motors, running water, rakes. He spent days at the task. Hobbled himself in the sound recorder room; what was what?

Could be as many as twelve trucks. Maybe a bulldozer crunching trees. Faint whine of a motorcycle. A toddler, speech suppressed instantly. Cautious creeping down hills, house doors left ajar.

Some hurling themselves off balconies, falling on dirt, slipping through weeds. A door that couldn't budge.

This had to be a treacherous crime.

Roar of a river, water splashing. A flood? Water flowing in, four knots an hour. It ceased after fifty minutes. Someone flailing about. Trickling water from a high place. Sound of an oar in a kayak.

A building collapsing under pressure. Clinking pipes bobbing on water. An unhinged door slapping an inflowing tide and submerging. High pitched voices. He separated each syllable. Forget the suitcase.

Kill the lights. Trees being uprooted, crunched. The same bulldozer? He'd have to match the motors.

Wood wrenching, car toppling, garage caving in maybe. Possibly five people walking through four feet of water. Rifle shots fired into the air. A car sinking in water, motor sputtering. An airplane.

After two days straining for nuances, he had a headache. He walked around his tiny studio comprised of a closet Magnusson, kitchenette, dining and living area with fireplace insert, and two Armstrong sofas and dining table. He lit a balboa fag, lightly aromatic, as he sipped a Mai-tai, always cognitive of developing issues, comfortable in woolen polyester. Five small meals a day, most often Brie or cheddar and kipper on stone wheat cracker, not infrequently red caviar and boiled egg on sashimi; some rare occasion bite sized sesame wafer topped with kelp and papaya, all accompanied by Chinese tea.

He fell asleep listening to Beethoven's Fifth and awakened to an alarm on his dusting equipment for an incoming message. By an odd occurrence the dust sound record for a late call recorded over the lake plashes. Weary with sleep he poured himself coffee and sipping it sat at his computers and turned up the sound. Tommy was impressed that a dispatch had set up the roll herself and in doing so crossed into a Department Of Justice splice of a dozer moving down a hill. He wrangled apart the rolling steel of the dozer over midnight tea. The subject sounded like he was dragging bootleg in casements up a rough drive. The movements contained confidence as though it were a chore he'd done many times, beating a path to the door of someone who would find the presence of dead a humiliating if not outright embarrassing experience.

He charted for any earlier incident which might explain the deaths of the dead. To do this, he convened probable address areas for them. The region the bodies originated in lay on the southern side of the ice caves along the shore. He went through half a dozen filters before he came across even one tape with peculiar noises. He made notes.

There were one too many sound bites. He reversed the sequence and slowed it down. He listened again for about twenty minutes. Caught the quick sound followed by the long drawn out one.

In the distance it arose, a sort of rustle. He matched the noise to a general file in an attempt to define it.

The sound produced a long erratic line, definitely

recognizable. Somewhere along the water's surface bulldozers were plowing a few rows of houses into mud washing them into the lake.

It was ten-twenty Saturday night, but he gave it a try anyway. If the Supe was out dancing with his wife, he'd pick up on his cell.

Lt. Jay Don Jims

Margot was fixing dinner chopping green and yellow melons, strawberries, boysenberries, kiwi and grapes. Jims stood at the stove frying up diced vegetables, bell peppers, green, yellow and red, leeks, cilantro, Chilies, oregano, chard and purple onions. They each sipped dry white wine in goblets. Dinner on Saturday was a marital ritual born of no children. High school sweethearts, at fifty Margot was a teased blonde with blue eyes, five foot ten in black spiked heels, usually in denim khakis and blue billowy blouse, and at fifty-nine Jims was jet black hair, crew cut, devastatingly dreamy blue eyes, black silk shirt, white linen pants, grey cap, thongs. Cooking and eating, they discussed his cases at the Cook County hospital precinct, before they went out dancing at ten at the jazz club Freight Yard Club in Westside near the train yards. He was assigned homicide, green card verification; erotic graves, most of them drowning by toasters or lamps in pools, some girly nude stabbings, and garment bag mining suffocations. They ate off fine, bone white porcelain in the all wood dining room at a long oak table at which he sat at the head and she to his immediate left closest the kitchen door. On their joint salaries, his forty-five and her thirty grand a year as an administrative secretary at the hospital, they owned a two bedroom house, open kitchen living room, one bath a hundred and forty square feet done all in gold tile, outside a spacious deck he built and narrow rose garden, blood reds, yellow tea and white, that she planted that extended between two streets. He drove a black Lexus sedan and she a brown Corvette sports coupe with the hood down. Their dream for retirement was to reside at Wisconsin on the lake a mile from the sanitariums in a lake house, but they had four years to go.

They prided themselves that of their ten best friends they had succeeded in staying youthful. Their voices to each other were still affectionate, non authoritative, with lots of eye contact. She had decided years ago in her twenties to always be adoring of him and she had never bitten her words in their thirty-two years of marriage. For his viewpoint she was a resilient bride as inventive as the year they met. He borrowed on his enthusiasm for the job, having promoted twice.

The call came on his cell at ten-thirty. He and Margot were slow dancing to Porter Coles. Jims told the detective he could be at the Emergency Ward in fifteen minutes.

He and Margot sped through town in his Lexus, red light silent alarm flashing atop his vehicle, she nervously contacting the men in his unit, all the while smoking a Dorval as if she were on a jagged edge herself. They headed through the last lights to the parking lot.

Technically every stiff in the state of Illinois was sent to Cook for final resting diagnosis and evaluation. Yearly their general hospital saw several dozen; sometimes sixty. Most dead could be awakened after trauma. The staff comprised fifteen regular docs. Cook was a lively place, average diagnostics took a few hours; they didn't touch up or do reconstructions, predominantly just X-rays, carotid arteries, glimmer glass, mask; ghost skin, brief thermal, reflex. The fractured limbs were released after less than an hour; standard bull was that burns took up to an entire day, drowning victims as long as two full days, suffocations were the worst, often five days.

The first pile-up pits off the rail mounds left no body hair growing, recession, chin marks, urinary tract shortened.

In roots in water these bodies were seen barely visible above water, mud had caused their knees to crack, not bend. These were bad ugly deaths.

It didn't say much about circumstances, if skin was not charred, there was no fire. Water moved fast, too swift to stand.

No one had a chance with moving earth.

They were ushered quickly to an O.R.

The emotional toil had begun. The anxiety of waiting culminated pretty damn fast. This was a physician defined process, a necessary undertaking he felt a need to stand watch over before he had an idea as to what had occurred.

The typical questions since the crime occurred after dark were, were they eating, taking a bath, or watching trees fall when they died? These were things to consider while taking a look at a body for signs of severe trauma, raised or corpuscle flesh, torque twists, neck dislocation. Eating, the body often retained undigested material; naked inside a tub they might be drowning; but watching a tree, there was no sure way to steer clear of a bad tumble, a falling tree might land anywhere. The condition of the first group of fifteen bodies certainly accounted for bizarre and scenic death masks, although the occurrence of dead sipping river water seemed to fetch for other crimes; as if a battlefield had come visibly to exposure.

There were going to be problems once the crime was identified. The knowledgeable guilty convened around their dead as if to retain an acquired possession, and he had to protect the public from the vultures. The task of finding human remains often caused trained concern. Margot would routinely denounce oddity saying a body in any pasture or hillside field got there due to human interaction. Lost people weren't always escaping the devil's evil.

Jims gathered his staff to advise them. First the suspect

had to be apprehended. He approved fourteen of his twenty police officers to make the arrest. Next there was to be a shut down, no computer entries of any information, no labs details, no actual names, investigations all denials; court orders to obtain a complete media blackout. Finally an on-foot investigation of any area that had been picked clean for evidence of destroyed homes and cars.

Captain Conrad Quibble

A basic man for any death scene, Quibble was himself a British first and a Russian transplant after. Tall, distinguished, peppery brown hair with a bash that fell forward when he gazed downward, bony even in a well plied haberdashery dark brown trouser suit, starched shirt and vest, comfortable ruddy leather penny loafers, always a notepad in tow on which he wrote copious essays that were immediately transcribed, he oversaw eight districts for death detail in Chicago and a hundred detectives. Since his precinct office had become situated from downtown where it sat inside the Amtrak building to the third floor above a ship dock on Superior Lake that looked out over the jagged coastline at three wharf fronts, petrol gasoline stations and warehouses and storage, previously frequent vandalisms to the police vehicle garages had almost ceased. The third floor contained two other offices, one halfway down the hall wedged between Quibble's secretary stenographer and four central district accountants belonged to the wharf captain who boarded each and every ship and one office at the opposite end of the hallway where the Canadian constable assigned to Illinois worked, a large five room office with a lit hearth in the private desk room where the constable wrote his reports and met with state medical examiners and contractors. Quibble's interior took up two thousand square feet, beginning with a cozy receptionist office with three upholstered couches with flocked tree and snow designs, next his brick walled office which contained his massive desk situated against two large sash windows, two tweed brown and yellow sofas and two yellow tweed easy chairs, in the next a conference room with long dark teakwood table and twelve matching chairs usually for discussing tip finder colloquialisms, and last a small corner room for his state coroner, a medium height thin silver haired male named Headley who was approaching seventy-one, whose primary purpose was to provide expert testimony in state gravesite hearings.

After reviewing listings on the cases known as the last sip, open air gravesites, Quibble in his dispassionate dislike considered the testament motivation to have been a planned attack on the prison quarters of the city's jail maximum security guard families. It would appear the teen children were shoved off embankments. Why else would a construction team ditch those youth into pits in dirt mounds some fifty feet deep and then cover their houses with so much dirt to build up mountains of over a quarter mile in length? It seemed quite rational to consider that once that ground was saturated people had clawed their way through mud until they surfaced above ground.

There were four pits discovered with each burial between ten and fifteen victims nearly all dressed in short shorts and plaid tops, average ages fourteen to nineteen or seventy-eight to frail ninety. Most had deeply red skin, looked to be Asian or Indonesian of some type, hair texture was similar, dark straight black Japanese maybe, definitely not Chinese; and were restaurant take-out order clerks working in lower class neighborhoods jointly co-habited by Blacks.

No one claimed their bodies; no one wanted inheritance for them.

This was someone's private war.

Of course, when there was a black-out, the public had

no notion anyhow; the near dead entered wards on stretchers with toe tags attached, often IVs implemented in the throat or collar. Wrists too damaged to accept fluids, these wounded lay senseless for days before they showed any awareness of time. Quibble sent an Examiner in daily to the hospitals to conduct rounds. He used the notations to gauge levity. He had his clerks pull every file as to dirt under the fingernails to compare crimes to what he termed scenic morphology. His methods tended to be as simple as he could manage. His units worked long hard shifts, often back to back half weekends, and he didn't want them caught in a no win bind where exhaustion rode the helm. Their instructions left no room for speculation, on the lower right hand side of the file, labs and test evidence including dusting for gamma rays; on the middle of the file attached to clips, observations of scene and body; and at far left upper peg, court inquest, and lower left, orders. His men had to visit the patients, their families, significant friends, and tap phones to find any discussion as to death risk; every week, every month, turn over every weed. Once the file established probable suspect, he moved the file to his police analyst group of four senior officers to put together the arraignments and from there the cases were transferred to the District Attorney for trial and impeachment. On these burials, he had the one question that had to be asserted to, did the assailant intend to cause bodily harm. An answer in the affirmative struck the suspect dead.

Quibble himself visited the labs seeking any flaw in entrenchment that might indicate if an overall plan had been undertaken. Chief chemists were forthcoming; and he filled his notepad with a dozen or more indicators. Hand prints on clothing documented shoving and pushing; caterpillar rotary track markings revealed type of threat; fingerprints on the nose or mouth to suffocate gave an enormity of evil purpose. Undigested soil, bark, leaf particles and amount of dirt caked on the skin revealed extent of risk. There was no yellow tongue so none had been shot, held down forcibly in dirt or water or subjected to pipeline gas or emissions, and no cartilage damage anywhere so none were killed first by moving extractors. That at the least was reassuring. Those who did the best could breathe freely. When each body was finally accounted for, Quibble called for aerial dislocations for any overview possible, except these were very incomplete showing tiny squares of infrared in blue and orange for imminent threat.

Usually he felt damned if he couldn't obtain enough information and queerly depressed if he did get it, and often he slept the first few weeks inside his comfortable office on the couch in front of a lit hearth where his secretary sometimes awakened him, showering in an all black and tan tile elegant hotel style bathroom outfitted with sauna, hair dryers, shave razor and steamy shave, and a dozen black bath size towels neatly stacked in wood shelves. He detested a slow grind of progress and soaked his impatience in gin, neat or martini. If his succor left him bleary eyed, no one said a word and he didn't either succumb to apology.

The girls in the hall liked to rave on that in his young days he had wed a famous British actress popular to the silver screen. Her bulimia ended the relationship after six short years, but he didn't try to replace her although he dated and liked to show his girls off at the bars especially at The Seed in New London on the cleft and at The Priory in proper cheese Chicago. Otherwise he admitted by cab across the border to The York in Toronto where he stayed many an autumn weekend with a regular dining partner on the Sound, chasing the morgue weather, reading an upper gent's Cheever or Merkel, and shot a few tables of dice or kept to the cranberry and walnut Brie on toast with fried pickle. The dates took up a savor he liked to think kept him constant. In a seldom garden digging with the collegiate cronies of his era, he shoveled a row or two of petunias and cockle bells. The dance cotillions were filled with dapper horsemen like him, stitched up in wagon boots and a frilly, long sleeved blue shirt and debonair dark blue tweed pants, and he whirled his gals in their pastel apricot Cinderella gowns under chandeliers as good as any of them.

When he sent no mortal man to the scene to examine the grossly steeped marsh, they returned, sacks filled, competently assisted to argue their keen observations with cold wit. Death had gone down slower than might be expected, mud doing the drowning in very little water. The rigor stiffs couldn't be pulled out quickly, roots grabbed and held fast. Each man figured more than soil sank the victims; some were strapped to bedding, others put into deep closets. Any detriment of description was not regarded as a promised land. On a legend a far off pit contained nine, each body some twenty-five feet from the others, like Death trailed men on a bicycle.

Constable Franklin Streeter

Streeter gave no interviews, never had, and resolutely believed the public had no right to know what went on inside his Quebec City precinct.

He was fifth down on the structure chart for government below Chief, Lab and Morgue, Finance, and Prime Minister. He supervised seven constable lieutenants for evidence verification, homicide, narcotics vice, city patrol, hit and run, homeless indigent and shelters, and guns, and each unit hired nine to thirty fulltime officers. Referrals came in over the dispatch hotline. Depending upon immediacy dispatch forwarded calls to the respective unit which assigned to the next officer on rotation. Cases were allowed up to ten days each. Completed paperwork went to the supervisor for review and then to a secretary for data entry and last to the captain for closure. Those investigations requiring trials were routed to the Chief

Constable Office for decisions as to inquests.

His submission to the irreverent file on the marsh headlands defined actual whereabouts. Not so in warehouse district of lowest Chicago, US; technically another state over even though six stiffs were driven over the Ohio boundary and given rest inside a detonated watershed. Streeter was street smart, typically born Montreal in appearance, scanty snub crew cut and recalcitrant disposition; a gray streaked brunette with high set temples, stone hard mien, capable of climbing thirty miles a day, bone up physique, nothing amused or made him happy. Even less so at home in Quebec City where he resided in the castle hotel on the twelfth floor on the boardwalk of which he strode evenings and took a late meal at nine in a century old lounge nursing a bon aperitif sherry high wagon, nothing and no one to get in his way to cause disruptions although life kept him to a frequently disheartened morale. He had locked up many of his friends' teen kids, misguided youths who wanted knowledge of crime to facilitate their back breaking fathers. He'd heard it all from long term hardened addicts to girls for whom prostitution put them through college and bought them a husband. Periodically he had a photo taken at the lounge with a pretty girl who he passed off as a wife. He wasn't of a mind to have a private life. He liked to keep the work pristine, but the reality was he wouldn't share his living with anyone. He had earned his successes because he left the relationships to other men.

He believed the men found dead on the strait or by a river, mouths filled with mud, had escaped a carnival camp where they saw a crime go down, not the pit fifteen along the railway or the pit nine unearthed in swamp conditions both which he credited to gangland kill. Historically the Indochinese had wandered to the conservative bays from far flung Miami port and crossed the border to lay sand and plaster; teach or run a lunch and dinner menu although the Canadian government did not as a rule sponsor green cards. He'd have to say the subjugation of dead in all likelihood emerged because they interacted with cruel males toward whom no sympathy was possible anyhow. Time would tell where the victims began when they met up with their end. Psychological deprivation was his guess. Perhaps they rotated to many cities supplying labor to a hectic resort business until some unanticipated trouble occurred.

2

THE CRIME Scene

An aged, somewhat disgruntled Police Coroner Headley of slight erect posture affixed in police overalls, thermal shirt and marked jacket, silver hair needing trim trudged through the watery marsh in Vermillion, Ohio on the Erie shoreline trampling over burned wood smelling insidiously of acrid putrid arson. Five officers accompanied him. The day was cloudy with a gray tinge of imminent rain; but otherwise windy and cold, still iced over on the lake and beach. He moved slowly across an area of several acres, marshy gunk sunk to his lower legs, the patch of land enlisted of a presence of Underwood trees, hedges, sod and ground cover to a crusted charred vehicle inside which a body had collapsed in the worst of circumstances, either soundly asleep when the car began to fill with mud or already dead. Headley peered into the front seat of a Marquis where the driver had been allegedly found with the telltale skin imbued with purplish orange red chemical typically the chemical interaction of keeper's embalm fluid and gasoline mixed with short change, a substance used to rid storage of feared animal plague. He left the car with an officer who would arrange for transport to the forensics garage and continued walking methodically through the disparate soggy area every so often crouching to pick up an article of paper, pushed over wood, plant or cloth.

The call came in at four for the discovery of nine bodies confined in prisms of ice on the marsh of the eastbound railroad. The morgue staff arrived by four-fifteen and began chiseling the bodies out of ice, loading them inside the morgue van and then transporting them to Chicago to the university basement in Romeoville. Although there was no real evidence to define the scene as intentional – and he couldn't see how a crime would have gone off with the entire military sitting so close by – it was already being referred to at the warrant exchange as homicide weather which had to mean the Supers had evidence of criminal pursuit. By seven when Headley completed his turf evaluation, he was prepared to say only that the decomposed scene was at least an eight month origination. He would not know for perhaps months if he was looking at a crime.

In a freak snow storm, a deep freeze with record ice hit the lakes and buried the entire west side under forty feet of hard snow. The Lakewood Park lab chief had been up since three o'clock having worked since the prior night examining the samples taken off the nine dead whose bodies were wrenched from the Ohio headlands.

"What is this piece of wood?" he asked Headley when the coroner entered with his bags of debris.

"I hoped you could tell me. The headlands were filled with hundreds of them dug deep in the quick mud."

"You simply entered a dump deposit site; stuff has probably been sitting there since there was a higher water mark on the lake."

"Well give it a look, won't you? Diatom algae micro orbs would be helpful."

"Was it a bad site?"

"A second turned up this morning. There's some thought they weren't camping out when the tide came in."

"Could be they originally succumbed under blizzard frost while taking out the garbage."

"A spouse would've gone looking for them. My firm guess will be killed during a previous summer. What do your cell stains say?"

"Sloughed off skin, two months or more."

"What does that indicate?"

"Bodies held underwater for a lengthy period of time."

"What do you suppose took them outside?"

"Yeah, that's got to be the question."

The tips were coming in hard and fast. Youthful, energetic, blond crew cut, Sgt. John Conner from the base had barely kept up with the onslaught, sixteen on six lines in an hour, more coming in.

A male caller wanted the facts known. The county refused permits to build on the basis there was no space to build in the requested zone to an Asian group out of Singapore known as Pan Pacific Corp. who owned hotels who wanted to build on St. Clair shores.

A scared female: they are out there hiding.

Fake cops stopped cars at road to bay from Glen Oak.

Six cars bombed Indonesia Styx style.

An eye witness reported two vicious stabbings both to Indo.

Drivers retrieved the dead from dirt and stuffed them into their trunks.

A man had strung a young boy from a city light.

A bulldozer had plowed over seven small wooden buildings along the St. Clair headlands.

On the coast of the river the storm weather had battered

remaining district housing causing roofs and walls to be blown away.

The nine dead in a mudslide when last seen in May were de-planking off the American Mariner on Piney Dock at Ashtabula in Ohio.

So they finally had a reference.

Because John took the information it was his task to handle the background on these men. Piney Dock had registered nine men from Combat, Minnesota, all forager construction for a new subdivision building project in Vermillion, a pretty situated inlet in a lush garden shaded paradise setting on a beach. The project called for three docks, a leisure camp, a connecting highway and a hundred and forty modern houses. Project equipment had been delivered to the site. The land was grid with flags posted and separate sewage and water pipes laid, when a devastating snow castrated the entire area.

The Pan Pacific Corp. owned two forest shares in upstate New York in the late 1950's and sold them to the state for a half million to build a string of hotels in Indochina and three in New York State. Their board of directors said they were six physicians from Malaysia who had acquired shared houses which they eventually liquidated to fund a financial base for operations. They also bought a hospital in Singapore and trained surgical physicians. Vermillion city turned down the request to build on beach lake front land saying that the land was a mostly sand marsh that frosted over in winter and would freeze and break pipes. They were invited to reapply or modify their request. As near as Connor could determine on the strength of the tips themselves, the city that denied the permits to build on unstable land lived to pay the price; but where in hell the killers came from was an unknown.

John Connor fielded his information upstairs to the first available collection analyst. Bob Mac Umber was an account specialist who handled all info requests by phone. He had never been seen and therefore no agent knew who he was, if he was tall, short, dark, black, white, curly hair or straight, a kind or menacing face.

"I've looked over your noodle," Bob said in less than an hour later. "The city denied based on percolation tests which showed less than four hundred feet to well. In order to build on icy wharves requires firm dwelling to raise foundation, acquittal notice that ravines have not shouldered burn outs or been capable of spawn, nor settled ground over shifting mounds."

"So how did they get there?"

"Someone got their wires crossed, approved after a denial."

"What might the racial composition be for the killers?"

"As to the group they are none Indo. Nothing says they are or have to be. The pertinent photo out-takes view four white Africans of varying stature manning two dozers, a centipede shovel, and a pit drill water chute mud extrapolator. The equipment was owned by Bremerton Drill Drivers, Co., Inc. It was formerly used for trench drilling to build a shallow river basin offshore containment."

"Does the company lease its equipment?"

"No, but it doesn't mean they didn't line up a work order."

"Have you sent out your photos?"

"Yes, I sent them to a volume identifier for mix."

That meant Tommy Siren at Maelstrom. He was by far the best contract.

"Do you know who gets a wise guy itemization?"

Bob mused, "That will be Clandestine Operations."

"I will send my report."

"Good show, let me know if you see more kill."

Counsel Styron Kellie, a dapper red head Scot, sat behind a massive polished desk filing his nails while he studied five of seventy reports on the chill ground dead discovered at Ocean Bay, Ohio.

The area had been thoroughly combed for the lectern, as far as he was concerned; every precaution taken, each area staked by flag indicator to verify the body removed, green, red, white, yellow, black. Oddly the two creek bed dead had not been categorized. The ten iced male stiffs lay scattered as though they had fallen from the sky, vertebra and joints cracked, heads toggled, presumably as the snow fell and encapsulated them. Otherwise nothing gave a hint at cause of unnatural death. They had lain down and fallen asleep. The insanity that followed the removals convened at the lab and morgue; even finance had its twitter. The reports said shoeless so naturally it was thought shoes were taken to assure death. The idea that dying occurred in summer owed to a preternatural scant clothing, denim pants, swimsuits beneath garments, silk shirts, light windbreakers, but no woolen wear, hats or gloves, boots, or backpacks, no canteens or foods. Then again, no surfboard gear, lotion, tents; it was a guess they ran to the Sound to get help. Strong well developed pectorals, muscular femurs, solid abdominals, as a group they looked squarely able. Inside the barf room he had conducted the initial go round, saltwater adhered to the skin, eyelids looked glassy indicating commiseration with water to the upper face although minor amount of barf in the mouth and no fluid in the chest cavity ruled out drowning, hands were sodden with dirt, and mud up to the knee suggested standing for hours in wade. Time of relevant death occurred at low tide. Once the bodies thawed in four days he took nail and hair clippings, mouth cultures, Blood, swiped for urine and for three semen, and hair follicles at the groins.

Lab results pointed at over hydrogenation which occurred under conditions of unusual fear. In addition semen resulted in one male whose oxygen suddenly was restricted too severely to breathe. Hair follicles revealed subordination indicating blood stoppage for up to an hour. Saltwater minimized this effect. Knee bone became conclave in ice, duration less than a month. Lake deaths while often the worst producing an abundance of open pores which were absent here signified lengthy low tide.

In forty years he had stood by as hundreds were examined. A taciturn man of impeccable credentials, Kellie was wont to say he understood the criminal mind in its intricacy. Half dozen footprints in the high grass in trailhead creek mud nearest the rail track proved the criminals waited for the fled victims to emerge. Rifle barrel arms marred the ground. The easiest explanation resided with a strong confirmation that fifteen people getting off a train were killed along with witnesses and others nearby who assumedly ran into a thicket of trees and stood quietly to avoid detection and never left.

Kellie almost never went home. His gigantic studio opposite the inland train collected its fair share of sunlit dust over bare maple floors and brick walls, a full bed, desk stacked with active files, a lone red couch in front of a brick fireplace and modern, all appliance kitchen with long table and six chairs. Nor did he really feel sorry for himself, a man without sentiment for living and dead, conscientious, he considered he was married to the work and spent seventy hours a week at it, typically thirty of it on a crime scene with one of three inspectors. Since he turned sixty-three he had taken up with a middle aged secretary who lived across town on the water in a condo whom he moved into his office more or less fulltime; a graduate in forensics, forty year old son; she was a sleek blond bun named Kathy in tight bodice black and tan pant suits.

"You saw the reports. What did you think?" he'd start off each morning.

"Apples, the entire lot," she responded, glancing at his handsome trim posture from the prior day's dictation on his summary of his work, already preparing allegations to submit findings for the eventual prelim injunction against the builder, bangs falling forward.

"Rotten, would you say?"

"Do you think the train dead were involved?"

"I do. Why else stop mid track?"

"Could be they lived out that area."

"Did you look up last known address?"

"Not yet, haven't had time."

"Don't forget. I have to know in order to make my case."

"Who is opposing?"

"Charworth. Can't wait; the man has a finger up his ass."

"He's always been the anal retentive type," although the counsel all were when it came to details. Never enough proof to suit any high magistrate, thank God.

"Commissioner Retticon asked for you. He said there's bound to be a contest as to why discovery was not imminent."

"It won't be problematic. The evidence exists. Ice imprisonment takes minimum five to eight weeks. "

"He says it places death prior to January."

"There are the hostile impressions in mud. Low tide flowed in August. The train was stopped at gunpoint." Then realizing Charworth might try for late October tide and whittle down probable instrumentality, he conceded.

"What's his number?"

Over the endless agog of inquests there was such an extensive parade of information about crimes that any barrister associated to legal pronouncements viewed each new accusation as another index in a library of archives such that one felt stultified in a procedural procession, demanded of, inspected and at times placed on the rigor slab under the knife. The chores of exactness imparted a rather stubborn block of obstinacy countered by wimps and fornicators alike. To achieve gain Kellie had always maintained succinct but reasonable brevity. Technically the lakes fell under the maintenance of the navy base in US jurisdiction because a navy ship spied a body drifting on top of ice. The ship crew would form the initial investigation as a result of encountering the other bodies during a coastal search. Their course of finding took a night and a morning. They wrapped each body, took it on board and departed to the Cook County Hospital in Chicago's port of entry.

Four impartial declaratives were routinely admitted to at inquest. Were the bodies injured prior to post mortem lividest rigidity, upon surgical procedure were any found to possess severity of final rest, had any been found in an environment pertinent to hostile threat; and could death have occurred by human hand. Once basis was established as to unnatural death, cause had to be found to have been medically induced. After this, the hearing commenced. The court then set forth a term of no greater than fourteen weeks to tie in facts found during a fuller investigation.

"How does the Department of the Medical Examiner plead?" The Superior high court judge pronounced. He was a seedy little man who had charged India with mortal terror in the obscure obscenity of five young thieves killing three dogs in an empty swimming pool in a Surrey college.

Inspector Kellie stood to address the magistrate. "We seek an adjudication of homicide in the first degree. A total of forty-two predominantly Indo men were murdered by bull-dozer and waste drill in Vermillion, Ohio on shore in a doy-ennes of mud scaling down some twenty feet, the first group after getting off a train and three other groups because they witnessed the first crime.

"Based upon seven photos the first reveals the train was stopped and conductor shot with train left abandoned. The second demonstrates fifteen men detained were forced to cut trees when a truck loaded with soil dumped load onto them causing them to fall into a loosely covered recession. The third that a bulldozer flattened the area this group lay covered by; the fourth a wet drill mixer spattered wet soil throughout the depression; the fifth that increasing higher tide tossed seven bodies onto shore; sixth onlookers who made a line of defense were killed; and a last photo addresses by date that an early permafrost set in doing further damage. Bodies reveal displacement of distal bones which bears to fact that undue force was used.

"This was a brutal crime against alleged seasonal workers. The hiring company was denied permits after a soil test affirmed land was subject to drift. Despite this, they plotted grids. The court won't without being asked extend time. I am asking for maximum allowable time to conduct a further investigation to bring forth facts that crime was intended, not accidental."

The Court brought in a swift approval and allowed the maximum time permitted for any continuance of thirty-two weeks for investigation.

A scolding rattling chill had bitten the mast roofed gables shaking the interior. The task of bringing forward calls meant an agent had to enter a nearby den to collect correspondence which might cause a problematic reaction that necessitated additional support, and he had newly assigned it. A university was the more suitable to alert colleagues to most tasks. Once transcripts were produced, the allegations were flying and an unseen enemy situated, if only to thinly apprise the kill. Law was not fastidious employment; more eyes and ears than a console or steno tape.

He responded to a guard call at midnight. His pan fried noodles were left untouched in the Styrofoam box on his desk but otherwise it looked as if a cyclone had come through an open window. The overhead ceiling fan used religiously in summer was going. A specter of photos, all his selections, flashed on the computer. A thief broke into his office and turned the place over leaving a mess and stole the exhibits, obviously the photos were what they were after. The only assurance he had was because Mary took the computer home every night the thief couldn't read it.

But the scene upset him. The assailable murderers were everywhere bonded by some unusual brotherhood that seemed to confirm the situation had indeed been non-accidental. He had solicited for hundreds of cases without a single disruption.

Thus a disquieting hunch was impolitely asserted to. He called Detail Squad for a dusting unit. They arrived in the middle of the night and began a methodical task of dusting for prints and smudges, and with laser light searched for cigarette ash, pry entry, spit and boot marks.

By mid morning they had established earmarks of two burglars, both six feet one, swinging mallets, one man smoked Cools, the other ate Rollo's, outer wrapping torn by teeth marks sent to the lab for identification; one of them had shed bronze brown wig hair; they wore plastic surgeon gloves which left nearly invisible smudges on book manuals, drawers in the two desks, and on flung pages; and mudded soil consistent with the outside walk up.

At noon he took Mary to lunch. They sat in public view on the Marriott Plaza over squash soup and romaine salad and iced coffee looking precisely who they were, a top notch primer barrister and personal secretary over a dictation which she took on a notepad in shorthand as fast as he talked, a hundred and sixty a minute. The fanfare had to be close by, and he intended to milk it for all its worth. He described the situations he thought the break in went with and had her read each paragraph back to him as he compiled a squire's list of points. There was a zoo death accompanied by an odor of rubbing alcohol; a chase through Manhattan courtrooms, a maligned mailbag left on a park bench; a shooting that left a child in Lake Park in Ohio incapable of speech; by now these children were in their thirties, attorneys or counsel themselves.

They sat through a few handshakes from other court appointed attorneys, most of them for defense; a judicial officer for a commissioner shared that mornings admonitions as to an abduction case that Kellie had hoped would land on his desk in the rotation; an actor and his wife sipped bar drinks and a group of finance department lapped it up at the outdoor bar counter. He had represented similar cases not all that long ago; HIV children admitted to a private sanitarium for school, a bruised child who tested for epidemic caused by butane, a mother and adult son who lived on a feed unit after having survived an incident of mutiny; a bunch of odd cases not permitted interaction with any public; he also wanted South American refugees who escaped landslides in a major earthquake, but the Court assigned them to female lawyers; and to visit incarcerated adult clients for no contact, behind the glass interviews as to armored van, bomb witness and child abduction.

He had experienced bouts of agitation over being overlooked. The High Court for rationales misunderstood leaned in favor of a resonant barometer of good mediocrity from Harvard grads whose promises were made to a modern weapons technocratic scheme, a sin Kellie regarded as highly improper. But for westerly winds skittishly skimming a surface where a few hundred feet below were the rewards of a nation at war gravesites of gravel and powdered stone were uncovered on a breach of coast like illicit ruined headstones.

In the late 1970's amidst a flurry of liberalism, the military courts gave over their gavel to counties especially in an obsequious design of denial and abrogation. Thus whatever criminal act took place on port land became the prevue of a new aristocracy. Had the nine been found prior to this accommodative change of law, the military court would have read in the crime and deadlock sentences requiring underwater hangings sought. As part of trial preparation Kellie asked for the strictest penalty. He wanted a thorough discussion about imparted waiver of rights when a ship that usually travels the locks brings in workers for military owned land prior to government control.

The ground on which their bodies lay dead came under a few laws. As of the Fifties the land did not yet exist for a natural contemplation nor was it rising under water. The ships that would deposit disposal would leave what would in forty years extend the bluffs out to sea. The ground today surfaced sufficiently on the previous ocean side of the rail tracks to now be in its jurisdiction. Any body found buried along the railroad or on its land was under vast international protections. The idea of wilderness in Nature no longer had priority for body found in the woods which last sip did. The other law that bore merit was in fact an older water law that said if the entire coastline had formerly been military docking use then responsibility to make the bodies whole went to the military at sea.

And a final law governed bodies in ice as intentional, because ice generally did not expand below four feet in soil. For that objective he had to establish chosen ground.

In order to gain command order Kellie had to prove the dead had actually been murdered on previous military stateside controlled sites. Then he had to demarcate in what methods any of the bodies might have been killed by a military enemy to allege why their lives ended there.

The bodies had turned up convincingly in a plethora of medical conditions typical of camps having obviously had their bodies leeched. Veins were distended by severe cold, bones fractured, eye sockets shrunken, digitals too bruised to keep flesh adhered, shoulders caved in, legs grasped. The pile of huddled bodies found beneath twenty feet of dirt typified being pushed off a high embankment into a ready-made ditch. This all suggested planning. He thought it would be easy to establish physical evidence pertinent to the blood, for which he was hopeful he could obtain stringent penalty.

He revisited the windowless morgue. The stench of disease was sickening. On five tables lay five bodies. Flaps of skin like pages were peeled back from the intricacy of lung sacks and veins; hearts peered up from bluish shiny film of musculature. As the bodies had thawed the external skin began to corpuscle and sag in unusual places.

Telling torture was strangulation indicated by a dark mark indicative of a neck grasp, removed. Feet appeared to have been bound, straps also gone.

He stood under Examiner Gregory Gee's light and watched the clean cut small Chinese seventy year old poke around and cautiously scrutinize the skin for other marks, cuts, tattoos, and scars. When Gee found a wound, he circled it, lowered the lamp, and took a photo. He felt for limbic rigidity. Each inflexible area was measured by hand held ruler and noted on a chart. Massive bluing also diagnosed.

This had been no game except Kellie thought the victims were cold bloodedly taught life saving procedure.

"Their killers took life for something they were presumed to have seen."

"How did you arrive at this conclusion?"

"Oh, that's simple. Your dirt pulled in two heels that go to regulation boots."

"Which says jumpers?"

"Yes. Should a jumper's heel fall off, he has to replace it because he can't touch ground without it or he'd shake his brain. Look at this," and pointed to large marks on either side of each five heads. "Maybe they were blindfolded while on board. Material for leg binds is refuse holdings most possibly because of irregular perforation. I haven't had time to make winch tests."

"Where were jumpers coming from?"

"That I couldn't say nor how many occasions they baptized the land. Since there was no trace of parachute fiber, it's possible they wore plastic size lifts that would've kept them in the air ten minutes. Those run a fifth of a chute and pack up inside a small bag."

Maybe the military took photos of land from the air prior to building on it. Maybe it was simply a procedure for surveyors to chalk out the coordinates as to where an extension of a town could be purchased.

"Canadian?"

"These are neither Canadian nor American; they enter for a month long weekend and leave. They are believed to be Tibetan snow plow."

It was an impossible lunacy. "Why do they do it?"

"No one knows."

The curly waist length dark haired glamour girl walked across the plaza in long leggy strides in a shoulder bare silver sheath making her way to the BBC studios. Kellie watched as she disappeared into the aqua glass building.

He took a breather from the intensity of work which that morning began with loading down State Intel and matching vehicles from any of sixty sources.

The Intel gave the four of the fifteen dead having boarded in West Virginia; six from Lima, Crestline and Canton; the rest in Chicago. All who got off the train at Vermillion fell into the pit. The equipment for the leveling of trees and land was leased in Crestline and hauled by eighteen wheeler to the site per day of use. These two men arrived in personal cars which they parked on the shoulder of the coastal road, one car was a Chevrolet coupe was black and silver with the top down and the other, a Mazda white hard top and blue. License plates were registered to Mitch Cornwall and Steve Lowell, both Caucasian married residents of Crestline, Ohio in their early forties. Kellie tracked them to their houses, single family dwellings a block apart, and ran the pictures but found none of the dead.

As to the fifteen flung about the restricted beach off the tracks they were collegiate grammar having a picnic on a public cove with outdoor grills. They had flown a kite for an hour. Eaten roasted hot dogs, drunk soda, fell asleep in the sun, came to the area a few times a week in good weather.

Kellie wouldn't know what to make of any scene; the day was a breezy bluster streaking up a bit of casual wind near the bay field.

His first question was, what conditions of snow created embalming? Was a profusion of bleeding necessary? Next, were the nine hidden to avoid detection before ice could embalm? Condition to succumb inside ice were no greater than a milliliter of fluid and food in digestive tract in combination with over exertion; but there had been that early freeze three days later during which a system of low air was joined by a warmer system of high air which produced a premature winter storm with blizzard snow, sleet causing a lot of problems.

Grass was known to create extreme allergy. That end butt of summer the field had grown quite tall afar off the start of the grid for housing.

The two other burials found near the creek when uncovered were dry but were below thirty feet. The question, where else had this situation occurred, haunted him. Could the dead have met their killers? Since they worked as short order clerks for take-out eateries, maybe there was trouble in the industry; maybe a group of the coast guard decided to do its own thing. Anything was possible; after dealing with hundreds of stiffs each crime year, there conceivably were several who ran the numbers.

He looked back on the bygone era when he took river cruises on the Mississippi before it salted over in a few river ports. He was much younger, a physician's attorney who pled malpractice for youthful men who arrived to the O.R. drunk, hands shaky, unable to reconstitute memory as to procedure, all bad cases conducted by misfits who nevertheless put in five shifts in four days, his pessimism and rancor hard to put to bed. He lived for those trips to China and Pakistan, a chance to meet students, see the working world of the church, business class a polished diamond far from rough; more food than he had ever seen served up at once. The females were young beauties anyways, band shell concert waltzes under moonlit starry skies, each night for the drinks at a dollar each, thought wedded to its bliss.

He earned his visa to be judgmental and slips of the tongue fell loosely to the ship deck. While pride and authority stood on shore, he grassed about in khakis and silk shirts and loafers, momentarily indignant the maid came late to make the bed or freshen up his cabinet. Twice he took Mary and they danced all night to Louis Armstrong, rising late to caviar biscuit and tea, otherwise they strolled the decks arm in arm, sunhats, shawls and gins, the ocean air fluffing their hair.

It wouldn't be a first that he viewed a matter with unjustified cynicism. Booze did that, soured one's speech, put longer stems on favorable goblets. He had his dress rehearsals, his angst. He viewed the world dimly; there was often too much murder.

He hated. He loved. Emotion wasn't always consistent. He had ideas and reworked them. That was the flight of pigeons, one moment they slanted the ground in their shadows.

He kept Mary's confidence daily; no one else bothered.

After a seven day cruise, he felt enthused, gay, a conversational live wire. By the start of the subsequent month he was already in a whirl of activity, in sessions, bartering with opposing counsel, it could be on damn near anything including should a prisoner be permitted to enter court wearing a hat.

So here he was, long into work years without so much as a week to himself. He could feel the pressure heckles rising. He was repressing again. He was left to one emotion, numbness.

Deadened or dulled.

He went through his personal checklist. Was it dread that masqueraded behind a mask of inattentiveness? No. he knew what he must do. Was it anger? No, he wasn't actually attached to the situation although he sorely resented the break-in. Was it disgust? Not yet. Was it feeling menial? Not that either; tasks were just tasks. Did he want to win? Well, of course, he always wanted that. He was a lawyer; court always meant there was a win or a lose.

Foreboding? Fear? Horror?

He couldn't identify the feeling. It was just there consuming his energy. Could he shake it?

He didn't know.

3

THE FIVE floor plan lay on the Commissioner's desk unapproved. A steely foundation already laid sat unobserved in the weeds on the beach with cement stairs rising along a hillside where an observation deck to the green waters of Oak Glen took in the entire coast in a single beckoning. The State Recorder Office listed a Canton Chinese man Norlan Sorgi who owned parcel forest sections who was killed alongside the creek that ran parallel to track. He was a good Mitch, meaning someone who loaded coal into a train engine. He had as a physician notary accompanied dead bodies to Cook County for disposition. In all things fair and just it was train law that oversaw all new land rising above dock water is train for fourteen years; but this legality was missed by a narrow margin of nineteen years.

The impetus seemed the killers had planned past this law. Rushing water gave lake military agreement to enact the train law. Otherwise the federal government retained counsel.

Examiner Gee went over each body looking for prints of disposal. The killers had been careful herding each dead man by force of a gravel truck to his end. That truck was determined to have been driven by Michael Lowen.

Kellie spent days at the Intel. Lowen was on tape unloading rock matter, his prints captured at a horse and trough, although it was presumption he was inside the haul when these people were pushed into and fell to the pits. It was a weakness in the case. Neither Lowen nor Cornwall dug the pits. It didn't seem evident that anyone had. All fifteen in the first pit had been stabbed by a sharp point like a gang dagger in the back. Each mark was barely visible less than a percentage of a fraction in depth.

As a precaution Kellie farmed out the verification to a state bureau consultant who had access to still lake water camera taken by air and long distance lens from the high tower at the dock. The lens revealed three men with bayonet rifles who stood guard on high ground all night. A shot from a stadium during a baseball game took a photo of a two haul truck bashing the group of old men at the farthest burial. In this group was Sorgi, a stiff legged ninety, and seven other parcel section retention district owners for Boston to Montana.

Longevity of law practice placed any counsel over the top. Despite years at the sacrum, he still relied on voice analysts to produce weed. His preferred junk analyst Thomas Siren worked in Chicago, a long thorn in stabilization and pontific calibrations. Tommy Siren's deductions produced a quick bed durst of saddleback racing, speedy gallops which sounded like punctuated thunder at a distance. Since there were no local downs, it stood to reason the sound derived from summer sport. True to form Siren had sent the imprint which read like a studied polygraph, bands produced evenly in the first measure with sharp crescendo gathering strength, along with an actual sound clip. Kellie spooled it in a sound room and let it play the full minute. Out of a need for exactness, Kellie ordered up any similar photo files in archives.

At five end of day the printer downloaded two rows of

photos of dozens men, women and children being marched to their deaths by three men at gunpoint into flowing muddy waters at Desolation Point, Pennsylvania, west of Erie. He studied the atrocity of adults succumbing to the quick of rising moving water onto grass and streets, no way to stay afloat while children on the stone stairs of schools played, oblivious of calamity. The sight left one aghast, there was not a policeman or boat anywhere.

He took a collection of photos and threw them to Mary to red pencil any oddities. She returned the stack with red circles on a few. A group of Cossacks riding at hoof speed was caught in a corner of the stadium photo. The picnic group scattered. They fell onto sand and mud. She enlarged the picture until she identified the brand for the stables on a hoof underside making out a queer OGS for Oak Glen Stables situated on the St. Clair River. When she retrieved a photo for the stables she had the five Cossacks. They were chunky men under six feet one who when they weren't grooming horses for the Baltimore Opens ran at ice hockey on the frozen river.

The last circle was a long shot: a rack of ten bayonet rifles couched in a coffin marked Reject, not for sale, which meant they were defective, had to be rescinded and either destroyed or sent back to the manufacturer.

∧ ∧ ∧

Jake Long was certain she had the proof of a lifetime. The similarity kept her spellbound. It seemed a damn shame to come across a dead next of kin; but to now have a second man die in the ground who was brother to last sip was to cousin an odd fate.

Of course it was readily apparent that eighteen men clawed up into open air.

She was a shy thirty, mild mannered, albeit a self starter

who upon acceptance of the job required no training having come from Cook County records closed files, dressed impeccably in a pantsuit, usually black silk sheath top, black linen pants, a silver choker, thin silver wristwatch on her right hand, black pumps; her gold blond hair tied back plainly from a small forehead, jarringly menacing cheekbones and heart shaped chin, in every way her coroner records father except he played chess and she, a mean round of checkers; who relied on a flamboyant set of secretaries for weekend evenings on the town at the glitzy neon yellow, orange and pink Clove to listen to Shirell's Lesley Gore rock 'n roll . Although she said no to every man who asked, she was inclined toward lonely boredom and usually drove to her dad's apartment to talk cases.

She got to work at six and left at seven after tracking histories of dead men. There were stacks of dead files, most came with a morgue photo, prints, last known address; dozens of never married. She worked painstakingly inside a closet sized, ten by nine, green room with a narrow window to the hospital and high ceiling, desk and four computers, one for Intel, one for records, one to communicate to analysts, and one to write files. Rarely interrupted, almost seldom a phone call, acutely sensitive to the least sound, being she was as unlike the other office employees who in her opinion chatted at their desks all day putting in a few hours work a day; she went home and dreamed dreamless dreams.

The file had appeared for one of the elderly men who signed his way through watery mud to the river. While he was not considered last sip, his entry was tossed in with the last sip dead such that the two files bearing the same last name came up side by side on her console. Meekland. John, age 44, and Mathew, age 82.

At first she thought there was an error. That they had been buried together. When she checked she saw the variance in years. They died eight years apart. The first died at Erie,

Pennsylvania; Matthew at Vermillion, Indiana.

She scanned for any earlier crime and discovered the Desolation Point massacre of 1978. In that year John Meekland resided in upstate New York close to the border crossing. His brother was living in Lima.

As a child Jake had grown up in Lima and sailed stateside with her father to Canton to the lab where he spent twelve hours a week for his job. She stayed a block house away with an aunt who periodically took her to the lab materials supply office where she had worked in her twenties. Off the canal corridor between two rivers, Canton was situated below Meyers Lake in Stark County; Crestline above highway 30 and below the turnpike where an hour north Portage River fed into the lake, and Lima, all buildings pink, was a half hour from the Lake Michigan and was the site of a gigantic oil refinery explosion set by turgid arson youth who had killed the Erie twenty-one.

She studied the two Meeklands; the younger one John had the signature of rifle blast through a door in the orange tinge to the skin; the elder man had crawled through underground weeds typical only to a pipe forest and there were only three such forests in the world where flood waters backed water by route uphill to the crest line; removed ability of flat land to stage a flush out for long; lakes were different, land was wet, whereas rivers were dry in numerous places.

Both had had to crawl through the soil of their property.

She had to assume there were heirs to both men for the extravagant extent the killers went to. Each industry one by one terminated by murder and flood or bomb until all that remained were offices and houses and schools. Once the difficult to supply factories were replaced the city left a costlier gain and demand thus reducing a previously high excise tax but eliminating high salaries.

She looked for who was contacted for each death; both

comments read, next of kin deceased; amounts in banks, stocks and deposits went to a special fund in the state. The special forests were drained of all soil and rock and replaced to another parcel and sprayed a purple pink emollient to kill off seeding and the state received twice the value of the trees to industrial factories.

It must be that the people who committed the crimes benefited by the additional factories in a manner not immediately obvious, but it wasn't her task to determine, only to verify the near dead and dead.

She had her opinions though once she had the two Meeklands. Crystal clear.

These were ugly men with ugly ambitions whose greed once released might not be easily contained. Perhaps as foundry tile for rooftops and their replacements diminished, these men traveled west seeking employment unless they encountered restrictions.

She raised the first seven dead of last sip on her profile base. Usually there were medical notations for similarities as in referenced for date by circumstance which were absent despite the rarity of grave. She found each of five given the remark erotic with crusted ejaculate on the penis gland. Eroticism was possible if in near death the body awakened as a result of external disturbance. In these men's attempted murders the soil contents had been retrenched permitting them to crawl out of cement into fresh soil. Their ejaculations allowed them to breathe.

It struck Jake as very odd, if merely because rifle blast created also instantaneous ejaculate.

She decided after a good minute to think this over to get medicals on the parcel owner and his known relation.

She filled out the request forms on the computer and faxed them across town to Records.

Records called her within an hour.

Yes, both Meeklands had crust pore sugary looking semen. Each man met all conditions.

There were five contexts that could produce semen: rifle blast was the lead; lead poisoning by swallowing running water from building pipes; by losing air quickly in an underground; chewing arcane found solely in roots of pipe Stillwater trees; and by climbing across dead bodies.

This seemed none other than a forest crime by erotic grave. While for this crime category the Army took precedence, in Ohio where there was a pipe forest, the county but not the state was permitted evangelical rights to trans-dispose liens and exceptions.

Records also told her that the attempt to lock in any death by similar description could take years, but one fact was certain, the men had to be related in some will to the pipe forest because the trees themselves produced ejaculate rubbery material at their roots during trauma.

"How often has this been a motivation for murder of parcel?" she asked the physician at the Cook morgue.

"Damned if I know. These are facts, peculiar or otherwise."

"It seems persuasive by relational predominance."

"If you take a liking to your facts, then yes, you may be looking at a same type of grave. The hard stock says only one thing to me. It's because the worker comes by train. By air or car, much more difficult to pull off the erotic. Breathing gas fumes declines the body, drowning takes membrane."

"What did you think when you diagnosed?"

"I didn't for the first one. I thought for the others land gauge on river passage. That's how much land may go below in a flood."

"All four at Erie?"

"On the watershed for Erie. It's not that atypical in watery sloughs. The body succumbs on part wet after inhaling too dry dirt."

"How are the near deaths doing?"

"I suppose as well as anyone can after a major ordeal. You might ask Headley."

"Thanks for your time."

"Sure, happy to."

She called the police coroner straight away. His message said he was in the field and was likely to return in a day. She left a round-about explanation for her call, and thought he'd probably call in a year.

Ohio's Free Port Law held to counties only on jurisdiction. This was possibly the reason so many killers lived in the state since the laws for other states tended to be legislated inadmissible. The Free Port said a man wanted for murder in any other state who was a decent fellow in Ohio was a reformed redeemed individual. Acts of sedition were discounted. Thus, a mariner could seek work without a prison to object.

In his assumptive office in Chicago tending to his hundred officers Chief Quibble gave no charmed eye to the fornication laws of Ohio, one state over, on its merry jingle to the death swamps of Pennsylvania State orgiastic lamb beds. The squad room was in its entitled uproar, three homicides having posted in a drug sweep in Upper Valley. His lieutenants were still puzzling over the Vermillion near dead, especially on the finding of a pipe dweller forest owner. Illinois was no to train laws, never to forest, state usually.

The problem with Ohio was even with suspects it would never convict. The other problem was no murderer had ever gone to Death Row. Ohio's little problems were if a man killed a worker, he might get off since it was assumed the worker was property. A wife could kill a cheating husband and a philandering female live-in.

Most law makers thought distinguished brown haired Quibble had the right to do anything. He kept the conscience for Cook County.

Not only for Chicago, Cook could take pre-eminence over Vermillion under one eventful discovery, if there were a relation between any dead and any killer, then a change of venue could be demanded.

Vermillion had a river which often dried up to the roots and thus Ohio would say the killers meant no substantial harm because long before winter approached the river would be mostly dry.

"How will you get around this, that they were all Chinese Red?" Quibble put the matter to Kellie over a full plate lunch at the university MacMillan Law Center amidst a lit hearth and white tablecloths with burning candles and waiters standing closeby beneath columns of Doric wood like ivory.

"The tractor shovel is the parent of parcel. He did it so he could have fourteen factories in the nearby Lima."

"Do you believe you can ask for negation of next of kin under relevancy standards that technically parent separated at birth of infant?"

"I have an even more precise law. The idea of a pink brick Lima city may be referenced under an exception if need be. Pink is byproduct in soil from tanning, also cinnabar ore known as Chinese red. Roots at Crestline were pinkish and rose mud turning it brown and cloudy and suppressing the actual ground placing bodies far down by over four to seven feet unable to be seen or to adequately determine a entrance of burial. That condition of soil had to constitute the choice as to where they were murdered."

"Can you make a case for pink?"

On the grounds that of any group in which clear and convincing evidence existed, if one was guilty, all group members could be prosecuted under Ohio law; and therefore Kellie sought a separate law state.

Kellie petitioned the court for change of venue to the liberal Pennsylvania because the state had penalized the similar situation of the Bramston Twenty. Not only that but the hospital there was ordered into the post office to assure safe service for the population of its muddy waters. The superior court denied venue to the eastern state. With regard to the neighbor Indiana, although venue was consulted upon, Indiana was known as the state that denied tuberculosis treatment due to the state's severe snowstorms; in addition religious bias broke bread over Shiva's and did not as a rule favor families for which terrorist burial had occurred.

Kellie countered with change of venue to Illinois on the basis that Ohio did not have a history of prosecuting train law. The convicting information would be to demonstrate that a purchaser who could not buy Vermillion land had killed train administration physicians in a watery grave dug beneath the tracks the moment the nine planked.

Ohio denied venue to its conservative lakeside neighbor Illinois on the basis of its jurisdiction of medical control over all bodies, although County law stated that a city hospital capable of diagnosing tuberculosis and stiff joint spiny bone was essential to elucidate medical motivation for the crime.

4

THE VERMILLION stone out-cropping with white
tops rising from the lake hosted each like-iceberg
arches hundreds of ash pine white barked saplings
which were readily seen in numerous inlets along the Erie
shoreline. From these frosted pink, salmon, crimson floating
bergs the planks of moored mast ships clung to sandy bays
along with Turkish light barge ships whose iodine medicinal
tinctures had rusted on shorelines and a smattering of islands
and become absorbed by a contagion of wild fruit trees causing the roots to look succulent; history of the Great Lakes
gave an in pushing tract of branching soft cola brown mud
creek beds. Despite sanitarium and settlement problems
for schooners to docks, the grouping of flooded ships were
replaced by factories which produced small cures. The advent
of opium poppies gradually replaced sweet potato sugars; and
numerous clinics prospered on Wisconsin shores well above
soda-lite foundries for bicarbonate salts and cranberry pulp
mixtures for the treatment of its sailor economy for forking
ice down rapids. The resulting mud flowed on incoming tides
building up the shore with continual medicinal properties too
acidic to be of much value, even to its forests of lush wild

beast, Ashford pines, and cranberry farms. Yellow soda bake caused the durable sweet potato to look yellow.

Ohio had to contend with rugged coal Appalachia Mountains of Pennsylvania and West Virginia to the east, Indiana and Illinois to the west and far west, and an encroachment of emptying soil contaminants to the immediate north, thus minimizing growth of its basic crop.

The world was on the verge of a malcontent happening. Nothing warned, except for the missing group of post office lab coats. Twenty tall, very thin incorrigibles descended out of burning airplanes on ropes floating on billowing thin white wisps of air balloons to the federated post office for worker's badges and coats, then returned the next week and found the doors locked. They were understood to be stealthily loathsome, a group of Tarantula parachutists in a felonious wind storm in summer dressed all in black tights and head hoods; and believed to be jungle warfare trained, possibly as helicopter aquatic rescue teams, from Khuzestan mostly from high mountain ledges having flown downed airplanes.

Tommy Siren donned a casual white collar stiff shirt and black trouser for his weekend at home in front of the lit fireplace, about six reports in progress with narratives on the findings of both the Ft. Wayne post office attack and the eventide debauchment. As usual he had posted for photos and was just shocked as to the abomination of nine unit generals, all in charge of packaging and delivery for five states; not only that he had photos of their relations who had disappeared along rural routes between Pennsylvania and New York on the strait. He didn't much care for the suggestion of it, nor for the stillborn cradle of lake weed that choked their breath. A latest finding was that they succumbed to rampant coal taking hold at cliff line designations but he knew that a fateful galosh filled with rare appointment and struck to the fact that their authority was destructible. He had studied the material assiduously and allowed himself a grouping of questions;

Did these marauders train for rescue on bridges, buildings or schools dangling by cables, zipping over rivers, and securing pilots from wreckage before their return to terrorize an entire work force?

Did they fly low over roiling floodwaters and lift stranded people off rooftops?

Were they a rescue mission for shaft mines?

What created the need for their skills?

Tommy zeroed in on any night jump off any height for conversations obtained. He picked out a first occurrence at Cape Fear frontage wharf and asked himself how they knew which warehouse building to fly to and perhaps not yet seven years later Ft. Wayne. He was given one photo of these unusually tall people dressed in black mask and tights lowering off helicopters in parachute gear onto trees, letting themselves onto the ground, and lifting through opened windows inside the distribution center for brochures. They seemed large boned but very thin with atypically long fingers suggesting a work force linked to the Iraqi who allegedly traveled to Fez to work in Oman prisons, all in spindly skyscrapers, and flew out from their beaches.

He submitted his report over dateline MIAMI as follows: Staging by parachutists entering off the Atlantic Ocean in Stallion helicopters into N. Carolina for grievous purposes on government land. Question: are they leisure fliers?

5

INDIANA WAS India North America, relief state for people who had lived in India born most usually in Norway, Finland and Denmark; they transplanted to Vermillion Indiana and Vermillion Pennsylvania to work labs only testing bloods for testing of the sickly tuberculosis, tetanus and yellow fever. In town plants where effluent was treated with sewage salts later placed on land in shallow rows, the river port marine corporals processed pink rock in Erie mines and constituted a relatively large work force that was hired to work bays on the lakes.

The dialogue reads came in as follows, "We want you to take a look at the pasture rock where the theft of nine bags were found."

Minutes later, "That's not rock, it's waste efflux. The bags contain paper mill. They are sapped in crimson, not cola."

"Yes, those are vermillion roots toward the last. Can you step down and see how far back they are?"

From somewhere below, "this is a creek, it's mostly dry, a tangle of roots everywhere, no mixed mud."

"This is the way the lake hill starts. Can we remove it?"

"Probably shouldn't until white rock can be mined; may

require permission in Vermillion, Pennsylvania."

There were seconds of missing wording, too far away.

Finally a plea was heard clearly. "Don't leave us here. Come back."

The squad room was hustling for a Friday afternoon. A related report had been called in on Meekland alleging at least one senior Meeklund had applied to work the sulfur bench at spiny fin on the headlands in Vermillion, Indiana to test soil deposits captured in tree roots along the lake base. The early retrievals revealed M.Land was not M.Lund; that Meek worked ore on the strait and had had to categorize some rather odd fish, literally. Meek of course had been tracked to New Pennsylvania deposits on the lake, so now they had a lead to his bizarre death. M.Lund on the other hand was a pro who recognized the differentiation between mud and tree emollient. He proposed to scoop up disintegrating bark matter for mining and lay bare the coastal inlets for dumping; for this he would receive seventy, an unheard of wage. Once accommodated map makers would sketch the bay starting at New York and then mix and restore segments through Ohio with every intention of providing Motorola Red.

Laurence Arles in the Toronto Gardens squad room assigned a two person team to language for the last train. He was in a dull mood, feeling trapped in his square corn and punch dibs, a fruity martini. He was promised manager of the new Indianapolis 500 which would open in 1981 for which he had given a tentative approval hoping he could obtain a river sluice dungeon, but he felt like a traitor in his profession. He himself had asked for every hospitalization of ore red, and he had a stack of them, no pictures. The next task was to verify any discussion about the deceased train engineer staff. He had a police team sort for phone conversations as to discussions about the Erie disaster, grouping emergency personnel from lake cities including border and marine and cosmetologist reports. He passed on the reviewed tape for unintelligible gibberish to private consultant Maelstrom Thomas Siren. He also asked Director Stubby Randolph, Finance, for cancelled shoreline chemical plant operations due to solidifying salts.

By the final twilight the army base was flying in bottled leg victims from Coroner Headley's marsh, which were announced to be nine bodies at one site beneath the pasture and twelve youth at another site on the hill, all from between the Crestline to Lima junctions. The Lima plant had shot two gigantic plumes into the air in what resembled earthquake temblors. Toxic waste deposit employees ran to their vehicles. Some drove straight for the lab, others fled off the hill road onto an island. Engineers fled over parking lots on foot, one ran into the storage closet in the hill itself and was knifed. The waste plant continued booming. Oddly an on-site guard arrested three men for setting off dynamite and tossed them down a shaft into the brink. The plant waters dried up in moments cackling as if under pressure. The internal building that measured toxic chemical collapsed. Airplanes were instantly in the sky. A cargo ship, its motor a choking roar, left to pick up toxic waste handlers from the Canadian side. An airplane sprayed the flames with aerosol. Then subsequent booms from the tunnels were heard. Two men died. A cargo train filled with anti-rust tile rushing with the speed of wind approached in the distance. On the bay cars exploded in fire.

"How much impact occurred at ground?" Laurence answered Tommy.

"I shot it over to detonation analysis."

"When can I have it?"

"It'll take a few weeks."

Headley gave his report in person to the state inquest board. He began with the facts.

Nine propeller administrators arrived by ship from Monte vista, Ontario to Erie and boarded the B&O train to Ohio to work plat in a field seized by an under hill river bed on corporate land belonging to Two Tug Operations; Inc. Typical container met federal guidelines for a part lime and seven fluid, most a portion bass. Most lime was made from animal bones; but dozens of bird houses to collect bird droppings were located on the strait. They were shown to an inlaid chimney consisting of cribbed cinnabar rock and Dover pile foundry approximately a half mile long and a hundred yards across with fifty feet depth inside which red roots had strangled a river. They identified the docent as being in mine formation. The company collected warehouses of artistic paints and waited for drying to form varnish. All the rose, yellow, gold and green stemmed flowers were shipped to Kalamazoo or calamity harbor where perfumes were made, first into mine pools of red mud and from these to scents, the scent of death inescapable, a sickly sweet conflagration. While inside the rock, the hall was mortared shut and the nine succumbed at high tide.

At the other site twelve men from Wisconsin died in a blast set off in Vermillion, Ohio at the waste plant, less than five miles from the grave in which their near dead bodies were discovered.

They were fed vigor, unadulterated brown cola, straight despite its tendency to raise veins after a shower.

Placed in a shower for a minute; then they were shipped to New York where there was no threat of wharf explosion. When the disaster had set the land was far from lime, still a brown tincture softening carbide replete with the red pink surface for which the area was known.

Headley was excused.

The Ohio Superior Court found against Two Tugs and

admonished the builder. Because the builder owned a home in southern Detroit, Michigan, change of venue was refused to Illinois.

Tommy Siren had the only read ever produced. It was punctuated with lengthy swaths of grey sometimes alternating with sharp black very thin motion. He wasn't surprised that no color ever showed. This indicated a pre-planned irregular intent of graves to suggest a bygone society had moved on.

Three Bentleys sat outside the courthouse in Texas. The drivers were there to contest a lesser known law that said, if a man produced a perjured proof he could have his destiny reinstated. The drivers wanted a finding that the builders placed the dead in the graves in which they were found.

The case was still being compiled in 1980 when the general post office in Fort Wayne Indiana where four hundred people worked was set on fire as a result of a highly classified glass humidifier in a box in the handler section and escaped through a window producing the effects of a series of bombs.

The train did not advance to Wayne but passed to Toledo on its way to the immaculate conception of thoroughfares to Chicago station. Toledo possessed at a lake port the dome building with its two stories of offices lit up at night and shimmering on the bluest of chill waters. A First Congress Convention Center held the same judicial look of nine buildings in upstate Pennsylvania on the coast, while fast at Ft. Wayne a collection of photos revealed a death knell of library workers lying dead on a cement floor in the central distribution mail room, in dispensary, in back room off mail clerk stations in its main hall that weighed and stamped mail letters and small packages, each post office clerk who was hired because they knew rural routes, bridge crossings, FEMA distribution in floods, and mail to Congress building offices by letter delivery codes. No one had ever thought to require command mobile units with listening posts but new Parthenon entrances monitored by seeing eye which saw public offices and parks were installed at once.

6

THE SCHOONER passed peaceably over the still murky green waters of the lake on its entry to point of destination on the St. Clair. Just as it moved under the high bridge, within minutes a torrential gust swept in from the east, rising water flowed everywhere, people in boats, rain coming down in buckets. The wind struck with excessive wind force; toppling vehicles and fences, ripping off roofs, smashing through walls, yards and streets, wrenching up telephone poles, smashing pools, tearing and splitting apart trees; the waves rolled at height of the bridge, bashed the pier in startling aqua rollers; a flooded river over shot its banks and gushed into the lake. At Port Hueneme helicopters rose into the air pulling rescue ropes, three coast guard launch boats gunning around a bend put men in the river to assist people stranded in cars and roof tops. The schooner docked on crashing waves at a wharf beside a coast guard deck ship as rocking water rolled beneath the dock. It would be an altogether different objective to have to come to terms with a fact that while the city of Harbor Point prepared for the imminent storm threat, a team of parachutists descended from the thick darkened sky between lightning rips.

Alice Corpo stood on deck at the helm, wind and breeze wiping her hair from her forehead.

During this trip she had to piece together scenes from nature sounds so as to extract a bio for eight illegal parachutists off thirty tapes; her tasks were to comprise season, probable year, any edifice they climbed or flew to, and initial overnight stays, between required investigations she collected info on live-in shipping dockside condos. She spent a year in a rust and mustard color suite of seven hundred feet in Provence in southern France on tour drinking demitasses on the plaza every morning during summer; in winter watched the rains come down and took noodles and diced salad and green tea in her living room; and in spring toured the violet fields and tiny ocher apartments and landmarks of Parisian gardens and nymph statues, cathedrals, Pont du Gard aqueduct and elaborate statue-graced water fountains, living on burgundy, cheese palate and toast and caviar and melon pal ego. While there, she had to specify between a breathing spoon dutch and a life giving humidifier called white horse, the first was a cough, the second a lengthy wheeze. It was a distinction of tinny sound which produced resonance from ejector shrapnel.

The slightest substance sprayed on bark chip made it easier to suppress life was also white horse.

Perhaps the authorities in New York state might arrest the man for leaving the carnival piece in the grass in the park. Sometimes she was god; most of the time, nothing. Her goals were to retire with enough funds to travel and publish detectable sound sights of lakeside resorts, warblers, gusty wind, speed of waves, moving grass, speculators; once retired to shed work anxiety and unlearn anticipation, sit back and become adjusted to leisure. She feared the sense of awaiting any future would never go away. She was five years from retirement dreaming of what she would do daily and yearly, already considered a private detective firm for hatred crime on the water.

"We heard them descend off small planes, rip cords rising with parachutes blooming, the wind shift as they flew maybe a hundred and eighty feet dropping, then landing on roof tops with a thud, scuttles on flat land, billows of parachute cloth relaxing onto the ground, pulling at small boxes, tearing open plastic packaging."

"Where were the Rescue 4 command teams at that time?"

"They had responded to bridge, pier, high water and flood from rope, cable, helicopter and boat flood rescues."

"Was there a multiplicity of dual functions for which no one questioned the presence of the kites?"

"It should be relatively easy to determine where they were by photos of actual crimes. We also detected paddleboards and windsurfers for the ones who fell into waves."

"The real interest of course is for those who drifted down river inland."

"I think these people are so foul it's hard to believe. I heard they set a forest on fire and sank a tankard."

"Their acts were just astounding, upsetting. They had already invaded Manhattan coming down on high rise gardens stabbing residents. Some also jumped to streets. I don't think New York was in any way prepared. The jumpers got away with less than four thousand dollars primarily from stores and the subway."

It was another weekend and everyone she knew had taken off to go home.

She cleared her desk, arranging imprint storm tracker and dull files on four computers, and began a series of seventy comparisons. She compared ship lanes by year; water was tricky to discern by landfall, oceans raced uphill; lakes accumulated; rivers gorged, some trickled depending upon distance from scattered object. The plant on St. Clair had just been built; on Hueneme nothing was in yet. Hurricanes were infrequent. That year 1978 there were two followed by immediate blizzard, fast winds and severe crystallization of cubes of ice that bottled flora. Sixteen inches of rain in a night, ground too saturated flowed in mud cutting ditches alongside flooded roads. Major road intersections washed out evidenced by clogging mud and interminably running water filling vehicles and water that clanked, knocked and clunked as it poured out of radiators. The large cubes cracked with pressure of trapped water. Constable and National Guard drove in in trucks through floodwaters with boats.

At some point sixty hours later they were marched onto a small ship and escorted to prison by coast guard flanked fleet and tossed into the clinker to await trials for treason. Most were Oman and India.

Each served between nine and forty-six years, after which they were dispatched to live in a gymnasium.

Prior occupations ranged from physician, nurse, lawyer, fishing fleet dock hand and geologist. Many were brick layers for retaining walls and sand baggers during floods. They had lived simple existences when they were persuaded by mob deceit to take a ship to foreign shores to crack a peninsula to submerge a town. Promises of rebuilding masonry thronged with excitement every idea of honest wage to boys of thirteen. She wouldn't forget the only voices she listened to caught the sunsets of glee and of a lone wolf man on the run on the verge of producing children for a young girl of fifteen, life unlived by lack of proud fulfillment, too soon wasted on an immature illusion of honeysuckles not yet in bloom.

Life begins and then begins anew.

The red tile rooftops to the Doge's Palace ranked Venice its canals and port. So the pigeons inside attic corridors of St. Mark's Square chattering about occasionally flew sky bound and took perch on the basilica. Porcelain masks of Saint

Anthony with swirls of bronze gold and dark purple caps glided down the streets for the bacchanal creation of Carnival.

If she were going to stay for ten years, now was the decision. She considered the possibility of ditching everything until one winter night flood lines surged uphill in a ravage from the back shore leaving stationary plow heads in partially tilled brown fields, lacerations and risk buried deep in soil, reciprocal vineyard gardens left in an exile of pollution filled with compressed air. During its cyclonical bent, she escaped to the airport where a cylinder of light kept going on the blink.

Should the fluid that produced the white horse spray been emptied at sea along the coast from bins of Blanca Corsica, it made for a porous vulnerability to every edifice it touched giving a semi permanent dampness. Alice had to consider that here; where people crawled through wet bark mixed in damp mud to save themselves. There was sufficient haul overheard on the tapes to suggest the likelihood.

She told very few people she and an Ecuador man friend Kama had adopted and raised a Latin girl to adulthood in Bolivia; she had packed Rina on her back as a toddler when she worked sound tapes in Bolivia's Scientific Research Labs before she departed to the states when an aunt who reared her died. The Sound Department was located in an office on the lab campus and studied hurling monstrous waves along Argentina to the El Departido coast off glacial three hundred foot high Antarctica. Twenty-one years were spent naming each type of wave, plover, song, menace, moronic, and hurling. With each type came birds, mammals and fish, rocks, weeds, and thrust. The pull of ocean was not dissimilar to the billows of parachute or the pitter patter of light waves advancing up sand like shoes running on a beach.

The three of them vacationed at Santa Maria Cathedral in Spain twice for Kama's job as a mason contractor to repair older stone edifice landmarks. While there she recorded the peaceful coupling of sea laps and breeze, which became over time an erstwhile lament of future tidings. She fed her daughter, then a mere nine, Jorge Luis Borges' books in their native Andean Spanish, a song like adulation of miraculous breath, and a host of priest language Quechua taught poets, Garcia, del Granado, De Lorca, Machado, Moran, Guillen and De Vega, each pronounced in a religion of man descending to earth as bird. A religious warfare forever permitted Spain in armed opposition against the Portuguese; owing merely to the Inquisition. The separation of muscular skeletal structure in the dungeons where criminals who were mercenaries of light had disappeared was itself a depletive history. Alice never returned to live in Bolivia although the cost to her heart she felt as a traitor of sentiment feels when he turns his gaze in a foreign direction thankful at the last to be freed from an embrace too binding. Memories of Patagonia was not far behind, her blizzard ice in the trenches of a far sunk vast plateau of which its chill birth provided only wretched purple blue veined iodine salts and almost no water capable of being drunk for its human populations.

"So tell me what should one think about these deaths? " she put to the recalcitrant Quibble.

"Who can say except for the odd coincidence as to who they were?"

"I heard all men were stalked."

Alice and Quibble sat on the plaza drinking mint chocolates while piecing together the blandishments.

Quibble tasted his drink. "Worse than that, they were taken by force at a station after very nearly escaping the deeds and permit Ohio office. One who came across a kite was stung on the estuary and fell unconscious."

"Any evidence as to where they came from?" she asked.

"We are thinking a ship from the Sudan, that they came to work the oil."

"What causes you to think so?"

"Those are the only ships they've ever seen in their waters."

"What about the six in coffins?"

"Presumably physicians who treated the killers."

"That's quite severe."

"Make no mistake, this is a crime to the dust."

"Do we know why?"

"We aren't prepared to venture a hypothesis. It's still too early in our investigations."

"Could these people have known each other somewhere else?"

"Like where?"

"Oman prisons."

"Are you of a mind the victims were Fez spinneret prison guards?"

"I haven't seen the photographs yet."

"Maybe you should reserve your opinion until you have."

"Shall we order?"

"I'll have the rack of lamb. Why don't you order for both of us, while I go wash my hands?"

Quibble was rather at his best, she thought; pricked to the sides in chives. The case would sit in due time. Ohio had agreed to Illinois because the parent plant lay there. Lima was the prig for cola and although the weather had vanquished the group, there was reason to trust that the pink had set a boom over a drifting scurry of salted sands making their expedition to measure depth of land inopportune. They had all visited the Il Duomo the year she and Kama traveled to Milan, Rina on his back, the brocade stone the most exquisite of churches, each ave a separate throne tower. Quibble said of late he had become the sedentary mizzen opting to review each commoner interrogation for ship descent, and he sympathized with the various charters to redo their offices and duties.

Quibble was bitter and sarcastic in his aging years having seen far too much of sod crime among party conservatives who while toting a reason platform nevertheless were hounds for illegal demolition, barn burnings, church bombs, and various sundry illicit material for school building. He had seen so much of it he was professionally tired, a plaintive now in the pleading, vigorous in his dislike so much so he refused to vote and one after the next turned them over to the feds for being horse's asses. Any individual who made their bed wound up in it. As far as he was concerned the children of good friends had made it to crime and each and every last act predictable for imprisonment and deceased, dozens had stepped onto a bad path to seek immorality. He rambled on filled with whiskey. He had lived middle class and could retire middle class, and his men with him, their children having lived easy lives, a light on a stone post in the front garden, a spacious three bedroom home, winters in Havana, college and houses of their own. For each hundred people, usually ten survived fine; in his department of a hundred officers, thirty were undeniable successes, good solid careers, not a bribe, no internal affairs hearings, each had a straightforward honest life. That was just the odds; he trusted them all anyhow because the jobs were too damned consequential. Lots of men still went to wild summer parties, they were still surfers at heart, still snorted cocaine, still purchased Mendocino gold, liked to gamble, live fast, fly a sail, co-own an apartment or salvage yard. But there were plenty of problems. Still many superior courts were unforgiving in permissive thinking, a few turning out killers on the street. When could society be saved; no one knew and he didn't either. He told her his saving grace was not that he had to refer a massive stack of convictions but that regardless what internal affairs investigated most of his men had no failings. He was not in a position to say forget the world because it was sitting at his doorstep although on this one crime he wished he could when he came across the photos of the lot who burned down the Ft. Wayne Deed and Permit Office and with it the post and court, and three men were sons of his ranks.

In the late hour they dined on stir fried weeds of chard, mustard greens and rutabaga. He had polished off his rack of lamb over three glasses of Claret, and she let sit a delicate cut of steak and prawn. He said he lived for a well-made saucy glaze which came with soaked rum truffle and whipped raspberry parfait which they split. Like the gentleman he was, he picked up the check and walked her to her Corvette.

He was an undemanding individual who sought the politic in the manner in which people interacted, a facet of character she looked toward in order to better see the world. For years early in child rearing she felt stifled by not having enough adult stimulation despite having wanted a child and telling herself the twenty-one years would pass quickly, gone before she herself had come of age in her own confidence. When she and Kama began traveling with Rina, she enhanced her knowledge of the world. The world ceased to be an inveterate distant objective; rather, it contained boundaries and cultures which were supported by elaborate architecture and knowledge, which she took home, placed on her mantle and read whatever she could get her hands on. She would confirm her sense of life as different as people themselves with the unusual aspects being the task to discern so that as she took stock of what she perceived at any time she was able to sift through the experience. The fact that a parent ought to rear a child with curiosity singled out the frequency with which she slept through the baby's crying, grew depressed over the mindlessness of changing diapers, breast feeding, burping, rocking to sleep, feedings every three hours, endless laundering of baby shirts, pants, diapers, blankets, crib sheets, a plethora of suppression of just wanting to have a half hour to oneself each day. Whatever parents were about, she thought it possible in retrospect she married too young at sixteen and a half, in most ways unprepared for any responsibility outside herself, but that was life unforeseen, ambiguous, and unstated. She hadn't run away from her parents, she didn't dislike her mother; she had fallen in love and become pregnant and Kama did the right thing by her.

She retained that hunger for learning what someone thought about the demands of life. When the conversation wound toward the questions one posed for oneself – why had an event occurred, how did it come to pass, did anyone know in advance; was it commonplace, how did people from another society respond and what did she think of the situation afterward – she leaned inwards, her hearing prinked, senses straining to receptivity.

She started up the sports car waiting for the purr of the engine. Despite the intensity of their interests, she was not much like him in personality. She was an optimist, fortified by a call of the wilderness. She wondered whether perhaps he didn't wind up hurting himself inadvertently by his dissatisfaction. To retain hope, one had to think concern. But she thought he had seen too many of the wrong type of crime, of a nature that clawed one emotionally deep in the flesh to the bone. One too many of any glimpse of reality, no matter how familiar in its circumstances, once the knife was plunged, the wound of it existed long past.

7

THE SAYING was often presumed that if a person lives by honesty they will find the truth. This of course assumed that truth is a personal journey by which one can learn integrity.

Truth for a physician was a give-and-take understanding about as unlike any narrow margin of communication between a group of individuals aspiring to bust out of a substandard definition. For the physician what is true was also a determination of accuracy, a combined juxtaposition of immature delinquency with a governing principle of what was possible.

The county physician possessed three licenses for coroner, with medical certification from the Canada Medic al Association and Joint Accreditation of Hospitals for surgeon and lab chemist with clearances rated annually. Both Canadian law and Illinois and Wisconsin laws governed the waterways for dispositions consisting of medical problems which resulted from flood and blizzard diminishments. In limited capacity cases that involved fund medical safety administrators the law of truth stood undefiled; specifically should a person of fully functioning intellect and physical body be abandoned or neglected to disposable nature the court was ordered to make a conviction.

Dr. Geraldine Shores spent an entire morning processing suspicious tissues. The pathologies of sliced thin skin tissue of the Crestline group retained a stone look maladaptive to healthy cells. Her concern rested over the length of exposure to harmful, non-biodegradable chemicals as to whether a mutative trait could have formed in the cell structure in such a short amount of time. Three months was not a long time. Life dictated its own script on DNA. Generally even though a pre-cancerous state could affect normalcy, she thought some consideration might be given to the extreme cold dilemma for frost bite. Frost was a lonesome rider. It might kill, but lying in puddles of cola well beneath ground was contraindicated of dying, and most in the group had survived feeding on the elements. Hearing wasn't affected, in fact it was more keen; nor were taste altered as a result of starvation and eyesight and homeostatic metabolism tested in the above average acceptance range. It was just tactile sensitivity that had become impeded, distress having replaced awareness and recognition with uncertainty.

The problem for her as a researching scientist was that although standards were long established in medicine, there was no prediction for ways the body reacted under tortuous self-defense. Any condition was possible while the body restored to its former adaptability. She made conservative diagnoses, kept to a rigid guidance. Only one answer would ever be permitted. Any evidence had to conform to chain of custody in a court. She had to state in what order of sequential recognition the test proved conclusively.

This deliberate reasoning was her training and expertise and over forty years fashioned in her a steadfast authoritarian discipline. As a result she was thoughtful in all matters, a slight frown of consternation to knit her thinly plucked blond brow, high cheekbones restrained in tension, her light blond hair pulled severely back from her face. Besides being the sole chemist and having to oversee the work of a staff of five at each two labs, she breathed tension, held her posture erect, jotted down notes in an elegant cursive, maintained a polite guardedness; relied on her intuition when a test result was incomplete. She matched her wits against the inevitable. Living had to be accounted for in its whims of destructive malfunctions. It also stood witness to the inexplicable and only the panel of tests released that information.

Justifiably or otherwise, she had safeguarded her life against many a frivolity; despite being on her seventh husband with whom she occasionally imbibed, but never used recreational drugs, and since she had already lost six husbands who made up nearly every last coroner in the Toronto department to death by overwork and high cholesterol, they did not squire. If she felt twinges of being left out, she promptly put them aside. She knew she was the life of a party, but it no longer held significance. She had tested men's sociable natures for many years and having made several households returned to forage what she knew best. Whatever living had consisted of in youth of the proportions of gaiety, she had drunk her tonic for stiffer realism.

Geraldine rechecked her work on the corresponding bloods.

Nothing was overlooked. The stone appearance of the labs indicated the men had ingested a toxin capable of altering hair growth by stiffness, shrinking follicles, causing stiff pointed ends and possibly hair color to automatic very dark brown. Upon restoration they would look bedraggled. Normally the altering ingredient was called grey loose clay which was utilized to bury urine wastes, a common disposal method. A black stone look under the microscope which indicated crustaceans made the hair pile up. Both conditions took upward of forty years to derange.

In addition all nine men suffered beneath a pleat of

interwoven branches of trees which in freezing rising tide vascular tumors resulted in tears to mucous membranes formed by the dilation of blood vessels. This was a field seasonally plowed and it was not unusual for leach worms found in water soaked timber to exist. The other thirsty sucker was the kelp crab, tentacles like a spider that attached to animal or human flesh voraciously.

The entombed men had each acquired fractures. As the chill air succumbed them to forced entrenchment, leg bones fractured and broke again to the bone.

She considered the evidence carefully. There had been no mistake. The labs were consistent to osteoporosis-classic syndrome.

Then she picked up the phone and dialed Styron Kellie.

Barrister Kellie had obtained the two rows of photos that showed a man from the Deed Office in St. Louis pointing a pistol at the unsuspecting nine Chinese land surveyors ushering them to their possible deaths. Obviously he had joined them on the trip after allowing the six or seven fliers access to the halls of justice working with them throughout the night to torch four buildings to the quick. Be this Tammany Hall where the manager himself was on the flump, there was no one to neither intercede nor impede. He was of medium stature, jet black hair, a cruel mouth with too red wide lips, tan complexion, a tyrannical nature, a hush up man. The man had an aberration of the personality filled with spiteful hatred for which he had a need to hate as well as to kill and no doubt his assurance was characterized by inordinate indecency. No one understood what latitude people had who were of such subjunctive piss-y venom, if it lay deeply demised in envy or was of a natural inclination, a willingness even to spit at authority out of a beleaguered monocle or even of an endurance of malevolence. The rationale was hard put to to have to understand that they sided with evil as a life plan and took unkind pleasure in torment for the practical industry that it resolved their guilt of murder like a stepping Stephan Wolf of mythology.

Outside the skies over Ohio had parted from the heavens leaving behind trails of thick plumed clouds that reached across the civil libertine, plowed fields that made up the state's bounty. Under an embryonic enmity of light a piercing ray of sunlight shed a watery consistency over water lettuce, pond weed, cotton grass, bull grass and eel weed. Small agile deer trampled underfoot through the fields, clouds and trees casting innumerate shadows on their dark bodies. The sound of pages getting twilled could be faintly perceived in the distance like a faint failing motor. Further out near the river, flaps were flying, an injunction of obdurate persistence of perhaps a windmill and interspersed through those irregular sounds a man was crying or laughing having fallen prey with, hard to say which, the laugh of God.

Kellie had already decided prior to receiving Shore's typed report he would argue for change of venue on behalf of injurious harm and damage and hunger, distress and pain and provide a picture of a killer's infected introversion for which his impulsive act occurred in the same hour the headquartered Deed Offices were to have been set on fire.

In the department of Forensics, Raul Moreno carefully studied a grid of photographs. One photo each of two pages was blacked out which indicated content too serious to display. These were number eleven in the second row on a first sheet of four rows that contained twenty-four photos and number thirty-two in the second row of three rows on the second page adding to forty-two photos total. The first row of six photographs revealed two maps for Ohio at Crestline and Vermillion. The third to sixth photo gave shots of the nine men who willingly descended under the train tracks into a protected enclosure of some sort. In the second row numbers seven through ten and twelve discerned the cola plant was exploded at the same time as the Ft. Wayne Deed Office, post office and Courthouse in an emblazoned fire. The entire third row bearing numbers thirteen to and including eighteen viewed parachutists in the night that flew onto bronze slate rooftops and attached small packaged bombs that carnivore destroyed two statuesque pillared buildings. Where these parachutists dropped from was as yet unknown but Raul was still researching. They appeared to fall through entanglements of trees situated on the Great Lakes and therefore he sought a ship that brought in renegades.

He had numerous profiles to consult, not merely the two sheets that visibly portrayed three bad crimes, but he had to start with the identities of these six gliding wings.

They had first flown from small airplanes of unknown origination into Manhattan garden rooftops prepared to stab anyone who they encountered.

As they descended over other towns, Baltimore and Cape Fear, they tossed lit hand grenades onto government buildings igniting small fires.

On a separate sheet he had the six having hijacked a major airliner from Saudi Arabia. He thought they had all worked prison towers and were trained to knife, strangle, dive, and bomb. As a group they robbed, killed guards, and staged parachute takeovers of smaller airplanes, moving through a foreign country's coastline within days.

To date they had left five countries having unusually small populations, each less than five thousand civilians.

Based upon flimsy information, they escorted prisoners to towers some five to twenty floors above their Fez desert entrance hallways, having lived in Khuzestan in its high altitude mountainous region leading lives of winged descent to rescue snow plows.

From what he assessed the six were after building properties.

He wondered about similarities of each hostage taking. All areas they descended to lay on icy waterways; each town held a prison population.

At some point he could be required to compile a thorough chronology of criminal activities, contacts, and places lived and worked.

He had to imagine that at some past they were arrested and ran; were running often.

Kellie talked with Chief Arles on the phone for the better half of an hour. The Canadian morgue had already tracked human remains along the Osage basin in New York down through Wisconsin to Indiana and had derived several working hypotheses, the first and foremost that they had started as a relative group, many who reported the illegal activities of cousins. Some had served prison sentences of up to twenty years in a penitentiary. Arles thought the most recent dead deposited in coffin containers had died as a result of a bombed factory for human excrement waste on the Erie. They were dealing with a bunch of fanatics. Unwieldy floods, submerged towns, considerable erosion; the mess they left in their tracks seemed to have no other intention but to create havoc.

Arles said reasonably, "Chances are that Ohio will posit these nine men entered the enclosure willingly at their own behest. Since they didn't die in that miserable blizzard, Ohio is unlikely to convict. Ohio Court will say that was their error in judgment. Say what you will, threat to life does not occur."

"I'm going after contention of relations."

"I see. The Meeks who are killed are dead. Venue may or may not get established."

"The parachutists have committed the same crime five

times. They served time on a second try in Arabia. Now they're out having been in prison one of them forty years. You have to say why these Meeklands are dead, no other way to regard a case like this."

"The fliers bombed two Deed Offices."

"That's not your case. Ohio will put those perps away for life."

"I'm trying my appeal on injurious harm."

"You can't have it. Without dead victims, you have nothing on which to try a case; even with a goon there. Evidence is not overwhelming beyond a preponderance of doubt. He doesn't have a gun. There's no real proof he's there for a bad reason."

At a fundamental core, Kellie suspected Chief Arles was right.

Arles went one further. "Not only that, this goon hasn't killed yet; or bombed."

It was back to the armchair. He wanted the case badly, could feel how badly in his detachment brought on of disappointment, the salty taste on his tongue as he palpated hope that the nine entombed men victimized by a sadist should at the very least be awarded with the promise of safety. They ought to know that the man was apprehended, sentenced and in prison.

So he began over. He took up again with the Meekland murders. One died in New York in Yonkers, one in Indiana in Cortland; four in Pennsylvania in Erie. All were the same, buried in wet dirt, each tracked his way out of a quarter mile to a river to die, congested with bark, finally suffocated to breathe actual air. If life didn't make sense, didn't add up, measure across a knap, didn't render common sense, then it wasn't because it couldn't. In all likelihood it was because the facts didn't match, weren't restored or were impossibly contradictory, or even confronted by actual truth struck one as perjured;

the nature of testimony was to shed light, to infiltrate into confusion by which any non prejudicial individual might detect a
fraction of surmise. The labs had it, dead death, conforming to
white horse, an invisible liquid undetectable past twenty-four
hours, the clay gone as well were there any to have evaporated
off skin and clothing not even a trace; such were the conjec-
tures as to the killing substances. He ought to have more in
the way of evidence, not that the breath gave out or that once
life was glimpsed, the heart rhythm stopped. He dug in his
heels, clasped his hands behind his head, and surrendered to a
good hard thinking. Perhaps these men launched into the dirt
themselves to make themselves scarce having seen a murder
and nowhere to disappear to. He'd look into it.

When he consulted Records he found the trouble right
away. The six Meeks were related to two coffins, both uncles
who had tried to bust up a fight in upstate Erie with a man who
was torching trees during a lightning storm. He had never heard
of anything so utterly stupid. Maybe they thought to prevent a
bunch of Bolsheviks flying in capes but he doubted it. There
were too many inconsistencies, like their murders for starters.

He talked to the man in photo archives, Jacob, whose
familiarity with eastern seaboard murders was itself a volume
of unresolved complications. When people vanished into thin
air, they left their lives into the unknown and it was impossible to discern where they had gone. People who remembered
the reasons they had disappeared often outran all pursuers.
Jacob thought of several persuasive rationale for mis-achieved
near marks, each one a stranger.

Shaded photos, too dark and too bright, revealed peculiar
thumbnail sketches. The State Bureau of Crime Detection
had gone to lengths to restore viability, color reproducing
stills in iodine tint so as to see actual pictures of scenes. They
hired four color experts for scene restoration staying predominantly with grey to enhance shadow. Months into the task

they managed to elucidate a first print of a chartered federal roof in Erie.

The work was slow going. Frequently, daily they had too pronounced thick images too indistinct or faint to visualize. A modicum of unrecognizable images, streaks of light, no roads, houses, buildings or ports. They decided they were in the rural countryside somewhere with almost nothing to see but the night sky. In addition each technician worked a desk where they sketched rough angles, blurred long alleys, distant bridge lights, lit up store windows, but everything they produced resembled middle America of that era. They went after photo shots of ground, lake surface, starry skies, forested terrain, building sides, anything that suggested a place.

Finally the Bureau combined eyewitness statements with police narratives and attempted to match place. A light like a small office in the night sky had extinguished suddenly followed by sounds of great flapping wings in descent heard far off. The photos came in gradually. Streaming balloons, black high-laced boots lowering through air, childlike four foot ten inches high figures dropping onto peacefully grazing elephants; they pulled every photo they could warrant for interior India. An investigator contacted a New Delhi officer and received a frank acknowledgment their modern cities were besieged by adverse Am on peddlers' intent on thefts of ducats.

In the damnation of nights the artists struck at bravo on a broody, breathy clattering of sky divers floating buoyantly over brackish dam breakwater dressed austerely in black, clear precise face shots, lean bodies of medium height, gloved; their wind scattering the floury dust of flower stalks in a coastal shoreline meadow.

The place was Vermillion, Ohio.

Within weeks a mountain of pinpoint silver lights descended to the same meadow.

The distance by road between the sheltered river in

Vermillion to Erie was a hundred and seventy-five miles. That could account for slightly more than five hours traveling.

The Bureau sent in fifty agents of expertise in warehouses to interview resort managers and waterfront managers and set about to pool a collection of photographs along Lake Erie and a forty mile radius. They entered in a line-up of army trucks and covered the area on foot, a noteworthy obvious presence, men in dark blue suits carrying notepads, measuring tapes, surveyor tripods and stakes, cameras. They worked pre-dawn, morning, daylight and night, were relentless.

It became presumed the murdered men were from India, had worked Tibet or Oman,and had since the sighting of the first crimes moved to Erie.

Statistical hypothesis came up with a belief that all fliers possessed Persian black hair dyed silver blond and were white or tan complexioned.

The briefest winter extenuated into the wettest season mulching most valleys and pastures with an abundance of movable earth.

Unlike the other, more conservative jurisdictions that wanted compelling trials, open and shut for guilt, the State of New York approached Kellie on a contingency. New York had had to deal with an overt invasion for which there were easily a dozen cases already on the books. The situation had mushroomed to staggering proportions, none fair weather. The chief prosecution wanted the Yonkers murder tried and thought any similarity could come along for the ride.

Their foremost fact lay with the fact that the man who trapped them timed parachute clocks.

Then there was the issue of proximity of tenement houses. The ten seven floor apartment buildings sat on the shore of Lake Ontario at Osage. The Meekland victim was known to run a mile on the sand twice a month. On the day the victim dived into dirt the rainfall had been excessive and had washed out the hillside.

Kellie jumped at the invitation.

New York was far away, but it was the most liberal state of the union. It upheld a law of person familiarity saying that if a killer had seen his victim and stalked him to the death, the penalty was automatic for the electric chair.

This being the acceptance, the trial was set for April 28th.

On the racetrack kicking up dirt the nine horses were running neck to neck around the bend coming in for the home stretch. The broadcaster's voice had reached a frenetic pitch as he read the action: red Fancy Dancer ahead by a hair; the white ghost Stomping Charlie gaining by a fraction; the black horse Clear as Day pulling stride; a real blond beauty Bony Gal a speedy long shot; and it was Clear as Day passing Stomping Charlie, the entire crowd in the bleachers stood screaming for Fancy Dancer in the moment Clear as Day overtook the strident red horse and whipped the last post in a solid win. Teased blond hair for getting noticed, fifty year old Margot and her fifty-nine soon to be sixty husband Lt. Jay Jims, both dressed in matching black tops and trendy light green khakis and black tennis shoes, clapped and hugged at their successful bet for which they won five hundred bucks. They filed into line in back of a swarm of racing enthusiasts and slowly inched their way up bleacher stairs to the hall and ticket cashiers as the announcer led off the next race featuring a four year old colt Lightning Bolt new to the Downs. They collected their win and Jay placed fifty on the sprint runner in the Fourth turn for third to place.

Loping toward them with salient cheesy grin and holding a beer, the two Cook coroners Headley and Gee jaunted over to them, Headley's navy tie flapping in a slight salty air breeze, all in white uniforms they looked stylishly like captains at sea.

They shook hands, Jay introduced his wife, both men compli-
mented her vivacious vitality, she being lighthearted inquired
how the case on the strand was progressing and opened
conversation.

"Sick perverts," was Gee's comment. "Might as well as
dunked them for their checkbooks."

Headley was less accommodating. "Stood over them with
pistols, I would well imagine."

Jay excused himself momentarily at the lounge for two
rum daggers. When he'd returned, he found Margot had
affixed a black and green striped scarf to hold her hairdo in
place. The men were on their haunts to inebriation, now strik-
ing out at the severity of the earlier single deaths.

Headley was on a wig, huffily disregarding, saying, "Well,
the rather wanton promiscuity has by now occurred at least a
dozen times in the ejaculate. Lack of breath is granted, who in
hell breathes under dirt and kill plant weed?"

Margot took a languorous sip; was instantly swell. "But
you said you suspected locked knees."

"It only turned up when we opened up the rear end, the
extender muscles were still rigid. We haven't sent our finding
yet."

They proceeded into the profuse sunlight to an empty
bench about midway down in the section. They sat, Headley,
Margot, Gee and Jay; and rather instinctively each put on
shades. The horses had run for the Third and the jockey
perched on his patient horse was adorned with the gold cup
and a round of photographers and newspaper reporters.

"Are you planning to treat them for burns?" Margot asked
Gregory Gee.

"The ones who were catalogued in ice, certainly. It's standard. Of course, the retrieval grows wearisome; the frost succumbed flesh which placed introjective pressure on organs and
that shall require insubordination meaning no releases of any

sort. Also follicles have reduced and that requires adaptation and one can't have both without further regression."

The horses had lined up inside the steel box.

"Do you anticipate conjunctive stress?"

"There probably already has been a legitimate amount. The reflexes in particular."

The pistol fired, and the six horses dashed out, Pathetic Wonder taking a long lead. Headley said Wonder had the race because of his jockey who won any race no matter the horse. The sprinter Lightning Bolt fell behind at three hundred yards, a trollop on a pole. Margot and Jay polished off their drinks. The horses distanced apart, the crowd seemed ready to concede the race; halfway Lightning Bolt got into the spirit and shot out and rivaled the second horse all the way to the clock and the crowd went wild cheering him. Jay lost but said it was okay even though it wasn't.

"What does the high court need for these boys not to have died in vain?" Jay put to Headley as the racetrack plow made its way down the course.

"Two of one thing and half a dozen of another. I don't suppose we are much worried. The men who were threatened have the marks to prove murder."

"What about Ontario Lake?"

"Don't see any trouble there, he was stalked. He received cracked vertebrae from scalp to lumbar ten preventing movement."

"I'm glad to hear that there's a solid case. Who's shooting for the case?"

"He's a New York barrister. His name is Laird. I heard there's nothing he won't do."

"I heard the Defense complained of abuse of testimony and asked for a continuance."

"That is rather a bother. The fact has to be that the killers didn't allow anyone near for timely help to have saved life."

Relevance was a shot in the dark heard by farmers who witnessed downward drifting white lights.

The bating deduction came at a cost to chains and fetters, perhaps even to whips and knives; in the matters of appointment and examination the newest foundling on erosive material deployment was a bayonet clutch in aspic not merely a yielding elfish captivity consisting of emulous enigma. The yellowish substance found in rhubarb and seldom in wheat suggested an atypical profusion of digestible weed available at the root edge of rivers and could not be confused in living.

Thus the definitive process of endowing the deceased with a soul grouped an ensemble of old fashioned leanings and pragmatic sense combined with an industrious ingenuity.

A quick, hurried marginal abhorrence created from the inclined withdrawal of physical and emotional complaints and disorders could produce a backlash against reverent neo-dichotomy.

The photos in the final row thirty-eight to forty-two revealed an insipid clamoring footsteps with rifle gear, a precipitous drop, a man on the river banks, haul trucks unloading mud onto him and along the bank for several hundred yards masking the front. At the other end having insinuated through mud winding in an infantile, redundant absence, the man emerged. Attached was a note with the syncopations that read as follows,

"Shoot anything that moves."

"Pour it everywhere."

New York had tracked the assailant by voice to the dungeons of Harlem.

8

TOMMY SIREN walked the eight city blocks in Toronto to his inopportune office overlooking the placid bay. In the upstairs office he had a large walnut desk facing two windows on which he had his two computers for work files and his dictations; a series of three teak bookshelves filled predominantly with law books, a small sound room behind a tan opaque glass door having a synthesizer and six computers, and a sitting area at the back of the office of two upholstered abstract blue, red and dark green couches, two red high back chairs with arms and a yellow glass coffee table. Against the far wall was a Rodin of the Thinking Man.

As usual he stopped in to the café stand on the wharf and picked up a demitasse. Once inside his acoustics laboratory he began work. He had a long day ahead of him. His task was to identify by voice and physical characteristic the fliers who had parachuted to earth over the Great Lakes. The Attorney General for the state had served him with a ready to produce demand which read, Superior Court of New York, In the matters of Meekland and Meekland for the homicides of bodily threat, fatal disregard and intimidation as defined by malice and aforethought, Section 187 of the Welfare &

Institutions Penal Code.

He pulled up the picture of parachutes flapping in air, boots ready for landfall, lights on helmets like miners prepared for entry into an underground tunnel. A few seconds into the exposure, he had the group; sixteen figures in descent. A landing wind rustled their stability.

Upon touchdown they ran to gain firmness.

They spoke little to one another, but Tommy collected their words on dish.

"What first?"

"Find the man on watch."

"See if there's a question the bounty sprang loose."

"Look for the equipment."

Tommy studied the night sky in the high pressure zone from which they descended looking for a jump-off. He looked higher at any lofty object. First he got one person inside a chair made of basketwork being lowered toward windward groupings of trees. He squinted at any elusive shape for seconds before he caught the faint, almost invisible sight of turning helicopter wings. He froze the scene on computer first.

He waited for their faces to appear, but they wore hoods with unexposed eyes, nose and mouths. There was a hive of them, some sixteen falling figures dressed in all black. They were of a uniformity, a homology harnessed to floating whimsical silvery silk like cloth which in the night resembled jellyfish.

In the African language five humored one another.

Kama su katra, don't bless me beforehand;

Alare compost, express alms of judgment;

Kamas, as you may be willing;

Soma tu, I sleep thinking of you;

Chalma a bama, a child is recovered in a life;

Agape no low, love does not question;

Lu gam e, it is not time yet;

Des partame, we leave by any means;

Sha panga, I have departed.

They constituted a wake-up storm. He tagged them, listed each figure for clothing demarcation and boot size.

What gave them their notions of licherousness, except life must be already too mundane.

What gave them any keep of food and shelter; their comfort to subside or settle, such an odd legation.

Were they intoxicatingly fleeing, or controlled by a monetary inducement? Once on the slate roofs of the Deed and Permit Office, they scattered like small animals, hooked ropes over the sides of windows and lowered themselves inside.

Within minutes fire erupted and exploded the windows.

This was a malicious act claimed by hate, spite, vindictive malevolence, mean, nasty, lunatic, damaging, a provocation of infiltration, aggressive and brutal, foul, repulsive, unpardonable, ruthless.

Potentially murderous had any employees been at work. The voices of evil when Tommy had sufficiently produced them were matter-of-fact, with very little enunciation but definitely a rejoiced Tibetan accent, the males jocular, modulated and smooth, all had menace, nuances were gratuitous but unfeeling.

It took him four hours to make matches. He made a final identification on the man who imprisoned the nine bounty officials. With name identities, the case was ready for trial.

"Of course I was as shocked as the next man. Pennsylvania was a disgustingly bad crime and this one no less; same ugly face, bounties rushed out to Vermillion to survey the trouble and got killed in that insane blizzard."

Stubby Randolph, of Finance, nearly bald, was talking; enjoying a high lord's expensive dinner with Counsel Styron Kellie, flaming torch of law. The meal consisted of baked bass squares over a white wine sauce mixed of baby shrimp, diced broccoli and a rib steak eye strip.

Stubby continued, fiddling with his gold cufflink secured in a silken grey shirt, a cloth napkin draped over yellow and black tweeds. "I was relieved to see the Court make a fairly comprehensive response. It's been a most troubling affair, the deaths, these acts of aggression."

Kellie wore his usual, dapper bib of pink ruffles over brown garb wear. "I'm inclined to view them as minors in a major leagues."

"The temptation is money, I would imagine. Why else would one go to such lengths, although I don't see a single dollar proffered. It must therefore be for impudence."

"We were anticipating a pate of identity, but then the rush tide flew in. The photos themselves were unflinching in nylon stock."

"I explored those dandies myself," Stubby said good naturedly. "Not a heel on the course that isn't a hundred percent treason. All these bouts leave one scarcely digested."

"We took them on the sinks in upstate Rochester. Just a nature of quick sand to defy logic itself. The coast, as you know, bears none of its immaturity to cola."

"I have often wondered when a man slips, whose tolerance is it that concedes."

"They were encapsulated in rivers," Kellie remarked. "The deaths obviously were arranged with every consideration."

"Not the end twine of the matter, is it? These jumpers had already plummeted Manhattan in a night not straight two years earlier. The conveyance ports had a gigantic manhunt out. In reality they let them slip through their pull board."

"It's over, thanks. They're sitting in prison on death row if they don't fess up."

"My guess is they'll be out in fifty years just because the blizzard was a freak occurrence," Styron said after a pause.

"Their group killed six and stored them in coffins at

Edgewater Haven. That will run at least two horses to the hill."

"So it's a jump and a lead. We won't have more to think about. Dessert? It's toffee on the cream with scone."

9

AN INDIVIDUAL can only surrender to that which is possible. Pursuit of curiosity is human. The nature of flight is taught by the University of Crete in Greece for which an essential mythology is about Icarus and Deadalus who because they fly in wax wings maintain for a height which melts their wax wings causing fatality. It is not the extreme heat of day that kills but the winds of night. In the night lives sights and sound not meant to be abrogated.

The man standing on a beach gazing up at the starry skies wonders what life can be could he but reach out to touch its phantasmagorias. He is delivered in that moment to the realization that life is enhanced because he sees it; a silent fixed whirl of stars lit in the highest plains of endeavor. How many times shall he witness this sky only to come to terms with the Almighty and know in his own depths of awareness life is eternal? It goes on whether or not he is there. Thus, we have a keen sense of creation as life formation for air we breathe, for colors that induce living forms including plants we depend on, and a visual necessity of creativity as intellect.

The man on the beach has been here before. He has questioned Reason, himself, and his surroundings.

Miguel City sat on an adjunct committee for work to approve lake jobs. On it he studied factory, car, mine and farm primarily determining number of needed employees over eighteen years arriving at almost twenty eight hundred jobs in eight states, to include port, wharf and shipping. For each fifty a foreman and for ten foremen, one district manager plus a medical infirmary. It was a real headache to add up; he shook himself loose, poured a gin and went outside to sit on the sand to watch the waves roll up the beach incline.

Living should be romantic in the leisure sense of having a secure job that gave pertinent satisfaction, dinners on a terraced piazza, yearly travel to a European villa, often entertainment of movies, plays and ballet. Of odd ideology, he did nearly none of what he thought people might gain by his ideas of them; he stayed home every night, read books and watched TV, and strolled on the beach. His house was his sworn comfort and aid. Prior to arriving in Crest Hill, he lived out on the sound with a view of boats coming and going in an apartment of two rooms, both having a wall of aqua glass; kitchen with sitting room large enough for five upholstered gold chairs around a hearth and bedroom and bath, all rooms off a balcony on which he sat until all hours to enjoy the solitude of quilted snow and shimmering lake. He liked to tell work friends he was a loner who entertained once a year at New Year's; otherwise he saw no need to clutter his life with ambiguity, petty squalors, or convention overnights, a worse than bothersome patriotic ambivalence.

He was at once self-sufficient and placed to quiet leanings, a reductionist who sought mysticism as a scholar who questions the inevitable of human aspiration. He gave his all to any immortal scenery and lived in adequate distance to assure it. He neither disliked nor admired wealth nor lived to acquire an abundance of much of anything, and thus he possessed a week's worth of wardrobe and frequently washed his mostly black polyester trousers and white cotton shirts, basic color dickeys, pullover Scandinavian sweaters and woolen gray jackets. He was a tidy fashionable man of fair weather interests.

The man on the beach has been here before. He has searched the stars for answers to questions. He has sought solace, or he has decided upon a choice for action. He is inculcated with a collective unconscious in a need to learn from the great beyond in its mysterious complexities. Reality may be intangible; quests over time instruct. They discipline by repetition of daily rites and build into conscious capability a life plan.

Grief dulls, conflict abuts; voracious greed destroys, whereas looking to the stars to find one's soul reassures by constancy.

Who goes there? Is the light with which we hold to illuminate sufficient to clarify our understanding of life; or do we embark on greed to possess what few people know because these few do know? Are we a life-saving human race, ingenuous, capable? Are we salient in our deductions, or merely confused? It is assumed that for there to be human good, as a mankind of races we know the difference between right and wrong as well as when not to chase after a pursuit of destructive power; we have at our behest myths and religion that help us ward off inclinations of indulgence.

Man honors life transitions with song and calls it the entrance to the soul. He laments also when he feels himself lost or shorn. The cries he utters are made to communicate with immortality to which he shall one day return and reunite. He is fashioned by nature in ways he has never completely understood. He is a forever human, simultaneously capable and not adequate; reinventing his footsteps although they are often erased. Where he can acknowledge limitations, he is considered courageous; where he ignores or evades his distinctions, he is thought rash or hasty to attainment.

Miguel walked along the white sandy beach. Every so

often he paused straining to listen for cries he thought he heard emanating from the stars. The night sky was a vast dimension of stars and pinpoints of bright light, infinitesimal and oblique, a wind stirring above, not a cataclysm or a burst, but a flight of some sort of ordination containing heralded comings. Hearing nothing further, he moved on leaving behind an intuitive sense of recognition as though the wind bestowed an ingratitude of awakened grief. As he retraced earlier steps, taking into his body armor a wisdom of significance of the unknowable, he was aware his body acquired an idea that the cries stalked his presence causing his skin to feel prickly with agitation. If something were wrong somewhere, he did not know what it might be. He was just out walking. But instinct warned him. Someone was dying, calling for help, trying to impede tragedy. He gazed at the sky, hearing no other sound, he strolled to his beachfront house. It stood on a sand dune across the bay from the wharf and pepsin factory alit with rows of lights that dazzled in a shimmering reflection on the dark water. The house was a single story, all glass oblong property that consisted of five rooms with high ceiling dormers, lush dark green carpets, a loft mezzanine of empty space overlooking a sitting room having four white magnolia on yellow sofas, ebony tile floor and matching counters in a narrow kitchen, two bedrooms, and a bath that faced an outdoor shower attached to a stone wall. Upon receiving the codicil six years ago, almost four years into retirement from the decontamination plant in upstate Pennsylvania, he had installed five French doors extending the length of the house. Inside it, he listened to the soothing regular lapping of waves on the shore for endless hours. The house had stood in the family for decades handed down from grandfather to mother and then to him, having been a summer retreat surrounded by nature in the last half of his adult years.

His grandfather Jamon was an offish man who kept to

himself who built the plant. He had vivid red hair which he shaved to the scalp, a requirement for the job. By contrast his mother was a strident blond who cut her hair often for the same plant policies. Miguel himself was adopted and therefore it made sense to him that he looked Latin but in no way related to the family. He had kept his distance from them because they were small town while he considered himself cosmopolitan, a man of education unlike his previous relations, and having not married nor had children he had no worry he could not live in the small house indefinitely well into old age.

Miguel thought the issue of involvements to be a peculiar religious indoctrination. It wore on him that a community of employees should be a church ascribed work force as much as it should contribute its earnings to investment where the company later utilized its collection to finance aggrieved destruction. Certainly an individual could decide for himself the purchase of political power on his own if at all. He could ascertain to his freedom of speech when it might be deemed advisable the length and type of political usury he thought his workplace required. Although mining factories removed pay for housing costs, under law they were not allowed to control wage.

Miguel considered the matter of a company de-staging airplane a sort of vicious antecedent to the rights of honest workers. The fact that the coast guard hired its own deployment fliers to patrol its operating plants at night had often concerned him, but they were a steadfast government safety which in times of anti-plant activity was rigorously enforced. The problem as far as he could determine was that on spring weekends certain of their staff provided air flying instructions by parachute including descending in crash helmet, arm wrestling combat in the air, knifing one's opponent also in the air, landing free fall, overtaking a ship on the lakes, conducting a search not proscribed, and setting fire to masthead sails to attract attention of an unwanted armed combat. In other assailable matters they demonstrated flood deck by ascending engine reduction, where to find the radio and how to contact Lima on the bay for rowing counterparts. They were as a trained group considered armed and dangerous available solely to militant renegades for the purpose of setting off bombs and traps aimed at government employees boating across the lakes.

There was a rumor that was drawing considerable unfavorable press that these trained adventurists had murdered seven state managers who hired them as well as a designated deed and county surveyor and an assistant for the New York attorney general. A problem was that even as they entered legitimate work offices as rescue for bridges and highways in disasters, they were sometimes mistaken as an only rescue team handling river and bay crises and the coast guard itself was unable to distinguish between their own and these illegal patrols until having studied the photos of critical events, they realized their own work was co-opted.

To what edge of existence ought Man to travel in deep space? Should he attempt to penetrate barriers of the skies? Could he find a way to supersede himself enabling himself to leave the planet inside a spaceship, did he believe it was a proper attainment?

Well, certainly philosophy was all good and idealistic, but life deserved as much as could be put to action. There were many who thought that way, many who believed they were joining a political empowerment that would permit them to behave with as much violence as their impulsivity scored. The true nature of men at work was not essentially viewed as scholastic or often professional; they were prison departures whose anti-social acts had taken lives.

Let's return to philosophy as to why Man aspires to fly.

Because they can. He enjoys testing his wit against nature. He doesn't particularly worry he could die.

Life was too short not to take advantage of everything one could; or life was too long, was tedious as hell dragged out second by second; often the only relaxing thing to do was swallow a cognac so as to sleep off an afternoon and heat.

Where did all these power struggles come from? They just sapped one's energies, emasculated one by their insistence; Why listen to them, they were a bunch of kids waning in a cradle of the moon.

One couldn't do another thing to play at kiss and tell, the exhaustion made by stinking blaring car horns or a domestic argument followed by a rifle shot put one to defenses at the idea of what one heard. Not unlike whacks of mother to son heard on the other side of a wall.

In black he had a dark sophisticated somewhat whitened aging look, attractive and singular as though any combination of attributes proved a perceived spurn, or turning away from the attentions of an elegant available male.

Once one pursued the fantastic, after one was drawn into that web, the act overcame the person, was a much bigger project until its web was snagging.

This was pessimism, pushing one's will at a demand to obtain relief from it. Did one become more polite after these tirades; certainly not, one sank beneath one's dignity into a morass of biting hatred trying not to grow weary or become affected by name calling tactics; one reminded oneself that living could be thrilling again and erect barriers to preserve humor and one's adherence to conscientious principle.

He would ask his neighbor, "Do you think I tossed out my sandwich?"

"Don't you recollect?"

"I've forgotten. It's not in the cooler."

This forgetfulness might go on a few times a year. He was losing track; he made notes to remind himself by on the kitchen stainless steel refrigerator of his mother's house; still he kept forgetting. If truth be known, he was growing apathetic to the demands of being, feeling he was enough pulled from his center of intuition and weary had tried to withdraw to preserve himself but still felt over extended because the effort by itself required him to think beyond himself; so he decided once and for all he would sit still as possible and wait for life to come to him.

In one moment he recollected his mother sunning on the beach, her ripe perfectly shaped breasts naked in the sun and impossibly clad in a g-string bikini of black sharkskin, he remembered at age fifty he recoiled feeling he was an irreverent snoop and pulled back into the thicket hoping she did not suspect him of having seen her in her bohemian liberalism. He had not realized how provincial life could seem. He was aware she treated him as a man with a manhood despite the fact he did his utmost best to deter her thinking him so and walked about even after midnight fully dressed including shoes. It was not simply that his mother obviously enjoyed having neighbors perceive her as altogether attractive at her age of seventy-five to have a much younger man at her heels, but he found it nearly impossible to ward her off, and in some manner he felt sorry she did not take up knitting or read books or assiduously grow a garden so that he had some real way to commiserate with her.

Thus he abandoned her often in the midst of a weekend as she was getting comfortable. Not infrequently she served fresh brewed coffee at six, his favorite time of morning when he could feel only his own awareness; and he felt hemmed in by her. Or she walked around in a tight light green crepe dress and backless high heel sandals, her toe nails painted bright green, her preferred color. Every so often she tousled his hair much as she had done when he was a teen and he smelled her jasmine perfume that wafted in its subtlety of felinity. His school chums had gathered to be around her and so adapted to their habits, she had not outgrown hers although it produced condescension in him.

He had not actually given much to her personality of infantile premature rejection. She was after all his mother, a single unmarried mother adult. If she were vain beseeching of need of being thought of as youthful unable to be disposed of as she aged, she still wanted a son and not a grown man at her call. To that impervious reluctance he was loyal but maintained a necessary separation. Thus he awakened in a giving state, aware, conscientious. He prepared coffee and sipped it finding all to himself the day began in startling grey moonlight across the night sky like a flood light beginning to breathe air to dawn.

He possessed a sensitivity to dramatic skies, to quiet manhood, to a certain awe of seeing life unfold. He told himself not to intrude or be intruded upon. He created his disciplines just so considerate of the mental space of others. He saw into the horizon, into peace.

He knew many like him.

Many who tolerated few intimacies.

Who nevertheless dreamed.

Who possessed a sixth sense.

The idea of existence itself, a duration of life lived within the subjective and culture of an essentially farm and medical taught society, gave an individual a bedrock for continuity in unselfish thinking. The emphasis on medicinal product saw its way to ship fleets and their arrival every five days such that one held the world arrive and depart, dock ropes uncoiling at masts unfurling. Just the joist of salts on their way to river deposit lent to a notion that life was canonical. The bent breeze at the stern sounded far off along a mountain shore rising with each lap to rock. The knots in speedy succession held a cadent sleep as assured as the downside wind stirring the trees, tall petrified epistles that hushed even breakwater.

In the most private of woods the sense of the eternal became envisioned as a launch host of barely sunk ships, wood plank tearing off as beach sand took the lank into its trust.

Like a submarine circling the Med that no country could figure out where it came from. Had it been launched off a stolen ship at sea? There was no way in.

The current state of affairs was an attorney general who ran for president and the other was a general in WW2. The first was the son of an executive for the AAUW.

Douglas Brispol was on camera as post office clerk master of Naomi, Ohio who traveled the Sugar town Rail. "We join a union to save our lives and then die by the knife," said on the Union campaign trail in lower Wisconsin.

10

INTERMITTENT BREEZE drafted in through the grasses. The rain had long ago stopped and the trees had scattered their leaves across an inevitable field. Under the roar of the Illinois bound train, the group of nine had walked along the Dover hard sediment two miles to the river end where great wine trees collected their branches gathering them in snarled bases. The slight water level barely visible constituted no more than dregs of muddy brown water slipping through composure of sand. For no reason he could think of Miguel consulted the vast array of stars, a multitude of salt and sand in a logical destination of seemingly haphazard infinity. He went after anyone he saw who represented a father. To him they represented the soul of existences; although he knew in his bitterness it was a lie.

The hostility of females conjured up a placating sense of grief. Toxic shock syndrome, warm water combined with human blood wastes and driftwood, gave an immediate crawl through mud that extinguished breath. At his back came the finite sound of hoofs sailing on the sand, a horse and his trainer, tearing into the wind. They were practicing speed flying saddle-back at the intolerances that constituted the angst and thrill of life, an unnamed practice of taking the horse past his limit, both a private spirit of energetic freedom. Horse and rider charged past him like a single demon unwilling to be tamed and flew to the oblivions of time and immortality. It was an act of motivation, this flying with the wind driving the horse to the utmost of wind, a thought of being one mind with the speed, a man on the animal and man a single creation of the soul.

The chase was up. The sole sleeper in his dreams on the wind, no thought, no intention, only a winged marauder on a beach collecting a stampede of destination, sands flying, breath the same, the force of effort non exhaustive. Oddly the horse hovered his rider who slipped in the saddle and foot grasped by the stirrup the man's body bounced over pitch ford and rock in a tribute to undoing until grasping the reins he anchored himself back into the saddle. That might be a horse that in its foal wandered off to have its litter and then returned weeks later to its stable to be saddled for the race.

Miguel didn't think he possessed any real answers.

He had seen something in the night that he knew didn't belong; men drifting to earth from on high off a toppled ship that had crashed off Niagara Falls; boots coming through the night on the sounds of flapping cloth.

What these people acknowledged was an altogether unreason. They were invaders of a different commitment of immoral activity, descending like a leaf fluttering in a soulless wind. Were they governed by some madness or survival? Small men of small designations who knew they were wrong even as they barely accommodated shock and went out to commit murder. Nice guys who joined a rebellion after feeling terminally wounded, abandoned by very life itself. If they had spent a hundred thousand bucks on hiring sixteen people to bomb the three deed offices as was rumored, it was already too much money. They weren't here yet. They were children who had scored a big scene so as to call the shots in the new world, but each was a man who hadn't discovered himself yet, bastards of invention to play the odds until they were caught. It broke his heart to see them all land like pigeons on the inscrutable jellyfish of stinging catastrophe.

The rider was on his horse again. The sound of hoofs at gallop took him in an even cadence of soothing gentle relaxation. The coast had seen a rash of horses dying in their blood resembling the turned head apart from a saddled body.

The Mounties of Toronto uncovered data that the drug affected each breathing as well as constriction which was inexplicable, potentially a writhing and unleashing of nightmares as if attacked by metal beasts like Guernica. Then came their wrath in the realm of the pony express. So the question was, why would an entire crew be outfitted in parachutes?

Chelsea house entire house burned to ground by kids living there. They drove the train from Buffalo to Jupiter into Lake Osage sinking it. Rumor had it for the horseman that he was Jr Mounties on the half shell; could drive a horse through anything; like a Paul Revere pulling the silk on the sand. A stampede of hoofs across a vast tundra racing ahead of the screaming train, lightning speed mane, fast as the wind, the chill breathing into his lungs, cold whipping his delicate skin, eyes stinging, keeping cadence against the roaring train, all the way to Jupiter, man and horse a sole locomotion, a driving force of night, the train light bouncing ahead in its destination to the shores, mud ranging in a shallow plat of burdened wash, man grasping the reins, gripped by the final finger, gallop and hurtle leaning into the quest for a holy grail, a flying legend. The horse an Arabian stallion of trained temperament; a charger with only a sense of winning. A choir of hammered repetition, a key on the chords, as strange a sound as one might anticipate from some unseen wind rising high above any station or plateau on the great lakes along the eerie shadows. As unlike any Canadian roan speeding over the chords.

Miguel listened straining for what he did not know. A bridge song. Three hanging rigs lifted the train out of Erie and were still there. He trusted the images life had endowed him with. Had he to say that they originated because of his father, he wouldn't know what to think. There had been no father in his mother's house. No imagined lead either. But he trusted his instincts; no one carried a pouch on his body against his flesh and this horseman did. The image was almost inescapable. Miguel had lived inside a tormented love, not that he even remotely loved his mother, an utterly repugnant idea, it was the absence of the father that caused him to shirk her outwardly, that caused him to not ask of himself what is love when as a teen he had kissed her from his depths on the mouth and uttered knowing nothing yet of life that he loved her only to discover years later he was born of another female's loins who left him to pursue a man to hell in the unnatural terrain of Chelsea House and he mourned his forever feeling he had lost heaven and hell in eternal damnation.

Perhaps he dreamed he was on the cantering horse himself fighting off instinct and urges and soaring against the cries of howling storms relinquished his very existence. A crash of hard G notes on an organ arrested his thought. He had protected himself against depravity and blamed his mother for abandoning him to reform school in the middle of the great wilderness of barren land and ice where nothing was held sacred. If he hadn't left her, he couldn't; if he loved with wronged breath, he shut down as often as he could.

His father was an equally devouring parent, living out of state working for the port system in upper Lake Huron where he flew a ski plane over the water between the coasts transporting medicinals. A New Yorker he came to the Wichita Lineman prairie on board the coastal transport from Eastern Cape to the capitols to work their city courts. He was a faire doctrine man who believed the economy stood as the real goal of society. But after hours he hunted illegal's, tramps and ship departures on the lakes. Coming across any, often females of tender age, he took them to a hotel loft where he stabbed them and left them for dead, returning days later to haul a body to Cook. On occasion he brought Miguel's mother to bed her and they made love behind a locked hall door for days, their cries like agonized colts. Then he sat around, a man without a care looking out the window at the lake and its ash pine birch, a man non-consoled as to food and drink, at a society with hundreds of boat ways, misted vapor lamps, pink walls and cherry floors, and endless candles.

Of all the multitudinous generations he had known, he was thankful he had known the intellectual best, a group of college graduates who sat in the coffee houses and talked about psychopathology, geology, landmarks Uribe, Toledo, and Ann Arbor and beautiful places; and starry skies and astronomy, and Dumas, Sarte, Dos Pasos, and art and museums. They stayed for hours in courthouse restaurants at the edge of university lawns, everything wondrous, magical and endearing, probably the most constant of their new adult years; the physician interns in wards at the Cook County Hospital, a sandstone Holiday Inn looking facility of six floors, emergency entrance always lit up. Out on the pastures of Wisconsin the constables trained for disasters, tall Indiana men mounted on roans, the swiftest horses anywhere, their captain statuesque on a light yellow tan stallion capable of racing against train and horse stampede, roar or thunder no distance disruption to that horse's breeding despite any fracture of the rider on it. In that winter of 1959 when fires took all sanitarium mansions surrounding the north Michigan coast in a snowfall of burning tule fog, the stallion and rider broke painted barriers searching for the stranded. The horse knew no intimidation, a magnificent body of precision, the mane wild and ultra white, the rider himself a white looking ghost that sat solid on the saddle directing the search, and burning eaves like green olive leaves intertwined by tiny frankincense.

On nurses night out, all escapes kept their winters.

Miguel gave his remorse to the swiftly jostling lanterns of men on horseback. The factory took more of his mental energy than he cared to give, not that he had all that much anyways; since he preferred to sit on his balcony listening to the peaceful lapping of waves. The second incident of mansions burning in the chill spent his quiet containment, disposed him to an altogether slow anxiety that neither time nor nightfall belonged to the living. He was fairly certain once he returned to his beach solitude he could rationally comprehend that the Wisconsin alder pine peninsula was taken by a vicious enemy that had appeared out of nowhere who sought to obliterate the pony express taking with their burning siege towns, industry, church and hill alike.

The nurses came and went too soon after a year employment retiring to sanitariums with tea houses where old husbands languished about waiting out a youth. In six ports on the Ontario to the Saskatoon coast there were less than four high schools and three universities for job training and placement for two thousand seven hundred people who would vie for two thousand jobs, most in youth institutes as teachers or in building complexes for language translation coursework, shoreline factories for product manufacture and far out on the icy barren wilderness on farms shoveling for potato, squash and root. The size of towns determined the number of apartments, parks and trolleys. Cotton fields and clothing mills, rugs, food, vegetable fields and fruit orchards, for the markets, resorts on rivers, and offices for lending comprised even modern cities having art, news, ballet, theatre and speakeasy's.

Over years he borrowed on the idea that a stroll on the beach gave one a sense of an eternal history, living being tightly managed for quiet evenings and contemplative restorative thought. He would never understand the evil nature of human cruelty. Why so many clinics were set on fire in a blizzard he wouldn't be able to understand. When the mounted police finally apprehended the small group of church choir boys, Miguel having known at least one fifteen year old from Gladden, he still was unable to realize what behavior prompted their actions. Their families worked the cotton mills on the Glendale canal, all friendly Dutch; so now the Dutch were no good, a bunch of prize champions who were illiterate and sullen, baleful close mouthed thugs. That they lived five families to a ten room apartment lent them a subservient status of under employment although they were more well-to-do than anyone else.

He waited at the corner suitcase in tow while on the opposite corner in a black sedan his ride waited for him, neither aware the other was there. He had spent the weekend on the bluff walking two miles in the early morning and again toward sunset just prior to taking a rum scotch on the serenade walk at the yacht harbor to watch the boats come in. He had taken an entire two days over a Friday and Saturday at the horse races placing his bets to bring in a few chasers, worth a pretty value of three hundred bucks enough to pay off the affluent hotel he'd strung himself up to to pay the season for a mild tourist at the pink. He had ponied up a bet on the exacta twice and one 12:1 long shot which oddly enough on a prickled poinsettia in the gardenia he topped off between fish salsa bouillabaisse and mango and jumbo prawn cocktail in the dill relish at the beachfront cabana and parasol at the grass that fronted the bay. In between he had taken off to visit an older British friend, then jaunted off to sew the Jordan, finally brought back to his hotel room a stiff mannequin blonde dressed all in black lace fringed by light blue from the local weather station, and ended the au cockle shells on a hose line emptying across the grass and black sand into a sparkling aquamarine water.

When he was at last pungent in sorrow after a week of vacation he could have guessed how it would end, distilled and foggy, passed out on the sofa on board the blonde's yacht in the harbor, a mist having fried his mind and obscured the mast pole down to the deck. The bay was still in floating time winding through lapses of exhaustion, eddies coming in swirls in mud, cut free brown and squalors of mercurial silver, layered like delicate petioles, two layers froth, the main cloaks all shortage that the supply can't reach to; causing him to question who walked on foot in the fog where nothing was but errant light; somewhere a fog horn broke the opaque mist. Along the wharf a modernization of culture had sprung up like tangled roots of new Dutch condos, Old Navy, PF Chiang, Barnes & Noble, theatre, pubs, hotels, fronted a freeway where the rush of cars, dense at five in the evening offset the roar of tide, an exasperation of abrupt interruption of the quiet having risen unexpectedly out of momentary suppression.

Sunset walk on the headlands the next evening, the setting sun like a bright yellow orb scintillating like a planet in an orange sky, tall mast pole sailing into harbor amidst rows of decapitated masts at rest; bourbon drinks and calamari dinner alone again on the terrace; the usual call from his mother at seven which he let ring endlessly; a good night to watch a movie on the color but he probably wouldn't preferring instead to stare into the absoluteness of darkness; toward nine the wind had caught a whistle off the water coming off the hills in a low moan.

Miguel heard voices emanating from inside the ground like the dead rising from waters on the tern. He fled in sympathetic speed running to catch the wind to summon the Canadian Mounties.

When the sleet flew, it descended laterally with swift

damage of a tone-out. The grass froze in a conundrum of a puzzle, all gravity holding to fixed points until the brittle slate seemed at once to build hexagonal forms, some filled with the plum brown mud of the shoreline while other cube poly-gram shapes encompassed the bluest of icy water at draft depth, seen from an immediate distance as submerged aquamarine color captivated in trance. Once delivered, the sand beach and bottom roots lay ensconced in crystalline beauty, each form a miniscule cave sealed off from the whirling night air, globules raining onto the land from every which direction, an ice junk pile of gigantic rock pieces thrown together by an oddity of fate. If people were captured inside these glassy fixtures, they hopefully had not died a snappish sudden loss of air and strangulated as surely had they hung off a high bow in a shrill wind. From far away the terror of horse hoofs could be heard over the howling wind as a dozen horses stampeded in shallow water and on land. A small price would be paid for any steed that slid on ice and crashed to its death, whinnying in stunned pain, a glower-dom.

Much later from somewhere on the hill red headlights shone upon the marina and grass swathing the dock and boats in an odd golden crimson. Miguel fell asleep listening to a far off mechanical crane lift edging through the soil, relieved to be listening to some sort of rescue operation.

11

FROM A TREACHEROUS height off a cliff hanger suspended well above towering tree tops and a bilious calamity of waterfalls each jettisoning through myriad rainbows in shouting strength gushing over a rock plateau into a steep canyon ravine, the vociferous sound of soaring water was all which could be heard. A diver jumping off the concrete platform through this cavernous thunder immediately dropped into shooting sprays of infinite columns of falls within seconds and fell to the Niagara Dam itself in an underwater hurdle of shelling fierce streams firing out of some twenty-five gates in a torrential cascade. For the bombardier who survived this improbable feat, the fall through air surrendered him or her like drop weight into a three hundred foot depth pool. Any Canadian Mounties rigorously trained to perfect this act a half dozen times in all weather without a knife knit opening chute; in addition to sailing off jungle like precipices donned with headgear windowless glass bifocals, sharp descents into menacing wind from claw mountain range positions.

The diver fell to earth in a taut straight dive that in seconds had plunged him into a deep river in light green water to where a small upright ship lay, a sole wide berth mast still hung at a half fathom.

Drawn tight the held mast might never loosen and flag; such a tightly pulled mast cord would only supply to highest sailing mast kites; manufactured only by the Italians of Venice; for which six people rode inside a lengthy cabin and the airplane flew in air space above dense clouds, its small motor capable of flying one and a half days. From this candescent crest it clung to life although its treasures were some time ago removed and its chief log of citations in a water tight compartment was blank. Obviously the names had there been any would have been of utmost value. The foothold locker which ought to have contained chests of gold lay vanquished, empty. The diver swam between gigantic motor wings kicking up toward the surface of the glowing light and washing in with a tide to thin swamp trees on a ledge that regularly shed slowly drifting mud.

Once in shallow water the man waded up an incline rocky slope through the darkest of brown red waters to a beach head following the river mouth to its deposits until he entered between narrow embankments past docks on both sides to the end. There, aged trees, their bark turned almost purple, held the river in a clenched fist, two inch in diameter elephantine roots knurled like benches soaked up the water to reveal nothing more than an ebbed collection of damp recess. Up a sandy path between two conjoint pastures trimmed by whitish rock he found the sleeping place where the twelve land appraisers huddled against the encroaching storm.

The situation approached a funeral on a beach by the looks of it, three groups of people who lay destitute. No one witnessed their demise; the sole predicator as to who any were was they began in Indiana state and had witnessed the shell fire of the Fort Wayne post office hit by a very bad bomb inside its fancy, marble laid floor, decorous corridor where each of ten billet teller stations handled mail and packages and its chief section of dormant land development accountants were in the field in Pennsylvania busy approving new businesses that would ship parcel post by train.

Debris lay scattered about the beach as though something major occurred there prior to the train pulling into Crestline two states away. The death problem seemed not to have arrived west from Erie station where a hundred miner bodies lay dead at the train station after a bomb to a ship at Sleeping Bear mine on the Canadian coast. Instead, it came east out of the Indian state to fetch the money orders on the dead miners. The man climbed up the path all the way to the hill where a dark bay horse stood grazing and mounted it, grabbing its mane, kicked it in the sternum and rode it like thunder holding his body as close to the beast's neck so as to be one in mechanical flight to the wharf at Lima where the oil deck of a long step of oil field lay burning, its torrential leanings smothering in fire and smoke.

All the way to Canton horse and man jostled a light fare on the beach front of the Traverse across crest and vale up to where the sordid heap of bodies were lying piled up on the trail line, all dead, their final act to have been gunned down as they ran to escape a shocking enterprise falling from the skies.

This was to have been the second incident of invasion by air of towns along the Erie and Lake Michigan, a dearer price than even a life spent working collapsing shaft mines in the Allegany Mountains of Pennsylvania for an embittered ore for steel. The fact that the steel well often took lives from deep in the ground was overlooked by news and nurse camps alike because the tenuous nature of lateral depths recognized the deeper a group trenched, the worse the likelihood of risk.

There were ten men who cat walked down by rope and pitch fork into any depth that had at any time to listen for buried falls leaking interiorly that could fracture rock plate like ice. These men lowered on a belt along a tightrope to a base and measured each strata to haul out by sink-age.

Nevertheless he expected the case to be resolved within a year, all thugs identified and convicted, not even an adolescent remaining. He sold himself on the idea there was ample evidence including on the man with a tattoo on his left side of his face which made him seem horribly disfigured. It was a sick kidnap for any small group of men who seemed to want little else than entry badges into a building to lay their hands on deeds especially for farmhouses on the lakes and then blow the place to hell. If he himself worked too long hours, went without, lost track of them in forests, regularly came across their bombings and had to assign bodies and destroyed foundations, he had to press on, climb high into the mountains, set traps, scout by helio-land and ski plane, chart coordinates, surrender to steep ledges, walk the mile; hunt by scent, all exhaustive, tireless, thankless searches, often dubious. The mountains made up a vast terrain, descents over slate, granite, gravel and falling rock, clandestine, icy, riddled in lakes. They could be anywhere, buried in snow, high in trees, underwater, anchored to a herd of driftwood camouflaged by moving buck. A rifle shot spotter himself, he wore above ninety millimeter green goggles a very compact camera that could scan ten miles of dense high brush forests, his gunner release rifle, two pounds of fur over his outdoor woodman clothes, had a thick, hand held, non visible by ray cable line capable of a snap release for climbing terrain, left smothered campfires wherever he bed down; his mountaineer training had taught him how to survive in diving; he didn't worry that he fed himself on acorn and berry, nor that they burned every shack they left, or that they left speared fish on the beach to attract prey. He knew he had them, only so many trails, few ledges, the slick rock killed injudiciously above mining washouts anyways. On occasion he heard shouts and he clawed his way up hills to catch a glimpse of them, rowdy canoe trappers wading in very shallow rapids to hurdles to avoid the falls. He kept in tandem waiting out their food supply watching from much higher up thinking them seduced by over confidence and the lonesome wilderness, not just that the theft of money had chiseled awareness from instinct. If they had to follow the rising sun, they'd be dead; eventually they'd arrive to the granite narrow passes of impossible terrain, but down rock face they slid off dirt banks often into a river. They didn't maintain camp by day or night, but the longer they lived by their wits the easier it was to lose them; if they fed on snake and slept in holes, they reduced their own risk of capture. Predictably they periodically robbed a liquor store for pints of booze, cigarettes, camphor and steak which they used for animals, once he spied them atop a glacial rock at nine thousand feet. Once they showered in a national park and stole sleeping bags. When they entered a mine, he set off a charge at its entrance certain he had them until a month later he saw them again situated at a rapids soaking their feet, pants rolled up.

He had expected apprehension to take just a week. By the looks of it, he was in for much longer.

He cased his camera photos daily to bi-weekly looking for any human movement in tweed. He even checked charted course, left target light at points they traveled and automatically faxed wanted posters. A handy device, worshipped by forest ranger and bullpen alike, known for speed of chase in destitute climates, he was rarely without it. By now the parachutists were entirely on foot almost a week and had not written anyone. Also he kept a six inch powered telescope to assess sights by which could shoot a photographic description inside of a minute. He had to go in closer because his rifle didn't shoot over a hundred meter range at target.

The rain kept him cooped up indoors. He spent an

afternoon by the lodge fire keeping a gaze on who stepped inside and waited out the downpour which took two full days.

He could have been getting married or at the opera for a fundraiser attired in a suit and bowtie and dress ruffle instead of tracking these utter junkies to their paths, nothing so wanton as the numbers of people they had knifed and tossed off high rise gardens; he could be teaching his students how to wait porpoises in the murky depths, or at home the balcony doors ajar frying eggs and hash. He was in love after a fifth divorce to a student in his tracker course who was thirty-two years younger who hadn't lived enough to know what she was yet, a ballerina who danced Swan Lake who between seasons liked to curl up with him, a dichotomy of interests; and here he was on his sixtieth kill, roaming the ice and rock and streams like he was the oldest man on the planet foot trodden by rope and pick until he could hike the wilderness with his eyes closed. Here he was at sixty born of indifference, instincts honed to silence and listening for the smuggled sense of furtive escape. He stood sipping coffee in front of a cabin studio window as rain glazed the window thinking about the city district Croton-Harmon where he taught. It came to him from time to time he was not cut out for the classroom nor for the pent-up demands of a desk grading mid-terms; when he had a compelling need to be outside camping, being alone in solitude, unavailable to anyone.

Even as he assiduously plotted course off his camera lens carryall, even as he took note they flew downwind or traversed cross-country on skis, he prepared himself for anticipated confrontation, signaling by repetitive light, crossing shallow streams, appearing in heavy mist, always asking, how high was up? In private moments, alone on top of the roof of his brick stone apartment flat in a tenancy of twenty apartment buildings in Kingston, he asked of the quiet, strange questions for which he had no answers anyways; these were just arousing inquiries to invite intellectual provocation on the least explainable acts of humankind. What caused a man to turn a murder? Was he in sudden fear that someone saw him commit a robbery and debauchery? Or did he plan to kill, think about a death prior to choosing a victim? Was he in his right mind; did anything caution him first beforehand to abandon that act, or was it impulsive, hasty, an act of passion such as rape? Murder was such a base act as if the killer himself had no ability to enter a work force and conduct his life without the violence of short term thinking.

But thinking was an expensive foray. Nothing ever quite wound up in court as it played out in life. There were so many extenuating circumstances; some having prior convictions, some who only wanted a free ride to check out of a gang for awhile, do nothing, be fed, clothed.

The sound of blinds in wind sounded like someone running upstairs.

It was followed by an abrupt thud, luggage being lowered onto the ground to await an incoming train, maybe to Coney Island and the boardwalk.

What did he think had started all this to begin with?

A group of rich kids whose parents sent them to boarding schools at which they learned sky diving, crane piling, tree chopping, on their way to the rarest of professions but who wound up rotating in and out of jail for pulling house robberies.

He had been there, at home on his roof feeding the pigeons, watering the begonias and honeysuckle, when twenty black boots in black descended at once out of the night, slinging themselves from somewhere obscure on the wings of parachutes.

And then for days, weeks, ten, twelve bodies turning up, derelicts sleeping in alleys around the corner from cheap eggs restaurants along the waterfront docks, old men found in the lowest stairwell of brownstones; most stabbed in the gut, some chucked into the bay. Often a wistful emotion escaped his chest like a barely suppressed sob, uncharacteristic for a man he told himself, brought on by not eating, drinking for long hours, during which his only contacts with the world were the maid and his clerk, the rain coming down fast, sleet slanting across the city chasing after taxis and vans.

It was unknown whatever brought these renegades into the ports of New York, Erie and Hoof Town, Chicago.

With flashlights they descended in a light rainfall amidst a police force gunning at them from rooftops and the streets.

For the ones who got away, it was a round-the-clock manhunt chasing them on horseback into the mountains.

It was 12:13 am when he finally saw his opportunity.

He came upon them asleep in trees at sunrise elevation and shot five men in the back and left the one female undisturbed. His shots surrendered spines to inlaid fractures.

At minimum the dead deserved their deaths.

www.ingramcontent.com/pod-product-compliance
Lightning Source LLC
Chambersburg PA
CBHW020334120726
47904CB00002B/405